THE
BUTCHER'S
SON

THE BUTCHER'S SON

GRANT McKENZIE

The following is a work of fiction. Names, characters, places, events and incidents are either the product of the author's imagination or used in an entirely fictitious manner. Any resemblance to actual persons, living or dead, is entirely coincidental.

POLIS BOOKS

BOOKS BY GRANT MCKENZIE

Switch
No Cry For Help
K.A.R.M.A.
Port of Sorrow
The Fear in Her Eyes
Speak the Dead

As M.C. Grant

Angel With a Bullet
Devil With a Gun
Beauty With a Bomb

For Karen and Kailey
Who have been on this journey
from the beginning

BOSTON, MASSACHUSETTS

JACK HAD LEARNED a thing or two about body language over the years, not that it took a professional to interpret his. His message was crystal: *Piss Off!*

When the two men entered the bar, Jack kept his head down and his gaze focused on the unexplored depths of his pint glass. For this part of town, everything about the men was wrong: too well dressed, too well fed, clean fingernails and teeth, fresh haircuts and… Jack paused in his observation, reevaluating. Their hands belonged: large in span for wrapping around a scrawny neck, calloused knuckles from beating on slabs of whimpering meat, and trigger fingers obediently trained to squeeze without mercy.

Down here, they stood out like a pair of one-legged nuns in a titty bar.

The bartender kept a sawed-off shotgun and two baseball bats behind the counter, which was one reason he was seldom robbed. The other reason was that even bums like Jack didn't soil where they drank. Everybody needed at least one place that allowed them to be, to sit alone on a barstool and drink the years away. The same couldn't be said for the junkies, however. In Jack's experience, they'd shit in their own mouths for a fix.

The bartender's name was the same as the establishment's,

McNally, and he stashed one bat at either end of the long bar so he didn't have to walk too far in order to keep the peace. Through habit and well-earned paranoia, Jack always positioned his stool close to the bat at the end of the bar furthest from the door.

The two strangers scanned the threadbare crowd before showing a photograph to the bartender. McNally shook his head, which was the same reaction he would give if you showed him a mirror.

Jack tensed as the men walked the length of the bar. The taller one was more aggressive than his partner. Full of musclebound confidence that came when one was used to everyone trembling in your wake, he spun the drinking men around on their stools, grasped their chins in his meaty paw and squeezed their bones while scrutinizing each face. His own mug wasn't anything to brag about: a boxer's nose, chipped granite eyes, and ears that could be used as paddles if he was ever dumped in a lake.

The shorter man was more observational. He was studying the reactions of those patrons his partner had yet to accost, watching for that telltale twitch of panic that would spark a merry chase. His face was more Cagney than Bogart, and definitely the more dangerous of the two.

Jack remained motionless except for his drinking arm. It ticktocked slowly from bar to mouth, the black stout beneath its milky head sliding down his throat with no concern for slacking thirst. After years on the run, there was nothing left in this world that could quench Jack's thirst — except perhaps a blade across his throat. Even then, Jack figured, he would arrive at Hades' Gate and ask what time the pubs opened.

When the two men arrived at his side, Jack was downing the dregs of his pint, allowing a final swallow of that unsullied foam to accompany the tenebrous liquid down his throat.

The taller ape grabbed Jack's chin and squeezed, bringing his face close. Jack opened his mouth to show yellowed teeth and exhale sour, sickly breath.

The man's eyes flickered in revolt, but before he could pull away, Jack grabbed the back of his neck and pulled him even closer, as though eager for a kiss. The man's eyes widened in surprise as Jack's mouth lunged forward, but instead of landing on the man's lips, Jack's teeth locked onto his bulbous nose and bit deep.

The man howled in agony as Jack savagely twisted his head to rip the nose from the hired goon's face. Hot blood gushed everywhere as Jack shoved the freshly disfigured man aside before spitting the bloody lump of flesh into his partner's face.

While the shorter man recoiled in horror, Jack reached behind the bar and plucked the baseball bat from its resting place. With his first swing, he broke the man's right arm, removing the threat of him reaching for his gun. On the backward swing, he clipped the side of the noseless man's skull, knocking him into the vacant bar stools and down to the floor. Keeping his momentum, Jack's next swing glanced off the shorter man's left shoulder and sunk into his lower jaw and neck.

The snap of bone was unmistakable and the man joined his partner on the floor, twitching like a marionette whose strings have been cut mid-dance.

"Leave the bat," yelled McNally from the other end of the bar, "and go out the back."

As the curtain of blood dropped from his eyes, Jack focused in on the bartender. McNally rested the shotgun casually in the crook of his arm.

"What do I owe you?" said Jack, placing the bat on the counter.

"On the house, since you didn't shoot the damn place up."

Jack nodded his appreciation. "I'm gonna miss this."

"Well, that's about the saddest t'ing I ever heard," said McNally. "This place is a shit hole."

"Yeah," agreed Jack. "But it was my favorite shit hole."

"You better get." McNally tilted his head in the direction of the front window. "There's two more coming."

"Damn."

Jack turned and made for the rear exit, pushing aside a few empty crates to break through the fire door and into a narrow alley that stunk of stale beer, piss, garbage, creosote and salt. He turned to his right, but a sudden flare of oncoming headlights made him change direction.

As he ran, his heart pounded in his chest and his tired lungs ached. If he had ever been young, he wasn't anymore. The years had been anything but kind — not that he would have known what to do if they had. He was the punchline, life the joke.

Jack heard a vehicle accelerating down the narrow alley as its headlights caught his fleeing shape, but if he could make it to the docks there was a chance of escape.

The sting of a bullet caught him before he even heard the sound. It entered his lower back and broke two ribs on its exit. Jack gasped and staggered, but kept running.

This is it, he told himself. *Christ, how long have I been running? And for what?*

Another bullet whizzed by Jack's head, so close it cut a groove in the helix of his ear, as the headlights of the pursuing vehicle grew ever brighter. A third bullet entered his thigh, barely missing the long bone, but chewing through muscle and flesh. Thrown off balance, Jack staggered into a doorway, his leg going numb. His pant leg was quickly soaked in blood, too much of it...must have nicked an artery.

He needed to...ah, who the hell was he kidding? This day had been hanging over him for most of his miserable life. *Face it, Jack, your luck's finally run out, and the only luck you ever did have was lousy to begin with.*

Jack freed a disposable cellphone from his pocket and hit the redial button for the only number it contained.

"I'm sorry," he said when the call was answered. "Deliver the package. Don't wait for me. I won't be coming."

Jack smashed the phone to the ground and shattered its plastic shell under his heel. After bending to retrieve the tiny SIM chip from the rubble, he placed it on his tongue and swallowed.

"OK," he told himself. "Let's fucking play."

Cocking both thumbs and pointing his index and middle fingers straight out, Jack had a fleeting memory of playing cops and robbers with his young son. His boy was always the cop, a sheriff to be exact because he liked to wear his straw cowboy hat, and Jack was the criminal. How many years ago was that? A lifetime or more.

Holding up his imaginary guns, Jack burst from the doorway and rushed headlong toward the approaching men.

He only made it a few steps before a hail of gunfire tore him apart.

PORTLAND, OREGON

IAN QUINN STOOD on the lip of the freshly dug grave and opened his clenched fist. Instead of dirt, a half dozen colorful toy bricks rolled off his fingers to tumble into the open wound. Each brick made a hollow, clicking sound like the tutting of an annoyed tongue as it bounced off the flimsy coffin lid before coming to rest in the dirt that would soon blanket the precious cargo inside.

"What the fuck is that?" yelled a man in an ill-fitting dark suit who was struggling to break free of his brother's grasp.

Both men had been beaten by the same genetic ugly stick that left its mark in severe acne scarring, receding hairline and teeth as crooked as their career plans. The older one, however, was smart enough to know that Ian wasn't the only outsider attending the burial. Two uniformed police officers stood on the fringe of the sparse crowd, watching for any opportunity of a parole-violating disturbance to send both brothers back to jail.

"Lego," said Ian without looking up. "Your son loved to play with Legos. I keep finding these bricks scattered in my car, under the seats, bottom of the cup holders, like a secret stash in case he ever found himself without his sack of bricks."

Ian lifted his gaze from the pauper's grave. His eyes were the color of tempered steel with just a hint of blue, the creases around them etched as deep as knife wounds. "Did you bury his bricks with him?"

"Fuck that," said the man.

"Yeah." Ian sighed with a weariness that made the words fall from his mouth with the weight of lead. "I guess those six will have to do."

"Pick them up," yelled the man. "My boy don't need no crap in his grave."

Ian's stare locked onto the delinquent father. Even from this distance he could smell the alcohol on the man's breath and the distinctive body odor of someone who sweated too much due to the poison he injected into his veins, rubbed into his gums, and inhaled deeply into his lungs.

"Do you know what your boy's favorite movie was?" Ian asked. "Or what comic book character he wanted to dress as for Halloween? Or what books he liked?"

Ian gritted his teeth and strode forward, closing the gap between them. "Did you know there was a ginger-haired girl at school he was developing a crush on? That she had a slight lisp, but her freckles were cool? Or that he was scoring high Bs in math?" Ian stopped on the edge of the man's personal boundary. "Do you even remember his fucking name?"

With a primal growl, the man broke free of his brother's grasp and charged. But Ian wasn't the same person he had been even a few short months ago. Recent events had changed him, ripped the curtain of civility and stoked a furnace that hardened his heart into a block of weeping iron.

The child protection officer who the father remembered had been easygoing, if not a touch broken from the tragedy of his own daughter and the failure of his marriage. That man had been willing to turn the other cheek in an effort to broker peace between feuding parents for the sake of the children who were his charge.

That man would have raised his hands in supplication to halt the charging bull — but that man was no more.

Instead of backing away, Ian kept his feet planted and swung his elbow hard into the man's face. The man's head snapped savagely to the side as his cheekbone cracked and two meth-rotted teeth flew from his mouth in a spew of blood. Dazed, the man staggered perilously close to the open grave before Ian kicked away his footing and shoved him back to his older brother.

The brother didn't budge as his dazed sibling bounced off his chest and crumpled at the feet of his ragtag posse of mourners.

Staring at Ian through eyes that would be more threatening if they weren't so glassy, the brother wiped a spatter of blood from his cheek. The two uniformed officers had perked up and were moving in to see what was happening.

"You should leave," said the brother from behind clenched teeth. "This is a family funeral, and you ain't family."

"This isn't a funeral," challenged Ian, anger bubbling from deep in his belly. "This is your twisted family burying the only decent one of you, a boy who was tortured and beaten to death because his father bargained his life over a lousy drug deal."

"You got no proof of that," said the brother. "And you ain't no fuckin' cop, neither. You're nothin' but a glorified babysitter, man. So unless you're stickin' round to suck my dick, it's time you fucked off and left us alone."

The two officers broke through the cordon just as the younger brother was hauled off the ground by his friends. The idiot's eyes were still spinning, and strings of bloody drool dripped from his bruised mouth.

"Is there a problem here?" one of the officers asked.

The older brother and Ian stared at each other in silent defiance before the brother spoke.

"No problem, officer," he said. "My brother was overcome wit' grief is all."

The female officer turned to Ian. She moved in close like cops did to smell your breath and study the clarity, or lack thereof, of your pupils.

"You should leave," she said. "Let them do their thing."

Ian turned away from the officer and glanced over to the opposite side of the grave where two young women stood. With arms linked for support, they both wore black. The sympathetic friend had tried to downplay it, but when the entirety of your self-esteem was rooted in the cat-calls of low men, she couldn't resist tarting herself up with a touch of peek-a-boo mesh at the bosom, a too-short and too-tight skirt with dark nylons in a spider web pattern, cherry lipstick and bruised plum eye shadow.

The other woman's plain, shapeless dress looked borrowed from a scarecrow, while colorless flesh made her appear as close to death as the son she was burying.

Ian had trouble meeting the fragile mother's gaze, and she did nothing to help him.

"We tol' you to leave," spat the father, his words slurred behind broken teeth and stiff jaw. "You ain't wanted."

The officer touched Ian's elbow. "I'd do what he says. You're not doing anyone any good here."

With one final look at the reinforced cardboard box, barely four feet in length, lying on the bottom of a soggy dirt hole, Ian swallowed his anger and walked away.

*

Leaving the broken circle of mourners behind, Ian headed for a large tree crowning the top of a small, green hillock in the center of the graveyard. From there, he knew he could find his bearings.

Chin down as he walked, Ian barely noticed the damp, gray drizzle portend the approaching storm drifting in from the west. His attention was lost on the way each blade of grass bent under his weight before springing back upright after he passed. Nature was resilient, humanity less so.

"Were you trying to get him to break parole or just being an asshole?" asked a familiar voice.

Ian lifted his chin to see Jersey Castle, a detective with Portland PD, and one of his few remaining friends, sitting on a memorial bench under the willow tree. A flowery yellow umbrella was resting by his side, but the tree's canopy offered enough protection from the light rain that he hadn't bothered to open it.

"Mostly the latter," said Ian.

"Good, because if you wanted him to break parole, you needed to let him throw the first punch."

Ian allowed himself a soft grin. "Noted."

Taking a seat on the bench, Ian removed a dimpled metal flask from inside his jacket and unscrewed the top. He offered it to Jersey, who declined, before pouring a healthy swallow down his throat. Knowing it would take little encouragement for him to drain the vessel, he screwed the cap back on and returned it to his pocket. Out of sight, but rarely out of mind.

"Nice umbrella," said Ian. "Didn't know yellow was your color."

"It's Sally's. She left it in the car."

"Sally? She the one who caved in your skull?"

The hair was growing back to cover an ugly scar that ran across the top of Jersey's scalp, a war wound from an out-of-town case that he was still keeping close to his chest. Combined with the unusual streak of pigment-free white that nature decided added a note of character to his dark hair, all Jersey needed were a few neck bolts to be mistaken for the Son of Frankenstein.

Naturally, Ian wouldn't tell him this; his friend was usually armed.

Jersey grinned at Ian's quip, giving away nothing. "You didn't get enough of being a jerk down there?"

Ian turned somber as he pointed a finger down the hill, resisting the urge to cock his thumb like when he was a kid, back when justice could be meted out with a simple *pew pew* and forgiveness came with the announcement of "Wash your hands. Supper's on the table."

"Noah Bowery was six and a half," said Ian. "He liked to mention the half. A bright kid with an unfortunate harelip that made him look tougher than he was, and the only thing he ever did wrong was being born to a waste of space for a father. The mother wasn't much better, but she was trying at least. After she entered detox, I supervised visitation for both of them."

"The kid's better off in that box," said Jersey, his voice cracking slightly. "The officer who found him is still on stress leave."

"Any chance of an arrest?"

"Doubtful unless someone talks, and once word got out about what was done to the boy, nobody will. Poor tyke's body wasn't just a message to the father — it was also an introduction to a new player in town."

"Organized?"

"Not in the way you mean. This is someone trying to muscle in. No connection that we know of to the founding fathers, bikers or the nouveau Russian and Chinese."

Ian watched the funeral crowd break apart and scatter. No doubt the brothers were planning to get shit-faced somewhere — everyone invited.

Raise a glass, pipe or needle to my boy. His life was cut short, but fuck it, that's depressing. Let's party!

The boy's mother and her friend were the last to leave, although even from this distance it was easy to tell the friend was getting antsy. This was a difficult test of loyalty for her; she really wanted to join the party.

"The bastard used his kid as collateral," said Ian.

"And then he fucked up," added Jersey. "But we got nothing on him."

"That you can prove."

"Nothing that will stick, but assholes like him and his brother never get a happy ending. Let the law do its job and he'll be back inside before long."

"That sounds like a warning," said Ian.

Jersey offered a wry smile. "Just friendly advice."

Getting to his feet, Jersey grabbed his umbrella and popped it open. The cheery color seemed even more garish in the gloom of the empty graveyard.

"Feel like a burger?" Jersey asked. "I'm starving."

"Thanks, but Emily's just over there." Ian indicated a small copse of cherry trees on the other side of the hill. "She'd want me to visit."

"Want company?"

Ian smiled in gratitude. "No, you're OK. I prefer to be alone."

"No problem, but I've got a gig tonight if you feel like taking out some of that aggression in the mosh pit."

Jersey moonlighted as the drummer in a local punk band called The Rotten Johnnys. And although Ian stopped playing after his daughter's death, he had once been an accomplished jazz guitarist. The two men first met at an after-hours gin joint where Jersey went to unwind after his own gigs, and where Ian used to play. Still dressed in his punk leathers and chains, the heavyset man with the streak of white running through his hair had stuck out like a bad note. Intrigued, Ian introduced himself and through a mutual love of music, the two quickly became fast friends.

"You're still playing?" asked Ian. "Your new woman hasn't reined you in yet?"

"She'll have to pry the sticks from my cold, dead hands, which, if you knew Sally, is a whole other tale."

Ian laughed. "I'll need to meet her. Enjoy your burger."

Jersey patted his stomach. "Always do."

*

Emily's grave was well tended with fresh mown grass, while a glass jar filled with day-old flowers told Jersey that her mother, Helena, must have visited recently.

Emily was only six years old — the same age as the boy who now joined her in the ground — when she was killed outside her school. She was running across the road at the time, excited to see her father. Ian had watched it happen, had cradled her in his arms as the light left her eyes, and struggled to breathe when her tiny, broken chest went still.

He had never forgiven himself, and neither had his wife.

Ian crouched in front of the simple headstone, the dates carved on its face so close together it seemed like a mistake.

"Hey, Thumbelina, it's Dad." Ian paused, allowing the quiver in his voice to settle. "There's a new kid coming to visit, and he's likely to be scared — although he won't admit to it. His name is Noah. He can be a little tough to handle at first, but he's got such a big heart. I know you must have the most wonderful playgrounds there. If you could show him around, introduce him to the other kids, and find him some Lego. He loves building things and I can only imagine what amazing buckets of the stuff you have up there."

Ian reached out to rest his hand on the headstone. The granite was wet and cold.

"I love you, baby girl, and miss you so much. Be good for your grandma, and I'll visit again soon."

With creaking knees, Ian stood and wiped rain from his face.

He had walked just about every inch of these grounds since the time he was eight. It was where the Quinn family buried most of its secrets.

The first funeral he remembered attending was his grandfather's.

Augustus Quinn was a formidable and short-fused man with hands the size of ham steaks and knuckles made of gnarled pig bones. According to family legend, he could make even the bent-nosed dockworkers tremble when they stumbled from one column of his butcher shop ledger to the other. And yet a rip thinner than a hair had breached a blood vessel in his brain and brought the giant to his knees.

It wasn't the burial that marked Ian's memory of that day, however. Rather, it was what happened after, the way his father casually patted his shirt pocket when they climbed out of the station wagon at home and so easily said to his wife, "Nipping to the corner shop, love. Need a smoke in the worst way."

That was the last memory Ian had of his father. It was also the second time in his short life that someone he loved had vanished without saying goodbye.

3

WALKING BACK, IAN noted a tall man standing on top of the hillock where he and Jersey had stood not long before. The man's face was hidden in the shadow of a long barreled, black umbrella — the sturdy kind with a polished wood handle and a chrome spike at its tip to double as a walking stick.

Although he couldn't be sure, the man appeared to be studying Ian's progress through the graveyard.

Ignoring the stranger, Ian plodded across damp grass to the gravel path and onward to the parking lot. There were only two vehicles left in the lot, and Ian wouldn't have minded if his had been the one he didn't have keys to.

The immaculate black Range Rover, waxed to a mirror finish that had the rain dancing upon its hood, made his ride look even more tragic than it was.

Ian unlocked the driver's door of his used, fifteen-year-old Dodge minivan — one part of the fleet that flooded the used car market when the Boomers' kids took off for college and allowed their parents to buy the sporty vehicles they really wanted. On the upside, it had decent rubber left on the tires and, more importantly, it had been cheap.

Inside, Ian shook the rain out of his hair and switched on the van's heater. It took a few minutes for the engine to warm, but soon he was able to unbutton his coat and watch his hands turn from blue to pink.

Outside, the rain fell heavier, each droplet crashing onto the van's flat roof and filling the hollow cabin with a cacophony of sound. He hoped the grounds attendants were busy filling in Noah's grave as that cheap cardboard coffin would already be in danger of disintegrating.

Wondering if he should run back and check, pick up a spade and help, Ian was stopped by the unexpected presence of a small gift bag sitting on the passenger seat.

It hadn't been there when he parked.

The compact paper bag was a classy matte black, like you might receive at a high-end jewelry or lingerie store, except it was absent any ubiquitous store branding. The charcoal twine handles were tied together at their apex with a thin black ribbon. Someone had taken special care with the ribbon; tied in a bow, its loops were two perfect ovals of equal size.

Disturbed, Ian rolled down his window and turned on the van's wipers to better study the surrounding area. Apart from the tall man standing under an umbrella on the hill, a few thousand decaying corpses in the ground, and the parked vehicle beside him, the place was deserted.

Reaching over to wipe a film of fog from the passenger window, Ian studied the Range Rover. Its front seats were unoccupied, but the rear seats were hidden from view, shielded behind tinted glass.

Ian wondered about the two brothers who had just buried Noah, but if they were going to leave a gift it would be in the form of a flaming paper lunch bag with fresh dog shit inside — not this.

The lock on the passenger door was still engaged, but that didn't mean much, not in this vehicle.

After rolling his window up again, but leaving a small gap at the top for air circulation to help the other windows stay clear, Ian placed the bag on his lap, unpuckered the top and peered in. A small, square box in matching matte black waited inside.

Ian looked around once more, even checking over his shoulder to make sure nobody had snuck in the sliding door and was waiting to pounce from one of the rows of empty benches behind him, before untying the ribbon and removing the box.

It weighed practically nothing. Ian shook it gently, but there was no rattle.

Holding his breath, Ian removed the lid.

At first he didn't recognize what it was: an oddly shaped gray lump lying on a fluffy cloud of cotton wool. But then he saw the cotton wasn't all white; a crust of red hid beneath the gray object. Turning the box around in his hands, the lump shifted in his mind's eyes before falling into the slot of something recognizable.

Ian swallowed sour bile, feeling it burn his throat.

It was an ear, a human ear.

Whoever wore it last hadn't been too careful. Not only was the gray flesh streaked with a film of what looked like nicotine and soot, but a fresh groove had been cut in its upper ridge, exposing the brighter, virginal cartilage inside. Apart from the distinctive groove, however, it had no other identifiable marks: no earring or piercings.

Whatever the message was meant to be, Ian had no clue as to who had sent it or what it signified.

Without touching the ear, Ian placed the lid back on the box and returned it to the bag.

He glanced out the windshield again, but the only change was the man on the hill. He was no longer there.

*

Ian pulled out his cellphone and selected a number from his short list of favorites. When the call was answered, he asked, "How's your burger?"

Jersey laughed. "Awesome. Just the way I like it. Pink in the middle, crispy on the edges, and real cheddar melted on top. Sally says we should only eat white cheddar, it's more natural, but there's something about the orange stuff. I don't know; it just goes better with a burger."

"You're making me salivate."

Jersey chuckled. "And I didn't even get to the onions. These guys know how to fry onions. I think they may be using bacon grease."

"Where did you go?"

Jersey told him.

"I can be there in ten. Mind sticking around?"

"Sure, what's up?"

"Something I need you to take a look at."

"Okay."

"Will you be finished eating when I get there?"

"Yep."

"Good."

"That doesn't sound promising."

"See you in ten."

Ian disconnected and opened his door. Stepping into the rain, he turned up the collar on his jacket and walked around the van to the Range Rover. Pressing his face against the side windows, he peered through the tint. The two rear seats were as empty as the front, but installed directly behind their headrests, a steel cage protected the cargo area.

Moving around to the back, Ian peered through the rear window. The privacy tint made it too dark inside to see much except for several large shapes that could be anything from groceries to camping gear. He felt around for the tailgate handle hidden beneath the glass, but the vehicle was locked up tight.

When he raised his gaze again to the glass, Ian's heart jumped into his throat. Two Doberman Pinchers were staring at him from inside the cage. Both dogs were completely silent, their sharp ears at rapt attention and their dark, unblinking eyes focused completely on him.

"Sorry, boys," said Ian as he backed away. "Just curious."

Neither dog responded.

Ian wasn't a fan of large dogs; he had met too many ill-treated ones to truly trust they wouldn't suddenly turn from family pet to child killer. Then again, he had also known a family whose pet ferrets were responsible for the gruesome mutilation of their one-month-old daughter.

Domestication didn't always keep the wild beast at bay.

*

Arriving at the burger joint, Ian grabbed his disturbing package and headed inside. He found Jersey sitting at a red vinyl booth for four, sipping on a chocolate milkshake.

"A gift," said Jersey upon spotting the bag.

"It's not what you think."

"That's good, 'cause I'm thinking lingerie."

Ian squeezed into the booth facing his friend, and slid over the bag. When the waitress approached, he waved her away.

"Not hungry?" asked Jersey.

"You're lucky you ate already."

Jersey eyed the package with more suspicion now.

"Who gave this to you?" he asked.

"It was sitting on my passenger seat after the funeral."

"No tag on the bag. Was there a card?"

"Nope. Just the box inside."

"You opened it?"

Ian nodded.

"Looks too neat for the Bowery brothers."

"Agreed."

Jersey called back the waitress and asked if she had a spare pair of disposable acrylic gloves.

"We sure do," she answered with a smile, not put off at all by the unusual request. "But I must warn you that they can be a titch on the chewy side." The young woman laughed at her own joke. "Let me grab you a pair."

After the waitress returned, Jersey pulled on the thin gloves and opened the bag to retrieve the box. Moving the bag to one side, he placed the box on the table and lifted the lid. Staring at the object inside, he tilted his head slightly until its shape made sense.

"Any idea who it belonged to?" he asked finally, his voice filled more with curiosity than disturbance.

"None, but it's an odd message, don't you think? What's it supposed to symbolize? If I'm meant to listen to something, shouldn't they have included a cassette or a CD?"

"Maybe you pissed off an artist like Van Gogh. He cut off his own ear, right?"

"Historians are still debating that one. Some believe he lost it in a drunken knife fight with Toulouse-Lautrec. Over a woman, naturally."

Jersey smirked. "I like that story better."

"But the only artists I deal with are usually still at the finger-painting stage."

Carefully, Jersey lifted the ear between two fingers and turned it around to see the back. There were four numbers crudely tattooed in blue ink. The tattoo was faded, but still legible: it read 1976.

"That number mean anything to you?"

Ian thought about it for a moment before answering. "That was the year my sister went missing."

"Missing? I never knew you had a sister."

"I barely remember her. Her name was Abbie. She was twelve. I was only about six at the time, so I didn't know any of the details.

My parents never talked about it, at least not in front of me. She was just gone. Then my father took off a year later. Oldest cliché in the book, said he was going out to buy cigarettes and never came back."

"Do you think there was a connection?"

Ian shrugged. "When I think about how Helena and I ripped our marriage apart after losing Emily, I suppose the same thing probably happened to my parents when Abbie disappeared. They argued a lot, I remember that. My mother would rant and scream, and my dad would punch a wall and storm off to the bar. For a kid hiding under the bed covers and reading comic books by flashlight, it was…terrifying."

"Maybe that's what made you start Children First? To protect that frightened boy hiding under the covers."

Ian smirked at the psychological hypothesis. "Could be."

"Did your sister wear earrings?"

Ian closed his eyes, struggling to find a memory, but failing. "I don't remember."

"This earlobe has never been pierced," said Jersey. "My guess is male. The tattoo is crude. Could have been inked in a prison or military unit, somewhere men get easily bored and masturbation has become mundane." He turned it back over and studied the groove cutting through the flesh. "This looks fairly new. The wound is clean, but see how the edges are pointing in a uniform direction." He turned the ear to expose its profile. "Entry from the rear with a slight incline before exiting. Could have been made by a bullet, something moving hot and fast. A fraction more to the left and the top of the ear is gone; another fraction and the bullet is burrowing through skull."

"But what does it mean?"

Jersey shrugged. "Your guess is as good as mine. Let me hold on to it. I'll get it checked for prints and run DNA, then see if we have a match in the database."

Ian chewed on his thumbnail, lost in thought.

"Something wrong?" asked Jersey.

"It's just such a weird message. A nose, I could understand maybe: *keep your nose out of our business*. Or an eye for an eye, but an ear?" Ian paused, and grimaced. "Sorry, that was off-track. But can we go to a private DNA lab on this? I know your labs are always swamped, and I'd prefer to get the results back as soon as possible. I'll pay the fee."

"Not a problem. I know just the firm. And in the meantime, I'll send out a few feelers, see if anyone has shown up in hospital or the morgue absent an ear."

"Smart," said Ian.

"That's why I have a badge and you've got a business card."

Ignoring the jab, Ian asked, "You planning to finish that shake?"

Jersey grinned, plucked out his straw for one last messy slurp, and slid the drink over. Ian had a fresh straw unwrapped and ready to go before the fountain glass came to a rest.

4

DRIVING HOME, IAN checked in with Children First, the organization he not only worked for, but was co-owner, albeit a quiet one. The woman who ran the child protection service, Linda McCabe, was far more capable at dealing with all the government regulation red tape than Ian ever could be.

As a silent partner, Ian was able to concentrate on what he enjoyed most: his clients, the children.

Jeannie McCabe, his boss's oldest daughter, answered the call in a chirpy tone. It was good to hear the reawakening of delight in her voice. Jeannie had been absent for over three months, volunteering overseas in an elephant sanctuary, struggling to come to terms with a terrifying ordeal that fell firmly at Ian's feet.

Absently, Ian rubbed the scars on his stomach that had cost him a foot of intestine.

"Hey, Jeannie." Ian forced his voice to sound bright. "Just checking in."

"How did Noah's funeral go?" she asked.

Ian winced, not wanting to share the whole truth. "I left him some Lego. You know how much he loved it."

"He did." Jeannie laughed. "He knew all the characters' names from those movies, too. When he was in here waiting for you, he would test me to make sure I wasn't just pretending to like them. Did his parents place his Brickowski backpack in the coffin?"

"It was a closed coffin, but..." Ian decided to lie. "I'm sure they did."

"Good. I can't imagine him going anywhere without it."

"I was planning to head home unless anything's come up that needs my attention."

"Nothing urgent. Molly called in to say if you didn't want to go tomorrow that was okay with her. I assured her that you would be there. You also have that meeting with a new family in the morning. Judge Rothstein recommended you personally, so I have a feeling it's a tense situation."

"I've got them in my calendar."

"You also received calls from two different law firms. Both said it was important that you call them ASAP. I gave them your cell number."

Ian glanced at his cell. The phone icon showed he had 4 new voicemails.

"I had it on silent, but thanks, I'll get back to them."

"Is everything okay?"

"Yeah, fine. It's probably just more divorce BS."

Jeannie giggled and then quickly apologized. "Sorry, I wasn't laughing at your divorce. It's just, I was reading something the other night, and do you know where BS comes from?"

"Bulls?"

"Yes, but...the term actually comes from the Latin *Bulbus Stercum* which refers to 'anything said by a politician.'"

Ian laughed, knowing Jeannie didn't have a mean bone in her body.

"They were thinking too small," he said.

*

The neighborhood where Ian and Helena raised their daughter

contained everything a young family needed: walking distance to good schools, a nearby playground, duck pond and park, plus friendly competition to see who kept the most pristine lawn. Everyone had a fenced back yard, a cedar deck off the kitchen, and a gleaming gas barbecue. Once a year, the Good Neighbor Social Committee even threw a potluck block party. Bring store-bought potato salad at your own peril.

Pulling into the driveway, its dimpled concrete surface marred by an oil stain left behind from his previous vehicle, Ian noticed the *For Sale* sign had been resurrected and re-planted on his front lawn. Whoever had been charged with the task had added four tensile-steel cables for extra support just in case its earlier removal had been caused by a rogue tornado rather than a Scotch-fueled pity party.

"Well, I guess that's one voicemail I don't need to listen to," Ian muttered to himself as he climbed out of the van.

The neighbors, at least, would be happy to see the realtor's sign back in place. Its presence offered the opportunity for a whole and happy family to move in, thus restoring balance to the cul-de-sac.

Though they wouldn't say it to his face, Ian's continued presence scared them. His neighbors needed to forget Emily's death almost as much as he never could. No parents wanted to have a constant reminder looming over them of *What If. What if it had been my child? Would my marriage survive? Would I?*

Too much internal rumination can widen the cracks that lie beneath the surface of every relationship. Plus, even though they all knew what Ian did for a living, no family neighborhood wanted a single man living alone in a large, empty house.

Ian was stopped at the front door by a manila envelope taped to the glass. The envelope was stamped both *Urgent* and *Confidential* in red ink.

With a sigh, Ian tucked the envelope under his arm and

unlocked the door. Inside, he kicked off his shoes, hung up his damp coat, and headed for the kitchen.

The three-bedroom, two-story house was as empty on the inside as it appeared from the outside. Helena had bought most of the furnishings, knickknacks and assorted ornamentation that turned a house into a home, but she had taken virtually everything with her when she left.

Ian's only inherent possessions were an old rocking chair that had belonged to his grandfather — though why he kept it he wasn't sure — a box of favorite LPs, and his Gibson acoustic guitar. He didn't even own a turntable on which to play the records, although with vinyl's unexpected resurgence in popularity he had been thinking of buying one.

Sitting at the small bar table where a family-sized one had once filled the space more eloquently, Ian opened the envelope. Inside was an Order of Eviction written in Lawyerish, a language so overwrought and dense that dollar signs dripped off every letter; commas cost an additional five dollars per, while semicolons and bullet points could run twenty-five dollars each. This letter contained a lot of semicolons, but as a lawyer herself, his wife was able to purchase them in bulk.

After translation, the meat of the four-page letter could be summed up in two words: *Get Out.*

Although Ian's name was on the title, the house had been an overly generous, albeit emasculating, wedding present from Helena's parents, and Ian was no longer someone for whom they needed to hide their disdain.

Putting the phone on speaker, Ian rummaged through his food cupboard while the missed voicemails played.

The first message was Helena's lawyer, informing Ian of the letter that was taped to his door. In addition, the lawyer told him in a perfectly civil tone if he was to leave by his own volition and sign away his rights to the house, his client was prepared to offer him a generous and immediate one-time settlement fee of half its current value.

Ian found a can of baked beans, which he opened and dumped into a pot on low heat.

The second message was from Helena.

"So sorry about the eviction, Ian. Father really wants to get rid of the house. He says your presence is making it too depressing for buyers. You should take the deal and get yourself an apartment or a condo somewhere. It can't be easy for you living there. Emily would want you to be happy. Please think about it."

In the back of the freezer, Ian discovered a plastic bag containing the curled remains of two slices of bread. Carefully, so they didn't crumble in his hands, he removed each shock-white slice from its transparent shroud and popped them both in the toaster.

The third message was from a woman representing a law firm he had never dealt with before. Her voice put him in mind of silk cloth wrapped around a razor blade.

"This message is for Mr. Ian Quinn, no middle name or initial recorded. If you could please return this call at your earliest convenience, it's concerning a matter of some importance."

When Ian's toast popped, he laid both slices on a plate and spooned the warm baked beans on top. Normally, he would have buttered the toast first, but he used the last of it a few weeks earlier and had yet to get around to shopping for more.

The final message was from the same woman as before.

"Mr. Quinn. Sorry to be so persistent, but could you please call me as soon as you get this? The matter concerns your father."

Ian froze mid-spoon to stare at the phone in confusion, unsure if he had heard the message correctly.

His father?

Ian didn't have a father. As he told Jersey earlier, he hadn't had one in his life for more than thirty years. His father wasn't there when Ian bought his first car — a complete, oil-burning clunker that barely lasted three months before the engine seized; he wasn't there when Ian graduated high school or when he struggled to find a career that provided more than a paycheck; he wasn't there when Ian fell in love, or when he got married; he wasn't there when Ian, alone, buried his mother; and he wasn't there when Emily came into this world, nor when she left it.

The lawyer had made a mistake.

His father was dead. Ian buried him a long, long time ago.

*

"Quit fidgeting back there," yelled his father, the stress of the day making him tug at his eyebrow with manic determination, the bald spot above his right eye more apparent with every pluck and twitch.

Sitting in the backseat, Ian struggled with the collar of his new shirt, the knot of his tie so tight that it was difficult to breathe. He didn't know why he had to wear a shirt and tie to the funeral, his grandfather never would.

The only uniform his grandfather wore consisted of baggy brown pants of some indestructible material, a white T-shirt that always looked stained even if he had just pulled it fresh from the laundry, leather boots with the toes worn down so far that steel caps glistened through ragged holes, and his apron. The apron was made of durable brown leather and reached from his shoulders to just below his knees.

Ian was fascinated with the apron. The thick leather was stained by the slabs of meat his grandfather manhandled, its dense grain scratched by a thousand cuts from the knives he wielded like an Irish Samurai. Although Ian rarely saw his grandfather without it, he had once spotted the apron hanging from a hook in the back room of the butcher's shop. In the dim light, it looked fiercely alive.

Despite his fear, Ian's curiosity was greater. He approached the apron and attempted to lift it from its hook. He wanted to prove to himself that it was only a piece of clothing and not the magical creature the other kids whispered about, a demon skinned by his grandfather and worn for protection, an evil spirit that needed to be fed the souls of young women to remain loyal. They had seen those women enter the store, never to walk out again.

The apron's weight was far greater than Ian imagined.

Grunting with exertion, Ian used his legs to hoist the stiff apron skyward. For a moment, everything was okay. The apron had slid off the hook and he held its full weight in his arms, the weight making his muscles tremble, but he was happy. He had accomplished something great, something the other kids would have been too terrified to try. When his grandfather returned, he would be so proud to see—

Ian's legs suddenly buckled under the weight and he fell to the floor with the apron crashing down on top of him. Beneath the foul-smelling leather, the seven-year-old panicked and his imagination took over from reason.

He could feel the apron trying to devour him; to absorb his flesh unto itself; to drain his blood and—

His grandfather had pulled the garment off him with one hand and stared down at the terrified boy.

"How many bloody times?" his grandfather had yelled. "What I do here is man's work. You are not yet a man and if you keep mucking around like this, you'll never be."

At the funeral, strangers said nice things about his grandfather. Some even pinched his cheeks and told him how lucky he was to have such an important influence in his life.

It was in that moment when Ian truly came to the realization that adults told lies. He had suspicions before, but the funeral cemented it. He didn't have a single memory of his grandfather being anything but a mean old bastard with a fiery temper that could rattle the very bricks out of their mortar.

Nobody would ever dare tell his grandfather to quit fidgeting over a starched shirt collar that was trying to strangle him to death.

"I don't like funerals," said Ian. "They're stupid."

"Nobody likes funerals," answered his father. "But they're important."

"Why?"

"They're a way to show respect."

"But why? Grandpa isn't there."

"Your grandpa's watching."

"From where?"

"Heaven, of course."

"Grandpa doesn't believe in Heaven. He told me. He said he'd rather be cut into steaks and sausage meat when he died than be sitting on a cloud with a harp. He also said a bad word before the harp."

Ian's father chuckled. It was the only break his sour mood had seen for the whole day. "Maybe so."

"Is Abbie in Heaven?" Ian asked.

His father's sour mood returned, and Ian's mother turned away from her husband to stare out the window.

"Is she?" Ian pressed.

"Goddammit, boy, I'm driving. Give it a rest."

"I was just asking because if she is in Heaven, then—"

"Enough!" his father yelled.

Ian jumped in his seat at the forcefulness of his father's voice. Tears were building behind his eyes, but he refused to let them fall. He had lifted the butcher's apron. He was stronger than anyone gave him credit for.

*

Giving himself time to think, Ian finished his beans on toast before picking up the phone and calling Helena.

His estranged wife answered the call on the second ring.

"Ian," she said. "I hope you're not angry."

"No, it's fine. You're right. It's time I moved on. The neighbors can barely stand to look at me now, never mind invite me over for a barbecue. I heard Lloyd built a hi-tech man cave in his garage, big-screen projector system, surround sound, mini bar, the works. Dave across the street had to practically sneak over there last week to watch the ball game. He kept throwing furtive glances at the house as he skirted by to make sure I didn't see him."

"That's horrible."

"No, it's just life. Nobody wants to party with the dad whose daughter was killed. It's a downer."

"If you need help moving—"

Ian chuckled. "Thanks, but everything will fit in my van."

"Oh, I wasn't suggesting that I would help. I just meant for you to call a mover."

Ian laughed louder as Helena joined in.

"Send the papers over to the office and I'll get them signed."

"Will do. And, Ian? Thanks for not making this difficult."

"I figure I've done enough of that already. How's your father?"

"He's spending more time at the gun club than the golf range these days."

"Ah. Noted. So I take it you're not dating much, then?"

Helena's laugh was like dew — both delicate and magical.

"One other thing," Ian added. "Have you heard of the law firm Ragano and Associates?"

"Sure, real old school firm. Roberto Ragano is the founder, a tough lawyer who handled a lot of the top crime cases back in the day. His granddaughter, Rossella, handles most of the work these days. Why?"

"Nothing, really," Ian lied. "Just received a call from them about a work thing, but I've never dealt with them before."

"From what I hear around the office, the granddaughter is

quite striking, but she has very sharp teeth and likes to eat her prey whole and alive."

"So just a regular lawyer, then?"

"Ha-ha," said Helena dryly.

Ian was still smirking when he hung up.

*

After plugging in the kettle, a post-dinner ritual that had become reflex rather than conscious thought after a decade living with a woman who quenched her craving for chocolate with meditative green tea, Ian thumbed through his phone until the list of recent calls appeared.

He tapped the number from Ragano & Associates, and listened to it ring. To his surprise, instead of an answering machine, the call was answered by the same woman who had left the message.

"Ragano and Associates."

"Uh, yeah, this is Ian Quinn. You left a message for me."

"Mr. Quinn, thank you for returning my call."

"You piqued my curiosity."

"How so?"

"You mentioned my father. I don't have one."

"But you did, at one time."

"Thirty years ago."

"His name was Jack Quinn, no middle name or initial?"

"It was."

"Can we meet?"

"When?"

"I was just going to grab something to eat. We could meet in my office in half an hour?"

Ian hesitated, the strain of the day pulling him more toward a glass of single malt and reading a few chapters of a novel he was enjoying, but curiosity won out again.

He asked for the address.

5

THE OFFICES OF Ragano & Associates were housed inside a heritage building in downtown Portland. In terms of sheer mileage, the building was a short trip from Ian's office at Children First, but it was a much longer distance when it came to prestige. Ian's Old Town office sat on the less desirable side of the street.

From the outside, the three-story building maintained its turn-of-the-century elegance with Victorian moldings and lead-paned windows; everything restored and repainted in heritage colors. The front door was formidable, made from inch-thick panes of hand poured glass, the circular flaws within each panel giving it both unique character and added distortion for privacy, set within a solid frame of painted hardwood.

Ian pushed through the heavy door and entered a short lobby. A directory on the wall informed him the law office he sought was on the second floor. Ian climbed the stairs and located the office, its frosted glass door adorned with a hand-painted sign.

Since he was expected, Ian tried the handle and found the door unlocked.

When he entered, an attractive woman with solar-eclipse hair looked up from behind her desk in surprise. Her eyes were large and bright and a startling robin egg blue...they were also smiling.

The reason for the smile was, perhaps, the juicy meatball sandwich clutched in her hands and the smears of crimson marinara sauce dripping from the edges of her mouth.

Ian had caught her mid-bite.

The woman released one hand from her sandwich and held it up in apologetic greeting while she quickly chewed the large mouthful that engorged her cheeks.

Smiling in return, Ian closed the door behind him before taking a seat by the woman's desk. It took her a minute to finish chewing what was in her mouth as it had been a privacy bite — the kind you only take when you are comfortable and alone.

Ian enjoyed watching her eat. When she saw that he didn't appear to be judging, her panicked chewing slowed down and returned to savoring the sandwich.

Beside her on the desk was a half-full plastic cup of red wine with a lipstick smudge on the rim. She wasn't quite as young as she had sounded on the phone, closer to forty than thirty, but as Helena had intimated, she was definitely striking. Olive skinned with sharp cheekbones and a proud nose, she could have given a young Sophia Loren a run for her money.

While the woman lifted her plastic cup of wine to her lips, Ian took in the surroundings. Along with the usual law school certificates, Harvard no less, the walls were also decorated with framed newspaper articles about Roberto Ragano — founder of the firm and, judging by a resemblance to the companion by his side in some of the earlier photographs, this woman's grandfather.

Several black-and-white photographs showed Roberto with such celebrities as Frank Sinatra, Dean Martin, Jerry Lewis and Jimmy "The Schnoz" Durante; others Ian recognized as notorious mobsters Carlo "Don Carlo" Gambino and John "The Teflon Don" Gotti. The color photos showed four presidents: Ronald Reagan, George Bush, Bill Clinton and George W. Bush. Not one of the photos showed Roberto smiling. The effect was that it made him the focus, as though each of these famous men were the ones who had asked to pose with him.

The woman put down her wine and wiped at her mouth and hands with a paper napkin. She reached out her right hand, as bare and unadorned as her left.

"Mr. Quinn? My name is Rossella Ragano."

Ian took her hand in his and squeezed it lightly. It was warm, slightly sticky and surprisingly soft. He had an urge to touch it to his lips, but resisted the notion as more creepy than gentlemanly.

"That looks like one hell of a good sandwich," he said.

Rossella laughed, her eyes and lips in perfect simpatico. "It is. Want a piece?"

"Normally, I would decline just to be polite, but the look on your face as you're eating actually makes me envious. I would love a bite."

Rossella laughed louder and with genuine mirth. She opened her desk drawer to pull out a small switchblade. Pressing a button on the handle, a four-inch blade shot out with a powerful, spring-loaded click.

Grabbing a spare napkin, Rossella cut a large chunk off the end of the sandwich and passed it over.

"Wine?" she asked.

"Only if it's a screw-top. I'd hate for you to get the idea that I'm an expensive date."

With a coy smirk, Rossella grabbed a fresh plastic cup from beside the water cooler and filled it with red wine from a bottle hidden out of sight.

"This is nice," she said, taking another but much smaller bite of sandwich. "I normally eat alone."

"I find that hard to believe."

"Well, it's true. Sadly."

"Are all your suitors turned off by your eating habits?"

Rossella's eyes went large as she almost choked on the food in her mouth by trying to chew and laugh at the same time.

"That was cruel," she said after swallowing.

Ian smirked. "True." He indicated the side of her mouth. "You've got sauce."

Rossella wiped the sauce away with her napkin and took another sip of wine.

"You know what the best way to eat a sandwich like this would be?" Rossella answered her own question before Ian could respond. "Naked in a bathtub. Then you could really get messy."

Ian laughed loudly, choking slightly on his own bite of sandwich while trying not to picture the scene in his head. It was an impossible task.

"Now that was cruel," he said.

Rossella's pink tongue skipped across her lips in a gesture of playfulness.

"So tell me about yourself, Mr. Ian Quinn, no middle initial."

Ian sipped his wine, enjoying both the meal and the company. He normally ate alone, too. "Not much to tell. I'm a child protection officer with Children First, a private company that has an official mandate through the state government to supervise court-ordered visitation rights between feuding parents and the poor kids stuck in the middle."

"I know of it. Married?"

"Divorced, but it's amicable."

"Kids?"

"I had a daughter. She died."

"I'm sorry."

"Me, too."

"So you protect other children now?"

"I try to."

"That's noble."

Ian shrugged. "Some days are easier than others."

"Hobbies?"

"I play a little jazz guitar. Used to be pretty good."

"What happened?"

"I stopped playing after Emily's death. Emily is my daughter."

"Did she like to hear you play?"

Ian smiled in remembrance. "She did."

"Then you should start again. She would like that."

Ian sipped his wine, but didn't answer. Instead he looked over at the framed photographs and changed topics.

"Your grandfather knew some interesting people."

"People of influence," said Rossella. "Nonno is always teaching me that influence is the grease of civilization. Make friends on every side of a battlefield and your own chances of success are guaranteed. I'm not sure if that's necessarily true, but it certainly worked for him."

"Where is he now?"

The light in Rossella's eyes dimmed a little. "He stays at home. I have a full-time nurse looking after him. Alzheimer's."

"Sorry, that's a difficult illness for everyone involved."

"It is."

They both sipped their wine and nibbled on the sandwich for a few minutes before Ian broke the silence with a contented sigh.

"This might sound odd," he said, "but I'm enjoying this. Watching you eat."

"Watching me eat?"

"You do it with such gusto."

"I'm Italian, we do everything with gusto."

They both laughed.

"And," Rossella continued, "if you think watching me eat a

sandwich is fun, you should take me out for spaghetti one night —
that is a real treat. You need to hose me down after."

"I'd enjoy that."

This time the silence was a touch more awkward until Rossella
crumpled the sandwich's waxed paper wrapping into a ball and sent
it sailing toward a wire wastebasket nestled a short distance away.
Swish — didn't even touch the sides. Ian tried to do the same with his
napkin, but it failed to make the distance.

"More wine?" asked Rossella, stopping him from rising to help
the fallen comrade, showing him she didn't mind a little mess.

"Please."

With their cups freshly filled, Rossella retrieved a file folder from
a nearby cabinet and laid it on the desk in front of her. Ian glanced at
the folder, but the blank cover gave away nothing about its contents.

"Jack Quinn was a client of my grandfather's," Rossella began.
"This file dates back to 1978."

"That's the year he walked out on us."

"Yesterday, a letter arrived from Boston with instructions to contact you and hand over the contents of this file."

"A letter? Was it from—" Ian didn't finish the sentence. He
couldn't. The very idea that for all these years his father might have
been living another life on the other side of the country turned the
wine to vinegar in his mouth.

"The letter used a code word for verification," explained Rossella.
"That code word had been established with our firm when the file
was opened. I'm afraid the protocol put in place at that time was
only to be used upon the death of our client."

Ian sucked in his breath. "He's dead?"

"I'm afraid so."

"But he died recently? Not thirty years ago?"

"It appears that way. I'm sorry."

Ian went limp, his body melting into the chair's backrest in search of support, and buried his face in his hands. After all this time, all those years of wondering, of burying the bastard's existence over and over, and yet never being able to quite say a final goodbye. And now this. A random letter out of the blue announcing that Jack Quinn was dead.

His father was dead.

His Da.

Ian wiped at his eyes, cursing himself for the emotions that flooded through him. The abandoned son inside this adult shell was being torn in half, and although Ian desperately wanted to yell at the boy not to feel, he knew he would never do that to any other child under his care. And like it or not, this boy needed to grieve as much as anyone.

"Are you okay?" Rossella asked. She had moved around the desk and placed a hand on his shoulder. Her touch was light, her fingers gently probing the rigid muscle.

When Ian dropped his hands from his face, he was eye level with her generous bosom. A tiny splotch of red sauce was staining her silk blouse, enticing him to lean forward, pull the fabric into his mouth and suck.

"I'm fine," he said, clearing the emotion from his throat and lifting his gaze away from her chest, away from the gap between straining buttons that hinted at warmth, comfort and pleasure. "So what's in the file?"

Rossella removed her hand from his shoulder and returned behind her desk. She opened the folder and handed over its contents. There were three items.

The first was an identical pair of old-fashioned door keys with huge teeth and long shafts. Each key was tarnished with age and flecked with rust, but still appeared usable.

The second was a property deed for his grandfather's butcher shop. Ian had driven by the shop numerous times in the past, often wondering who had bought the place and why they had never bothered to tear down what remained of a garish tin pig above the doorway. His sister, in particular, had never liked that pig. Before she disappeared, Abbie confided in him that its sharp slash of a mouth gave her nightmares.

The third item was an envelope. Written on the front of the envelope were three words: *For My Son.*

Ian glanced over at Rossella. She was leaning back in her chair, sipping her wine and studying him with concern. The top two buttons of her blouse had come undone, and he wondered if they had always been that way.

For My Son.

What he wouldn't have given for those words when he really needed them. Back when the child was still a child, when the schoolyard bullies labeled him a bastard and he became a favorite target. When Bo Kemp and his minions chased him through the woods in junior high, throwing rocks at him when he tried to escape across the river. He had nearly drowned when a large rock hit him square in the back and the swift current swept his legs out from under him.

My Son.

Or when he wanted to ask Angelina out in high school, but didn't know how to act on his feelings. His mother told him to write a poem and give it to her. He had, but things didn't go as promised. Angelina shared the poem with her friends and everyone laughed.

Son.

When Emily was baptized, Ian remembered looking around at the congregation, his baby daughter gurgling happily in his arms, and searching for a familiar face. It was only later he realized whose face he had actually been searching for.

Would having had a father to talk to change any of that? And if it had, would Ian still be the same person he was today?

Ian opened the envelope and retrieved the letter.

It was handwritten and short.

Sorry for everything, son.

I don't expect you to understand or ever forgive. I tried to fix it, that's why I had to leave, but if you're reading this, I failed.

My heart is heavy, but I'm afraid it's your burden now.

— Dad

*

Ian crumpled the letter in his hand and squeezed as though trying to turn the paper back into pulp.

What the fuck did that mean? What burden?

Thirty years and all I get is a cryptic note?

Ian hurled the letter toward the trashcan, wanting to cause some form of destruction, some noise that signified all the hurt and anger he was feeling. But the paper bounced noiselessly off the rim of the wire basket with no more impact than if a fly had died mid-flight.

Tears rolled down his face and the salty tracks filled him with even more anger. Jack Quinn didn't deserve these tears, he didn't deserve this rage, he didn't deserve anything from him.

Rossella came around her desk and grabbed Ian's face in her hands. She pulled him close to her bosom, smothering him in her scent. Ian's eyes rolled and filled with lust. He pulled her down onto his lap and pressed his mouth between her breasts, tasting her.

Rossella gasped and elicited a low moan as Ian's tongue and lips explored her fragrant flesh. With his hands pressing her close, Ian looked up into Rossella's face to see her smiling down. He uttered a low growl as their lips collided, locking together in a vice of passion while an insatiable hunger took them over.

Their lovemaking quickly became a blur of torrid flesh as Ian ripped open Rossella's blouse and yanked up her short skirt. Her breasts filled his mouth to overflowing as her hands eagerly tore at his belt and freed his manhood. Ian enveloped her with all his being, body and soul.

Together they filled the office with noise, flesh against flesh as though this was the end of all things and they needed to be completely sated before release.

Ian's tears were kissed away and his pain transformed into intense pleasure.

*

"Well, that was unexpected," said Rossella as she picked her scattered clothing off the floor, unraveling each crumpled piece before slipping it on like a striptease in reverse. "Was it the sandwich or the wine?"

Half-dressed himself, Ian crossed to her and encircled her waist, pulling her body tight against his and kissing the nape of her neck. "It was all you."

"Flatterer."

Ian grinned and inhaled her fragrance deep into his nostrils before releasing her to continue dressing.

"Are you going to be okay?" Rossella asked.

"I'll be fine, but—" Ian stopped, a sudden thought making his throat dry.

"But?"

"I received a strange package today. I didn't know what it meant, but now…" He stopped again, clearly troubled by the scenario running through his mind.

"What was in the package?" Rossella pressed.

"An ear. Somebody sent me a severed ear."

"Not what I was expecting to hear." Rossella winced. "No pun intended. Was there a note with it? A ransom demand or—"

"Nothing. Just the ear inside a plain black box."

"And?"

"And." Ian swallowed hard. "I think it was my father's."

6

LEAVING THE LAWYER'S office, Ian stood on the street for a moment to embrace the night. It was wet and it was cold, but he didn't care. Rossella had pressed her lips to a dead ember deep inside his chest, and with a simple exhale of air made it glow again.

He turned to face the building and looked up. Rossella was standing by the office window and looking down at him. He raised a hand and wiggled his fingers. It was the same whimsical way he used to wave to his daughter when they both decided it was the very best technique after watching an old Laurel and Hardy movie. Emily adored Stan Laurel, although it was Oliver Hardy who perfected the simple wave.

Rossella waved back in the normal fashion, but she dressed it with a smile that lit most of her face. Only her eyes escaped the glee as they were too locked in concern.

Turning up his collar against the rain, Ian strode off down the street. Out of habit, he had parked in the lot at Children First. The familiar spot always gave him his bearings.

As he walked, Ian thought about his father. Was the delivery of his ear a warning? And if so, a warning about what? He thought about the letter. What was his burden? What had his father tried to fix? And why did that mean he had to abandon his family?

When Ian buried his mother, she was a broken and bitter shell, tortured in both body and mind. If she had ever known a reason for her husband's disappearance, she never shared it with her son.

A dog's bark startled him and made Ian turn to look over his shoulder. On the sidewalk a short distance behind, a young man was dragging a short terrier into the doorway of a coffee shop. The rough-coated mutt was straining against its leash, teeth bared at something across the street.

Ian followed the dog's agitated stare to where a dark silhouette was barely visible in the misty haze of rain. It looked like a tall, thin man holding a black umbrella. Two large dogs were sitting silently by their master's feet, ignoring the undisciplined animal on the other side of the street.

A shiver of recognition ran down Ian's spine, but he couldn't be certain it was the same man from the cemetery. Whoever he was, he had chosen to stop equidistant from two streetlights where the dull yellowish glow was at its weakest.

Not wanting to extinguish the warmth he felt inside, Ian turned his back to the stranger and continued walking to his van.

On the second floor of the building where he worked, the lights of Children First were dark. As they should be, thought Ian as he climbed into his van and started the engine. His partner had been known to burn the midnight oil on more than a few occasions as she struggled to keep the agency afloat in a time when government bureaucrats could find millions to renovate their art-deco palace, but didn't have money to spare a child from being torn apart in an ugly divorce.

A few colorful tents had popped up in the empty spaces at the rear of the parking lot, a small encampment of people struggling with mental health, addiction and poverty. Ian knew a lot of the men and women by name. A few knew him in return.

Switching on his headlights, Ian was startled again, this time by a rap of knuckles on his passenger window. He recognized the unshaven and deep-lined face peering in. Tommy the Tink was a connoisseur of the finest soup kitchens in all of Portland, and had memorized the schedule of every agency working both sides of the river.

Ian leaned over and unlocked the door.

"How are you tonight, Tommy?" Ian asked.

Tommy opened the door, allowing the stench of alcohol, stale urine and unwashed sweat to waft into the cabin. "Can't complain, although I do enjoy a good grumble."

"Don't we all? What can I do for you?"

"Nothing at all. I'm set for an enjoyable evening. Got a Sandford out of the library, snuck an extra slice of pie from the mission that I'm saving for later, a wee dram of the cheap stuff to ward off the demons, and my sleeping bag is only a touch on the damp side."

"You're still in a tent?"

"Prefer it that way," said Tommy. "Shelters are a nightmare. Men farting and screaming in their sleep, addicts shooting up and shitting on the toilets, it's not for me. I grew out of bunk beds at the orphanage."

"What about housing?"

"I'm on a list somewhere, but won't hold my breath. The thing is, there was a man lurking around your van earlier. I told him to piss off and he did, but there was something off about him."

"Off?" Ian pressed.

"He wasn't one of us." Tommy spread his arms to encompass the area as though decreeing his kingdom. "And he wasn't a thief."

"How do you know?"

"'Cause nobody in their right mind would want to steal this piece of junk. My tent's more valuable, and it's got a hole in it."

Ian laughed. "True enough."

"Just wanted you to know while I had it in mind. Likely won't remember in the morning."

"I appreciate the heads up. Anything I can get you for your trouble?"

Tommy's lips unfurled to flash twin rows of terra-cotta teeth. "I've been thinking of cheese. A hunk of something robust would hit the spot."

"I'll see what I can do."

Tommy grinned wider. "I may just dream of cheese tonight. That would be a good dream."

After Tommy drifted away toward his makeshift camp, Ian pulled the door closed and headed home.

*

In a dark doorway on the opposite side of the street, a tall man dressed in black watched the van's taillights recede in the distance.

With one hand clutching an umbrella, he reached down with his free hand and scratched the heads of his two Dobermans. Both dogs panted in appreciation, lifted their chins and raised their inky eyes to him.

The man was their master, their god, their everything. He only had to say the word and they would obey.

7

IAN OPENED HIS eyes and stared at the ceiling, his slumber disturbed by a creak on the stairs as weight shifted from the top riser to the upper landing. He had stopped using the second floor after Helena moved out. All it held now were memories, all of them good, all of them painful.

Sliding off the mattress that lay on the floor of what used to be Helena's study, Ian silently rose to his feet and absently smoothed his boxers like a butler straightening his tie before rushing to his master's side. A frustrated thump echoed from above, the sound not unlike someone punching or kicking a wall.

With a jittery surge of adrenalin flooding his veins, Ian glanced around for a weapon. The near-empty room didn't bear much fruit as the only things he could see of any use were the leather belt in his pants and a pair of well-worn shoes.

He wondered if he should call the police, but what would he say that didn't come across as suburban paranoia? "Operator, I heard a creak and a loud thump."

Picking up one of the shoes by its toe, Ian slapped its wooden heel into the palm of his hand. It stung — a bit. Upon entering the kitchen, he abandoned the shoe for the small pot he had cooked his beans in. At least its handle gave him a better grip.

Moving from the kitchen to the hallway, Ian crept to the bottom of the stairs and looked up. Everything was quiet. Knowing he wouldn't be able to fall back asleep without investigating, Ian climbed the stairs. At the top of the landing, he glanced to his left where the door to Emily's room was closed.

Behind the door, the walls were painted yellow, her favorite color, but the room itself was disturbingly empty. The decision to remove all of Emily's things had sliced a wound in his marriage that never healed.

To his right and down a short hallway, the door to the master bedroom was slightly ajar. He couldn't remember the last time he had been in that room, and he could think of no reason why the door wouldn't be closed.

Gripping the saucepan a little tighter, Ian crept toward the door. The light switch was just inside the room, on the wall to his left. If he reached in and flicked it on, whoever or whatever was inside would be caught by surprise.

The other option would be to call out and let the intruder know there was nothing in the house worth stealing, but if he was still in the empty room, then he would already know that. Everything of value had already walked out the front door, never to return.

Ian eased up to the bedroom door, reached his hand through the gap, and felt for the light switch. When his fingers found the switch, he inhaled deeply to steady his nerves and flicked it on.

Nothing happened.

Either the bulb was burned out or the breaker had been flipped.

With a roar, Ian shouldered open the door, metal saucepan brandished above his head. He had only taken two steps when he was stopped by the sight of a man standing in the far corner, his eerie face lit from below by a flashlight — like kids did at Halloween to scare their friends.

The man wore a dark suit and everything about him was wrong.

Moonlight glistening through the window revealed a small puddle of rainwater encircling his black sneakers, and in his free hand was a large and very nasty hammer.

Shit!

Ian had no time to react before something thick and hard slammed into his chest, cracking his ribs and taking away every ounce of breath stored in his lungs.

The saucepan fell from his grasp as he bounced off the wall and dropped to his knees, his eyes bulging as he struggled to breathe.

The man in the corner hadn't moved. Instead, he tilted his head slightly and opened his mouth to reveal a picket fence of crooked teeth lit up by the flashlight.

"I knew you was a loser," snarled the man. "But this's even more pathetic than I gave you credit for."

The unseen second man swung the bat again, clipping the side of Ian's skull and sending him spiraling into the edge of unconsciousness.

His body had barely hit the floor before the coward in the corner rushed forward to rain a series of hard kicks into his body and head. Ian's body bucked under the vicious blows, and the last image he saw before blacking out was his attacker's menacing, dirt-brown eyes.

He knew those eyes.

*

When he awoke, Ian was in agony. Alone in the empty room, his useless saucepan out of reach, Ian groaned as he rolled onto his back. His scalp made a ripping sound as a small pool of dried blood crumbled away between his skin and the hardwood floor.

Gasping from the pain, he cradled his injured left hand to his chest. Somebody had stepped on it on his way out of the room as a departing *Fuck You* to his unconscious body. The knuckles on two of the fingers had swollen to the size of plums. His undamaged hand explored the tender wound on his head. It throbbed worse than any hangover, but the pain of it told him he was still alive, which, if he was being honest, was a surprise.

He ran his right hand over his body in search of puncture wounds, but the only other injury was to his ribs. At least two of them were cracked and the bruising was already discoloring his skin.

It took a while to get to his feet, his head spinning as he clutched at a wall to steady himself. He inhaled oxygen into his lungs, careful not to expand them too much as his ribs protested anything more than a shallow breath.

When he felt stable enough, he exited the room and headed to the washroom.

The message was on the mirror. Made by a finger dipped in blood, presumably his own, it read: *Stay Away!*

Turning on the taps to wash the blood off his face, Ian was surprised the two words were not only spelled correctly, but that the message was so succinct. He would have expected a few choice profanities or a slur against his manhood, but the author didn't even add the near obligatory: *Or Else!*

Who knew the Bowery brothers were such eloquent communicators?

8

WHEN IAN ENTERED the offices of Children First, Jeannie gasped and rushed around the reception desk.

"What happened? Oh my God! Who did this to you?"

Ian winced as she hugged him.

"The Bowery brothers didn't appreciate my outburst at Noah's funeral."

"You should report them to the police."

Ian shook off the suggestion. "They'll have alibis from their fellow mourners who'll swear they never left the wake."

"That's awful. What are you going to do?"

"Heal?"

Jeannie smirked. "Oh, you're a tough guy now?"

Ian smirked back. "Getting tougher every day." He glanced over to the corner office. "Is she in?"

"No, she has a breakfast meeting with some political mucky-mucks about our funding bill. Other mucky-mucks keep trying to sneak in personal extras, which could sink the whole thing."

"There are no bigger crooks than elected crooks."

"I think your face would disagree."

Ian grinned, but the muscle movement made him wince.

Jeannie glanced up at the wall clock. "The Anderson family is coming in at nine, and then you're scheduled to pick up Molly at ten for a visit with her uncle."

"No problem, but can you clear my afternoon? I've got a few personal things to attend to."

"Like visiting a doctor?"

"I'll try to fit it in."

"You better."

*

In his office, Ian eased himself into his chair, exhaling in short, rapid breaths as he did so. Everything hurt and his attempt at bandaging himself had been pathetic. The stomped fingers on his left hand were now twice as thick as the others, and a dark purple hue was turning deeper and uglier under his nails.

He opened the Anderson file and read Judge Rothstein's notes on the case. It was standard divorce stuff — sweet soulmate love sours into vindictive bile — except for the woman's desire to transition into a man, and her husband's repulsion over that decision. The judge had ordered shared custody, but wanted the initial visits supervised because of the emotional and psychological nature of the rather nasty breakup.

In a short addendum, the judge had written a personal note that said he was more concerned with the husband's mindset than the wife's physical transformation. He wrote, "Mr. Anderson's refusal to deal with the emotional trauma that he is experiencing due to his partner's transformation is resulting in increased anger and frustration that I fear could pose a risk to the child. This child is, for all intents and purposes, losing both parents. One to a physical change, the other to an emotional one."

Ian lifted the phone and punched in Jeannie's extension. Their desks weren't that far apart, but his aching ribs didn't allow him the lung capacity to yell.

"Hello, Ian. I have ibuprofen or acetaminophen with added codeine left over from my dental surgery last month."

"Yes, please. Both. You're a doll."

"True."

"About the Andersons? Where's the kid staying now?"

"Cody is living with his aunt, the mother's sister. Judge Rothstein wanted to make sure neither parent posed a risk before the joint custody comes into effect."

"Am I seeing all three this morning?"

"That's my understanding."

"Send Cody in first. I'd like to hear his thoughts before the parents chime in."

"Will do. You want the painkillers now?"

"God yes. Bring the bottle."

*

Jeannie didn't bring the bottle, but she did deliver two codeine-laced painkillers and a brown, candy-coated ibuprofen.

"I use the ibuprofen for cramps," she told him. "It helps."

"Thanks for sharing." Ian downed the three pills followed by a water chaser.

After retrieving the empty glass, Jeannie told Ian to wait while she went to her desk. She returned with her makeup bag.

"You're not seriously going to try and pretty me up are you?"

"Shhh. The way you look, you'll frighten the poor boy as soon as he sees you. It's only concealer."

Deciding he didn't have the energy to fight her, Ian leaned back and allowed Jeannie to dab his throbbing forehead with a liquid-based concealer. When she was done, she patted it with a flesh-colored powder.

"How do I look?" asked Ian.

Jeannie wrinkled her nose. "Still not handsome, but better."

"I'll take better."

Jeannie playfully stuck out her tongue at him before returning to her desk. A few minutes later, the Andersons arrived.

*

Ian pulled up in front of Molly Flannigan's foster home. As usual, the twelve-year-old was waiting on the sidewalk for him. Although she wore her customary long-sleeved black T-shirt underneath a bibbed pair of denim overalls, she had recently talked her foster mom into updating her look.

Gone was the unruly dirty blonde mop of a child who hid her face beneath a ragged fringe. Now, her hair was buzzed on the sides and spiked on top like a hedgehog under attack. She had bleached it all a startling snowy white except for the spikes. Those she dyed a Joker green.

She had also added a metallic green beauty spot piercing in the crease of her upper lip to accompany the small silver ring piercing in her nose.

Although he normally disapproved of body modifications in anyone under the age of sixteen, Ian liked the look as it spoke volumes about Molly's increased confidence. Instead of hiding who she was, and allowing childhood trauma and abuse to rule her life, Molly was standing up to it with fists cocked and teeth bared. She was telling the world: *I am strong and I won't be a victim anymore.*

When Ian stopped the van, Molly pulled open the passenger door and climbed in.

"Yo, Mr. Q."

"Yo, Molls."

Fastening her seatbelt, knowing Ian wouldn't leave until she did so, she said, "I don't want to hurt your feelings, Mr. Q, but your taste in cars sucks balls. This is, like, even more embarrassing than your last ride. I mean, it's OK for me 'cause people can tell I'm cool, but you?" She shook her head. "You ain't gettin' nowhere with the ladies showing up in this."

Ian laughed as he put the van in gear. "I'll keep that in mind."

"You should. You ain't getting any younger, and—" she stopped talking as she focused in on his face. "Seriously? What the fuck you do to your face?"

Ian winced. Profanity always sounded so much worse coming from the mouth of a child.

"I lost my cool at a kid's funeral yesterday. The father and his brother didn't appreciate it." Ian had quickly learned that telling the truth was the only way to maintain trust with his young clients. They had lived with lies their whole lives and were experts at spotting them.

"You smack them back?"

Ian shook his head.

"You're too soft for your own good, Mr. Q. You gotta toughen up."

*

Molly's uncle was the leader of a motorcycle crew called the Eastside Wreckers, but he was also the only relative who seemed to give a damn about her. His criminal lifestyle meant he wasn't a suitable candidate for guardianship, but his request for regular visitation had been approved after Molly's mother fell in with another bad boy and ended up back in prison for solicitation and possession with intent to distribute.

Molly's father was nothing but ash, his memory scattered to the wind after a rival gang took him out.

Ian's crappy van looked right at home in the down-and-going neighborhood as he pulled up to a rundown bungalow with two gleaming Harley Davidson Fat Boys parked on the weed-infested lawn. Directly across the street, four additional Harleys had taken up residence, but their riders were nowhere to be seen.

On the front porch of the bungalow, a broad-bellied man in

a T-shirt and leather vest rose to his feet and casually swung a Remington shotgun onto his shoulder.

Ian kept his empty hands visible by his side and nodded at the man in greeting as he and Molly walked up the sidewalk to the porch steps. The greeter sneered at him from beneath a dark beard, but his expression immediately softened when his gaze moved to Molly.

"Hey, Gordo," the man shouted into the house. "Molls is here."

The front door opened and Molly's uncle filled the frame. He was a fierce-looking man with dark ginger hair and a vivid scar that ran across half his face. The scar was ragged and jarring, made by a broken bottle rather than a knife.

Molly grinned when she saw him and ran ahead of Ian to be swept up in the man's heavily tattooed arms. Gordo squeezed the girl for a long time before aiming his gaze at Ian.

"How does this work?" he asked. "You need to be with us the whole time?"

"Afraid so."

"Like you could do anything if I chose to say different."

"Except stop the visits."

The man touched his cheek where a smaller scar crossed his larger one. That scar had come from the butt of a shotgun the last time the two men crossed paths.

Gordo grinned, showing surprisingly white teeth. "You better come inside."

The interior of the bungalow had been spruced up from the last time Ian visited. It no longer held the cloying stench of marijuana, spilled beer, sweat, gunpowder and engine oil. Gordo noticed Ian's surprised reaction.

"This meet your inspection?" he asked.

"It does. Where's the rest of your club?"

"Nearby. We've recently found property to be a solid

investment, plus when you own half the block, there are fewer complaints from the neighbors."

Gordo led Molly to a couch facing a giant, flat-screen TV.

"I've got a surprise," he said before turning his head and calling out, "Birdie! Bring TC."

A skinny brunette in tight jeans and a crop top that showed off her muscled stomach walked out of one of the bedrooms with a very large and very fluffy ginger cat snuggled in her arms.

"A kitty!" screamed Molly as she leapt off the couch and rushed to the woman.

Gordo chuckled with delight. "I know you can't have one at the home, but he's all yours. He'll stay here and you can visit him anytime." Gordo glanced over at Ian. "Or when your dog here lets you."

Molly lifted the docile cat from the woman's arms and carried him to the couch. After she sat down, the cat curled itself in her lap and began to purr. Molly looked over at Ian and beamed. For a moment, her face was a child's again rather than the adult she had been forced to become.

"You can name him whatever you'd like," said Gordo. "We've been calling him TC for tom cat."

"I'm going to name him Snap," said Molly without any hesitation. "Like in Ginger Snap."

"Snap?" Gordo grinned again. "I like it." He glanced over at the woman. "What do you think, Birdie?"

The woman nodded in agreement, but her attention was more focused on Ian. Crossing the room, she took hold of his left hand and lifted it for closer inspection. Letting it drop to his side again, she reached out and gently stroked the area of his forehead that Jeannie had covered in concealer. Lightly placing a hand on his chest, the woman smiled ever so slightly when Ian winced.

"Birdie's a natural healer," said Gordo. "I've seen her hold a man's guts in one hand, while sewing up the gash in his belly with the other. Looks like she's found a few cracks in your armor."

The woman took hold of Ian's hand and led him to a dining room table near the kitchen. It was far enough away to give Gordo and Molly some privacy, while still allowing Ian to keep an eye on them.

After sitting him down on a wooden chair, the woman started to unbutton his shirt.

"There's no need," said Ian, grabbing the woman's hands.

With an unexpected gentleness, the woman slipped her hands from his grasp, slid the softness of her palms over the roughness of his skin and pushed Ian's hands back onto his lap. She then finished unbuttoning his shirt before running her fingers across the mottled bruises on his torso.

Her hands found a nasty protrusion in his ribcage that sent an electrical current of pain shooting through Ian's body when she touched it. Ian winced again as the woman fixed him with a mesmeric gaze and began to breathe in and out, encouraging him to follow her rhythm.

"You don't talk much," said Ian.

The woman placed a finger on his lips to silence him as she continued to breathe with a hypnotic rhythm. Ian did as instructed and joined her rhythm. On his fourth inhale, the woman pushed her hand on the protrusion.

Ian gasped and his eyes watered from the sudden attack of pain. Before he could recoil, however, the woman grabbed his right hand and placed it over the spot, indicating he needed to apply pressure to stop the broken rib from popping back out.

Gritting his teeth, Ian did as instructed while the woman left the room. When she returned, she was carrying a large First Aid kit. After tightly bandaging the area to keep his ribs in place, the woman went to the kitchen to fill a bowl with ice.

The crude bandage that Ian had wrapped around his left hand was removed before the woman plunged the discolored and swollen flesh into the ice. While his hand grew numb from the cold, the woman pulled a chair close to Ian's and began cleaning the cut on his forehead.

"Can you talk?" asked Ian.

The woman's eyes shifted to his and in their dark reflection he saw his own haggard face looking back. In the last two years, he had aged beyond the simple passing of days, and he hadn't done it well.

"Birdie doesn't have a tongue," said Gordo from the couch. "Her pimp cut it out for talking back. We made a trade."

"A trade?"

"He give us the girl, and he got to keep one of his balls."

"You let him off lightly," said Ian, his eyes still focused on the woman's face as she tended his wounds. He wouldn't call her pretty, life had sharpened every edge to a knifepoint and deepened every hollow to a pit, but with time and care she could get there.

"Not really," said Gordo with a throaty laugh. "We couldn't decide which ball to let him keep, so we cut off both and then let him choose. He was still clutching it in his hand when the ambulance arrived."

Ian winced as another dab of antiseptic bit into his wound before the woman puckered her lips and blew on it to both cool and dry the skin. Her breath opened a drawer of childhood memories that held his mother's smile from when he believed she could answer every question and solve every trouble — before the trouble robbed her of a daughter and a husband.

After covering his scalp wound with a clear adhesive bandage, Birdie pulled his injured hand out of the ice.

Patting it dry with a clean towel, the woman gently massaged the numb appendage to return blood flow. She watched the pathways of color return before reaching into her medicine kit and pulling out three wooden popsicle sticks. She placed one stick between the two damaged fingers, and one on each outside edge. She then bandaged the two digits together.

"Thank you," said Ian when she was done.

The woman nodded without smiling before packing up her kit and leaving the room.

Ian fumbled with his shirt, getting a few of the buttons in the wrong holes before finally getting it right.

Gordo and Molly were laughing as they battled each other for Super Mario Kart supremacy on the Nintendo Wii, while the cat lay curled on the backrest of the couch, one paw resting on Molly's shoulder.

Watching them from the dining room, Ian suddenly felt incredibly alone.

*

As they were leaving, Gordo gripped Ian's arm and leaned in close.

"You owe somebody money?" he asked, his eyes roaming over Ian's bandaged cuts and bruises.

"No, just an asshole sending a warning."

"You need my help, ask. I owe you for this."

Ian nodded, deciding that a favor from a gang leader was a valuable chit worth hanging onto.

9

THE BLOCK WHERE Ian's grandfather ran his butcher shop had once been a gleaming nugget of multiculturalism in the city. It was a cramped and noisy neighborhood filled with loud immigrant families from every corner of the globe where the Irish and Italians mixed with Spanish, Portuguese and a lone family from Ceylon.

The city's less-mottled families would flock to the neighborhood on weekends to shop for local produce, meats and fresh bread. As these were the days before the terms organic and free-range became part of the general vocabulary, all people knew was that it simply tasted better. As Mr. Capello, the green grocer, would tell everyone, "If it no taste like a tomato, it no a tomato."

Ian remembered his mother always forced him to have a bath on a Friday night to "wash the spuds oot'a'yer ears" so that he was "spic-and-span" for the weekend visitors. His job — if you could call it that, since there was no pay, not even pocket money — was to play on the street with the other kids to show what a safe and family-friendly neighborhood it was.

If any stranger happened to ask where the best meat was to be found, Ian was naturally meant to point to the tin pig hanging above his grandfather's shop and tell the good folk how it was the tastiest in the city and be sure to try the…whatever his grandfather had excess of that week.

Ian enjoyed those weekends. Everyone was in a good mood — even, on occasion, his grandfather — and he was excused from chores in order to provide color for the visitors. A safari park of poverty. *Don't be afraid, we don't bite.*

The difficulty was that not all the kids got along. When Bo Kemp proclaimed himself the boss of the street, he expected everyone to fall in line — so long as they were light skinned.

Except for a spatter of caramel freckles across his nose and cheeks, Ian was about as white as it got, but he wasn't born to be a follower. He also happened to be smitten with Shanthi — a beautiful Sinhalese girl with the most incredible eyes, so deep they sparkled with bioluminescent strands of amethyst and sapphire, and long, ebony hair that always smelled of jasmine — and enjoyed hanging out with her younger brother, Dilip, who had the unique ability to find a joke in everything.

Despite her father's stern vigilance, Ian was positive that it was Shanthi's face — and secret, stolen kisses — that triggered his early-onset puberty.

After Ian's father abandoned the family on the same day they buried his grandfather, Ian's mother fell behind on the mortgage to their house in the suburbs. Ian was eight at the time when they moved into the two-bedroom apartment above the butcher shop. The move was exciting for Ian as it meant he got to play on the street every day rather than just weekends — or so he thought.

But with a butcher shop as their only source of income and no men to run it, Ian's childhood skipped past the store window on a daily basis while he mopped and cleaned and helped out where he could.

Memories of his sister faded fast as there was nothing in the sparse apartment to serve as a reminder except for the lone framed photo his mom kept above the electric fireplace. No photos of his father were ever on display.

*

Standing on the street now, one of the keys to the front door biting into his clenched palm, Ian studied the tin pig that hung above the boarded-up shop window. Like the street it watched over, the sign had known better days. In fact, Ian was surprised that it had lasted this long — but only a little. That pig had fueled more than a few of his childhood nightmares and, even as an adult, he wouldn't be overly shocked to discover it held some dark, mystical power.

The rusted bolt securing its rump had snapped so that only one anchor remained at its throat. Instead of flying, it now appeared to be hanging. A stubborn blister of flesh-colored paint clung precariously to one leg in a final standoff against the overwhelming invasion of marmalade rust, while the faint outline of the butcher's name could still be discerned in raised letters hammered into its metallic flesh. You had to look close, but painted beneath the raised letters was the proud proclamation: *& Son*.

Unlike his grandfather, Ian's father had never fully embraced the art of butchery and had chased Ian out of the shop at every opportunity. Thinking back on it now, what Ian had mistaken for bad temper could have been his father allowing him to choose his own path rather than following in the family tradition. But when Jack Quinn disappeared, whatever good intentions he may have had went with him.

Directly across the street from Quinn & Son Family Butchers was a Chinese diner that had managed to survive the neighborhood's decline with all-day breakfasts, fifty-cent coffee and a famous Wor Wonton soup. A few doors down, however, the Bed & Breakfast Hotel that Bo Kemp's family ran had been turned into a halfway house. Interestingly, they kept the name: Raven's Rest.

Ian wondered if the current owners knew that it was named

after Bo Kemp's mother or that in all the years Ian had known her, she never once stepped outside its doors.

With anxiety filling his chest, Ian unlocked the door to the butcher's shop and pushed it open.

*

A familiar sound pealed from a brass bell hung on an iron hook above the door as Ian stepped across the threshold. Dust devils whirled upon the breeze, dancing as though in celebration of release. The decaying boards fastened across the front display window kept everything inside dark, but even with the lack of light, Ian could see the place had remained undisturbed for a long, long time.

His shoes sunk into thick layers of dust, leaving powdery tracks to mark his steps as he moved toward the empty display cabinets that once held hand-cut steaks, pork chops, lamb and chicken. His favorite had always been his grandfather's homemade sausage, seasoned with sage, onion, pepper and garlic. Occasionally, his grandfather allowed Ian to add the final, secret ingredient to the mixture before it was squeezed and twisted into links: Guinness stout.

As Ian walked the cabinets' length, he dipped one finger into the dust, leaving a snake-like trail across the curved glass, knowing his grandfather would have chased him out of the shop with a bloody cleaver if he had attempted that when he was a kid.

His grandfather ran a tight ship, instructing Ian that when one dealt in blood in the back room, the front needed to be spotless. "The customers don't need to see the slaughter to appreciate the meat," he said. "We are the guardians of that."

Reaching the master light switch, Ian flicked it on and was disappointed but not overly surprised when nothing happened. The electric bill likely hadn't been paid in decades.

It's your burden now.

It made no sense to Ian that this building should still be in the

Quinn family name. Even if his grandfather had owned it outright, who paid the annual taxes? And why had nobody sold it?

Guilt still made his heart thump uneasily. When Ian left for college, insisting he needed to be something other than a butcher's son, his mother told him everything would be fine. She had regular customers and a new manager onboard to run the store.

Selfishly, Ian convinced himself that she was right. And even when she called late at night, her speech slurred and her logic broken, she would try to sound happy, assuring him that she was simply enjoying a glass or two of wine after dinner. Ian desperately wanted to believe her, and so told himself it was the truth.

Less than two years later, the shop was out of business, the manager nowhere to be found, and Ian returned to Portland to bury his mother. At the time, he assumed the bank took over the building. It was never mentioned in his mother's meagre will and, to be honest, he was happy to wash his hands of it.

Ian glanced at the blue door that opened onto the staircase, wondering if the apartment above was still habitable. As he reached for the handle, the brass bell over the front door jangled behind him.

He turned to see a giant of a man with two raccoon-like eyes and a large splint tented over his nose. He wore an expensive, custom-tailored wool suit that didn't match his face.

"Can I help you?" asked Ian.

"What's your name?" growled the man.

Caught off guard by the man's tone, Ian's hands began tightening into fists, but relaxed immediately as pain shot up his left arm from his splintered digits. Swallowing the pain, he asked, "Why do you want to know?"

"Don't matter."

"It does to me. Why are you here?"

"Wanted to see your face."

"Why?"

"Makes it easier."

"Easier for what?"

The man grinned, showing an army of teeth. "I know you."

Ian added iron to his tone. "You don't."

The man's eyes flickered in reaction and he reached up to touch the bandage on his nose.

"You like my gift?"

Ian thought for a moment. The only gift he had received recently was a plain black box containing a severed ear.

"Who did it belong to?"

"I reckon you know."

"My father?"

The man's upper lip curled in a sneer. "Depends. What's your name?"

Ian tried to swallow, but felt the phlegm sticking in his dry throat. He croaked, "Ian Quinn."

The man's sneer deepened. "Now I know."

"Was it my father's?" Ian repeated. "Did you kill him?"

The man turned his back and pulled on the door. "We'll meet again soon. Maybe I'll tell you then."

"What the fuck do you want?" Ian snarled at his back.

"If I was you, I'd find it before I come back."

The door closed as the burly stranger exited onto the street. Rushing after him, Ian yanked open the door and yelled, "Find what?"

But he was yelling to an empty street as the man slid into the passenger seat of a slick, four-door sedan and was driven away.

*

Ian cursed and returned inside the shop, his mind whirling like the dust devils but traveling nowhere.

If whatever the stranger was seeking had been in the store, then he would have had years to search for it without Ian ever having a clue. Instead, he must have thought it — whatever it was — had been secreted away by his father. But upon his father's death, the burden mentioned in his letter switched to Ian.

The only trouble was Ian had no fucking clue what the burden was meant to be.

*

Climbing the stairs to the apartment above the shop, Ian wondered if he should call Jersey for some advice. He was still contemplating the idea when his phone rang. It wasn't Jersey.

"Hi," said Ian, trying to make his voice sound light.

"I was going to wait until you called me," said Rossella, her smoky voice like a snake's tongue in his ear. "But I'm a modern woman, so here I am."

Ian laughed. "I'm glad you called."

"You are?"

"Absolutely."

"You didn't say much when you left."

"I know and I'm sorry, but..."

"But?"

Ian reached the top landing and opened the door to the apartment. It was like stepping back in time, except, like *Gulliver's Travels*, everything was smaller.

"I don't want this to sound corny, but our...err, encounter... was..."

"Go on," she encouraged guardedly.

Ian exhaled noisily. "So fucking good."

Rossella laughed in relief.

"I was being selfish, but I needed to bask in it, you know? Wrap it around myself like a warm blanket. It's been a long time since I've felt that good." Ian cleared his throat. "Sorry, that does sound corny doesn't it?"

"It does," said the lawyer. "But I like it. Where are you now?"

"The butcher's shop you gave me the keys to. I lived here as a boy after my father left, but I haven't been back in a long time. It actually never occurred to me that I would see it again, and to be honest, that never bothered me. But—"

"Another but," Rossella chuckled.

"But I'm glad I'm here."

"Good. So are you going to ask me out on a proper date?"

"Yes. When?"

"Tonight?"

"Dinner?"

"Yes."

"Where?"

"You choose. Pick me up at seven."

"At your office?"

"Yes."

"I'll be there."

"You better."

Before she could hang up, Ian asked, "One more thing?"

"Yes?"

"Can you find out who has been paying the taxes on this property for all these years?"

"That's not a 'one more thing,'" she said.

"It's not?"

"No. That's business. When you are asking a woman out on a date, one more thing is, for example, 'Until we meet tonight, I'll be dreaming of your beauty.'"

"That's good," Ian said, a smile breaking across his face. "Will you be dreaming of my beauty?"

"No. I'll be thinking that you've got a lot of work to do if you ever hope to see me naked again."

"I'll start studying right away."

"Good to hear."

Slipping the phone back into his jacket pocket, Ian studied the main room of the apartment. Consisting of a galley kitchen plus sitting room, this was where he and his mother spent most of their time. Not that they had much choice. The two bedrooms were small, which was why they both had single beds, and the bathroom was just large enough to fit a bathtub, toilet and sink.

Oddly, nothing appeared to have been touched. Whatever the thug was looking for, he obviously didn't believe it was hidden up here.

Walking to the window, Ian looked down upon the street where he played as a child. It had aged even worse than he had, and yet it still held a million memories — some fond, others painful, but together they formed the skeleton of who he was today.

His grandfather loved this street and strode its length and breadth like a king. To his father, it was a prison, a barbed wire tether that held him too close to the ground and choked him whenever he tried to go beyond its borders. For his mother, it was the lid on her coffin. And for Ian, it was a playground full of adventure, skinned knees, bloody noses and stolen kisses.

It wasn't home. That was a place he lost when Emily died, but there was a connection here, a familiar energy that whispered in his ear and beckoned him to return.

Ian pulled out his phone again and punched in the number for Children First. When Jeannie answered, he said, "Do you know any heavy-duty cleaners?"

"Heavy duty?"

"I'm thinking industrial. People used to taking on a daunting task. Maybe a crime scene crew."

"Crime scene?"

"Yeah, but with murdered dust bunnies instead of blood."

Jeannie chuckled. "I can ask our insurance company, they must have people like that."

"Brilliant. You're a gem."

"Of course I am, but it's nice of you to notice."

Ian laughed. "How are we looking?"

"Your schedule's clear for the rest of the day, but a courier dropped off a large envelope from your wife's lawyer that I had to sign for. He said he could wait until you signed it and take it back, which is odd, but I explained that I didn't know when you would return."

"Thanks. I'll stop in and sign it shortly."

"Everything okay?"

"It's fine, just divorce stuff. Helena needs me to move out of the house because I'm scaring off buyers, which is why I need the cleaners." Ian looked around the sparse room filled to the rafters with a confusing muddle of despair and laughter. "My new place is a bit of a dump."

10

ON THE MANTLE above the electric fireplace, Ian lifted a framed photograph and wiped away a thick layer of dust. His sister was eleven, he was five, and they were eating ice cream. Or, to be exact, Ian was mostly wearing the ice cream, his face smeared in a vanilla grin, while Abbie held a perfect cone, methodically licked around the edges before the drips could reach her fingers.

She was always the serious one; he, the clown.

When he bugged her too much, especially when she had friends over, she would tell him that she wished Mom and Dad had never adopted him, that they had brought home a puppy instead, like she suggested.

The disparagement didn't work, however, as Ian loved the idea of being adopted. And even when his parents scolded his sister for the hurtful lie, Ian clung to the idea that it might be true, that his real parents were space aliens or treasure-hunting pirates or even secret agents, anything that wasn't just ordinary.

Ian wondered why this was the photograph his mother had chosen to keep. There didn't seem to be anything particularly special about it except, maybe, the smile. His sister's rare smile shone brightly despite the silly antics of her brother.

Returning the photo to the mantel, Ian heard the brass bell sound from below.

With a final look around, he headed back to the stairs.

*

Waiting for him in the gloom of the shop floor was an old man with a silver-tipped cane and an impeccable, three-piece suit that had been in style when he bought it and, remarkably, was now considered retro-chic again.

Despite the man's advanced age, Ian recognized him.

"Mr. Capello, is that you?"

"Of course," he barked. "Who are you?"

"It's Ian Quinn, my grandfather—"

"I know your grandfather," he interrupted. "And I know you, too, young man. You still owe me fifty cents."

Ian laughed. "I do?"

"You thought I'd forget, didn't you? You bought two bottles of orange soda, but only had money for one. The other bottle was for that lovely Indian girl you had a crush on, and you begged me not to show you up." He held out his free hand. "I kept my word, now you keep yours."

Staggered by the man's memory, Ian dug in his pockets for change, found two quarters and handed them over.

Mr. Capello slipped the coins into a small pocket in his waistcoat. After patting the cloth to reassure himself the money was safe, he lifted his chin and offered Ian a warm smile.

"Now we're square," he said.

"I'm sorry it's taken so long. Honestly, I had forgotten all about it."

Mr. Capello tapped the side of his head with his finger. "First rule of business, never forget outstanding debts, no matter how small."

"Good advice. Do you and your family still live around here?"

Mr. Capello shrugged. "Nearby, but I like to walk the neighborhood, check up on old friends, make sure my store is still standing."

"You still own the green grocers next door?"

"I own the husk. The store is long gone, but nobody is interested in buying an old, empty building attached to other old, empty buildings. Why are you here?"

"I just inherited the place."

"Ah. Are you a butcher, too, like your grandfather?"

"No."

A sadness fell over his wrinkled face. "My children never wanted to run my store either. Bigger dreams they said, but what can be bigger than feeding people good food? These supermarkets today have forgotten what food is meant to be. They sell us chemicals and pesticides disguised as tomatoes and peppers, but one taste…ah, one taste and you know, it is not food."

"I'm thinking of moving in," said Ian to change the subject.

"Why? It's a shit hole."

Ian burst out laughing at the sudden change in sentimentality. "True, but it feels right."

"I wish you luck. The street has not been the same since your grandfather passed. He was the fist that kept the rabble at bay. Your father was smart to run."

"Smart?" Ian said, his voice taking on a sharp edge. "He abandoned his family."

"A difficult choice, I am sure."

"A selfish one."

Mr. Capello shrugged. "Perhaps."

A thought dropped onto Ian's tongue. "Do you know what his burden was? Why it's been passed onto me?"

Mr. Capello paled slightly as he pulled a gold watch out of a vest pocket and glanced at the round face. "I need to be going," he said, suddenly displaying the weight of his years. "It's time for my pills and afternoon nap."

"Did he tell you what his burden was?" Ian pressed. "There are men threatening me and I don't know why."

Mr. Capello glanced nervously at the door behind him. "All I know, despite the stories, is your grandfather was a good man. Your father became involved when his daughter, your sister, disappeared. But your father was not your grandfather. People did not fear him as they feared Augustus. That is all I know."

"Then why do you look afraid?"

"It's time for my pills. I need to get back. Good day."

Deciding he couldn't push it, Ian said, "Can we talk again?"

Mr. Capello hoisted his walking stick in valediction as he exited the store.

*

Following him to the doorway, Ian's attention was diverted to a tall man standing directly across the street. Although he didn't have a pair of Dobermans at his heels, the man appeared to be the same stranger he had spotted at both the graveyard and in the street last night when he left Rossella's office.

Ian's gaze flickered to Mr. Capello's retreat before returning to the spot across the street.

The tall man was gone.

11

IAN'S PHONE RANG as he pondered crossing the street for an all-day breakfast, and to mull over what Mr. Capello had said about his grandfather. The diner looked exactly as he remembered it from his childhood with one exception — someone had tossed a greasy bucket of time across its facade.

The once bright white frontage with gleeful cherry-red swoops that made every child subconsciously think of strawberry sundaes or ketchup-topped fries was now a grimy beige and putrid brown that was less than appetizing. Even the exotic name had lost most of its allure as the first D and Y had been stolen off the Dynasty Diner marquee and never been replaced.

Ian glanced at the caller ID and answered his phone. "Hey, Jeannie."

"I found some cleaners. They're not super cheap, but I'm told they're good."

"When can they start?"

"The owner just had a warehouse damage job put on hold by the insurance company, and he sounded eager to go. I've texted you the number."

As soon as he hung up, Ian checked his texts and tapped the number. A man answered on the second ring.

"Legion Cleaners. Clark here."

Ian introduced himself and explained what he was looking for.

"I'm intrigued," said Clark. "Can you show it to me before I quote?"

Ian gave him the address.

"Perfect. Give me thirty."

"I'll be in the diner across the street."

*

The Dynasty Diner was empty when Ian entered and grabbed a table for two by the window. The murky view of the street showed him it wasn't just the eatery that had suffered. Every building on the block was either abandoned or converted into a lesser version of its original self.

Raven's Rest, the boutique hotel run by Bo Kemp's family was never, in reality, much more than a place where salesmen stayed for a night or two because it was cheaper than across the river. And the only time Mrs. Kemp received the level of gentlemen she was most interested in attracting, their companions were never their wives, they always paid in cash, and they rarely stayed the whole night.

But time had stripped the hotel of even that illusion, that wished-for possibility. There were no lace curtains in the windows anymore and the lobby reeked of sweat, cigarettes and desperate men rather than fresh-cut flowers and lavender soap. When an under-funded charity took over the foreclosed property to turn it into a halfway house, it struggled to run it with pride.

The promise was there, but not the money, and the building continued its decay.

Between Raven's Rest and his grandfather's store was the boarded up storefront of Mr. Capello's grocery. Without its green-and-white striped awnings, fruit and vegetable wicker baskets crowding the sidewalk, and Mr. Capello's name hand-painted upon the large plate glass window, it was just another crumbling brick husk without a soul.

"Do you see ghosts?" asked a woman's voice.

Ian turned to see a young Asian woman with a round face so youthful and fresh that he couldn't guess her age. She wore little makeup, except for a pearly gloss on her lips and a delicate pencil of eyeliner, but her height and body shape made Ian guess early twenties. A nametag above her high bosom read Mei.

"I'm sorry?" Ian asked, confused.

"The street," said the woman. "The way you are studying it, I assumed you must see something the rest of us can't, like ghosts."

Ian grinned. "No, nothing like that. I was…remembering. Remembering what the buildings used to look like."

"Ah, you grew up here?"

"For part of my childhood." He pointed across the street. "I've just inherited the butcher's shop."

"Really?" In her amazement, Mei moved close to Ian and leaned over his shoulder to peer out the window, as if wanting to see the street through his eyes. "What are you going to do with it?"

"I'm thinking of moving in."

The woman blinked rapidly, then realized that her bosom was practically caressing Ian's ear. She stepped back with a slight blush in her cheeks.

"Are you a butcher?" Mei asked.

"No, but the apartment still looks livable."

Mei wrinkled her nose. "Really?"

Ian laughed and shrugged. "Well, not yet, but I've got some cleaners coming down to take a look."

"I think you might need more than cleaners."

"Talking from experience?"

The woman blushed a little deeper. "My family has been in this location for over forty years."

This time it was Ian's turn to look amazed. "Seriously? Your grandparents are the Songs?"

"Yes. You know them?"

"Mostly the cooking," Ian admitted. "Their children were older, so we didn't hang out. I'm surprised they stayed, though. Everyone else has gone."

"Not everyone."

"No? Who else stayed?"

Mei pointed out the window and down the street a short distance. "A nice young man runs the corner store. He is third generation."

A smirk crossed Ian's face. The corner store had been owned by Mr. Palewandram, father to his childhood crush, Shanthi, and her younger brother. "Is his name Dilip?"

A smile creased the woman's eyes. "You know him?"

Although a different answer slid to the tip of Ian's tongue, an answer too weighted in history for the young woman to understand, he let it fall without utterance. Instead, he said, "We were friends once."

"What happened?"

The question caught Ian by surprise simply because he had never given it much thought.

"Time," he answered quietly, looking around once again at his surroundings. "It always leaves a mark."

*

When Ian saw the broad-shouldered man climb out of his white paneled van and stand in front of the butcher's shop, he paid his food bill and crossed the street to meet him.

"Clark?"

The man turned and offered his hand. "So this is your inheritance, huh?" He looked back around. "I'm surprised it's still standing."

"Me, too," said Ian. "Gentrification never quite caught on here."

"You hoping to change that?"

"No, this is just for me. Want to look inside?"

After the two men entered, Clark let out a low whistle and his voice took on an air of excitement.

"I can see it," he said. "The exposed brick, the hardwood. Hell, you've got solid brass finishings in here. We shine that up, acid wash some of the brick. Wow! This could look awesome."

"Seriously?"

"You bet, but it needs more than a serious cleaning. It needs gutting, some renovation. I'll bet the washrooms need to be torn apart and replaced with modern conveniences. You put some money into this, it could be incredible, but I wouldn't recommend it."

"Why not?"

"The neighborhood sucks. You'll never get your investment back out."

"What if I just want to live here? How much to make it habitable?"

Clark glanced up at the ceiling. "Both floors?"

Ian nodded and led the way to the second-floor apartment. After Clark looked around, he said, "First things first, get the power turned on. We'll need that. I have three four-man crews sitting idle at the moment until the insurance company signs off on a flooded warehouse. If I get them started on this straight away, I could have this place livable in a couple days. It won't look new, just clean. After that, if you want it to be something cool, I can recommend some great guys who would love to get their hands dirty on this. You got any money?"

Ian thought about the legal papers sitting on his desk at Children First. All he had to do was sign.

He nodded and handed over one of the ancient door keys. "I received a bit of cash, too."

*

After Clark drove off to fetch his cleaning crew, Ian phoned the local power company and set up an account to restore electricity to the building.

The moment he hung up, a midnight blue, four-door Lincoln Continental glided to the curb, and the goon with the nose bandage who had visited earlier climbed out of the front passenger seat.

He studied Ian cautiously before speaking, and Ian was surprised to note a slight ripple of unease in the crease between his eyes. *What is that about?*

The goon curled his lip into a sneer and said, "Get in."

"Just like that?" Ian asked, not budging. "No flowers, no explanation?"

The man rolled his shoulders and opened his jacket to show the black polymer grip of a .45 Beretta nestled snugly in a nylon shoulder holster.

"Leather would go better with your belt," said Ian, playing off the man's nervousness despite not understanding its reason. "The nylon looks cheap."

When the man bristled, Ian glanced around at the empty street. His options were limited: get in the car or run.

Breathing through his mouth, the man moved his hand closer to his holster, but a sharp tap on the window behind him made his fingers twitch and hold.

With an irritated hiss of annoyance, he said, "Get in the back or I'll stuff you in the trunk." His voice lowered to a barely audible growl. "I'd prefer the trunk, so keep pushing."

Ian unconsciously touched his bandaged rib, the dull spark of pain reminding him that when it came to being tough, he was more of a punching bag than a boxer.

He climbed into the car.

12

THE INTERIOR OF the vehicle was like stepping into a time machine that had glitched, blending all the overindulgent glory of the jet age with present-day tech. Despite its generous size, there were only two seats in the rear compartment. Midnight blue suede and leather recliners were separated by a wide console that combined polished mahogany woodwork with a pop-up video monitor connected to a hidden computer somewhere out of sight.

Ian had never flown first class, working in a not-for-profit agency didn't allow such an indulgence, but he imagined even that luxury couldn't compare to this. The plush carpet alone made him want to kick off his socks and shoes and sink his bare feet into the velvety softness, but he resisted the temptation. He didn't think the elderly gentleman sitting in the opposite seat would approve. Then again, he wasn't entirely sure the man was alive.

The jittery rise and fall of the silk tie resting on the man's stark white shirt told Ian that he was still breathing, but the man was so old he appeared to be in the pre-stages of mummification. Folds of bloodless, slack skin had lost their grip on his bones, and its wrinkled surface was so mottled that it was difficult to tell if he was originally white or brown.

When Ian told the Dynasty waitress that time left a mark, he could see now that he had soft-pedaled the concept. Time hadn't so much bruised this man as it had sucked the very marrow from his bones.

The man's paper-thin and blue-veined eyelids fluttered before opening, like a vampire sensing sunset, as the car smoothly pulled away from the curb on its twenty-one-inch, polished aluminum wheels. When he sensed Ian's presence, his head turned and alarmingly coltish brown eyes locked onto the newcomer. It reminded Ian of a cobra sensing that a lunchtime mouse had been dropped into its cage.

"Your name is Ian Quinn," said the man in a raspy voice.

He touched a button on the center console to open a hidden compartment that contained several small glass bottles of water. Ian didn't recognize the brand, but it looked expensive. Shakily, the man handed the bottle to Nose Bandage in the front seat, who twisted off the cap and handed it back. The man took a small sip before continuing.

"Your father was Jack Quinn. Your grandfather was Augustus Quinn. Your family appears to have a disdain for middle names."

"Couldn't afford them," Ian quipped, a familiar joke that he added to his arsenal whenever he socialized with Helena's family. Her father had enjoyed using his yacht club friends as a passive-aggressive reminder of Ian's lack of societal birthright.

A smile crept across the man's lips, but it was more disturbing than comforting.

"When was the last time you saw your father?"

Ian shrugged. "When I was seven."

"Your grandfather's funeral?"

Ian nodded.

"And never since?"

Ian remained silent, not seeing the point in giving the man something he already seemed to know.

"Do you know why he left?"

"He ran out of cigarettes," said Ian.

The smile returned, but this time a dark tongue followed in its wake. The disobedient muscle was returned to its dusty cave with another sip of water.

"Would you like to see him again?"

Caught off guard, Ian's reply escaped his lips with a sigh. "He's dead."

"True," said the man. "An unfortunate turn of events." The man inclined his head slightly in the direction of the front seat. "He did not go gently into that good night, did he, Munster?"

Nose Bandage turned slightly in his seat and grunted in response.

"It's one of the troubles of sending a sledgehammer to do a scalpel's work," said the man, although his voice held a note of affection, which was clearly aimed at the goon in the front.

Leaning forward, the man pressed a hidden button on the seat back in front of him to lower a concealed tray. When the tray was completely perpendicular, a tiny white laser switched on to project a keyboard onto its dark surface. At the touch of a button made only of light, the computer monitor in the center console lit up.

Running his fingers across the surface of the projection, the man brought a video clip onto the screen. He glanced across at Ian to make sure he was paying attention before pressing *play*.

The screen displayed the interior of a dark and dingy bar with a scattered row of men sitting apart and alone. It wasn't a bar where friends went to meet and share a laugh, but rather a place where strangers congregated to be together and drink alone.

The video was jerky and it took Ian a moment to realize that it was being recorded on a hidden camera stitched into someone's lapel. When the cameraman's large hands appeared in the frame, Ian recognized them as belonging to Munster.

He glanced over at the man sitting beside him and saw glee shining in his eyes. He had watched this video many times.

Ian returned his attention to the screen as Munster approached a disheveled man draining the last of his dark pint. A second goon in a fitted suit entered the frame and stood off to one side, although a suspicious bulge ruining the cut of his jacket revealed he wasn't simply curious.

The man in the video lowered his pint onto a tattered beermat with the name McNally stamped on top of a four-leaf clover. The clichéd symbol had been made unique with a bite taken out of one leaf. When the man turned to the camera, his face was somehow familiar and yet one Ian had never seen before.

"Your father," explained the man beside him. "You can run from everything but the ravages of time. That bastard plays us all in the end."

An unexpected swelling of pride filled Ian's chest as the stranger who was his father launched an attack on the two men. The camera's perspective spun wildly as Munster recoiled from the brutal loss of his nose and ended up on the floor. The video jumped mid-frame as Jack Quinn began swinging a baseball bat, and suddenly the view was of a back alley.

"It needs some work," apologized the elderly man with the slack tongue. "This is a rough cut." He pointed a bony finger at the screen. "Watch. This is my favorite part."

The alley appeared deserted until Jack Quinn suddenly launched himself out of a doorway and rushed toward the camera. The man froze the playback, his skeletal finger twitching with excitement.

"Look at his hands," he said.

Ian leaned forward to study the video. A smile broke on his lips, but also caused an old scar to crack open in his heart and bring moisture to his eyes. His father was armed with nothing more than his fingers, formed into pretend guns.

He was also bleeding.

Blood dribbled down the side of his face from a gash in his ear, while a greater amount soaked one of his legs and blossomed from a soggy patch in his chest, inches below his heart. Ian touched the spot where his own broken rib ached.

The living corpse beside him hit *play* again, and Ian watched his father die.

*

"I wanted him alive," said the man. "But what is it that rock'n'roll band sings? You can't always get it."

Ian wiped a rough knuckle across his eyes, angry at himself for allowing this monster to see any emotion from him. When he finally found the strength to talk, he asked, "Why?"

The man cocked his head to one side like a chicken puzzled by the sharpening of an axe.

"Why did I want—"

"Why did you kill him?" Ian interrupted sharply. "What has my family ever done to you?"

The man began to shake in his seat, his papery skin making a noise like dried leaves being crushed underfoot. Silvery white foam bubbled in the corners of his mouth and his dark tongue slipped out of its cave once more.

"Your family took everything." His voice was sharp and venomous. "Augustus thought he could challenge me, stand up and steal my legacy, but all anyone remembers is the monster I made him to be." An agonizing rasp escaped the man's frail throat and cloudy spittle flew from his lips. "Your father thought he could run, like your sister before him, but if you don't find her..." he stabbed angrily at the screen, "...pretend guns won't save you from the fate I have in store."

Recoiling from the venom, Ian only had one puzzling question. "Find who?"

13

THE OLD MAN'S face contorted in pain, his sallow flesh turning from vivid purple to oxygen-deprived blue, as the car abruptly pulled over. Ian had no chance to react before his door was pulled open and Munster's hand locked onto his shoulder like a steel claw.

Before he could comprehend what was happening, Ian was yanked from his seat and thrown onto the sidewalk. Cursing as he tumbled onto his ass, Ian watched Munster quickly take his place in the backseat and secure an oxygen mask onto his boss's straining face. The man's bulging eyes reminded Ian of that scene in *Total Recall* where Arnold Schwarzenegger's face helmet cracks and he sucks in Mars' alien atmosphere.

"Find who?" Ian repeated before the door was pulled closed and the car drove off.

Rising to his feet, his body protesting every inch of vertical, Ian watched in frustration as the Lincoln drove away. Not only didn't he know who he was supposed to find, he also had no idea who the old bastard in the car was.

"Was you in that car?" asked a small voice.

Ian turned to see two young boys sitting on a pair of much

neglected and much enjoyed bicycles. Their cheeks were wind-burned and their eyes were bright with curiosity.

"Yeah," he answered. "Any idea who owns it?"

"You don't know?" asked the one boy as he wiped his dripping nose on a well-used sleeve.

Ian shook his head.

"Then why was you inside?" asked the second boy.

"Didn't have much choice in the matter."

Both boys grinned at that.

"The big dude is Munster," said the first boy. "He's the muscle."

"And who does he work for?" asked Ian.

"Serious?" asked the second boy.

"Serious."

"Wasn't he in the car wit' you?"

"He neglected to introduce himself."

Both boys found that hilarious, and they grinned at each other as though Ian had just farted in church.

"That's Mister Zelig, dude," said the second boy when he finished grinning. "My brother says they used to call him Ice Pick, back when he was a big deal, but he don't get out of the car much anymore."

"Is your brother in a gang?" Ian asked.

"Biggest gang there is," said the second boy proudly. "He's in the United States Marine Corps. Got the hell out of this shit hole." The boy grinned again at his choice use of profanity. "He's saving a spot for me. I'm gonna drive a tank."

"Sounds like a plan," said Ian.

"Oorah," yelled the boy before high-fiving his friend in a signal that this conversation was no longer holding his attention.

Laughing, the two boys turned tail and took off down the street at warp speed — or as fast as warp can be on a rusted chain.

*

Looking around, Ian discovered he had been dropped off less than a block from where he started, as if the journey had been little more than a waking nightmare.

But illusion or not, he needed answers. Zelig obviously knew more about Ian's own family history than he did, and that needed to change if he was going to get to the root of this madness.

Ian crossed to the corner store and went inside. The bell above the door hadn't changed in thirty years, and its singsong chime awakened a Pavlovian response. Ian was transported back to his childhood where he felt nervous, scared and bursting with excitement, the way he used to feel when he wanted to ask Mr. Palewandram if Shanthi could come out and play.

Despite his short and lean stature, Mr. Palewandram was a brick wall when it came to his daughter. He made no bones about his disapproval of a gawky, pale Irish lad whose family butchered the carcasses of dead animals for a living.

"Can I help you?" asked a male voice.

Breaking free from his reverie, Ian focused on the sturdy man behind the counter. Although slightly younger than himself in years, the man looked a decade older in spirit. His darkly handsome face was lined with worry, his eyes baggy from lack of sleep, and starless pupils burrowed so deep that Ian could feel the cold distrust oozing out of them.

Ian broke the ice. "Dilip?"

The man blinked, his vigilant stare wavering slightly in confusion.

"It's Ian," said Ian. "Ian Quinn?"

"Bullshit."

Ian laughed aloud, a sudden memory of Dilip as a young boy dogging his sister's heels, never letting Ian go anywhere with her alone. Ian had used plenty of profanity in his youth, a freedom not allowed the Palewandram children, but it was this particular term that made Dilip laugh the most, and the one he adopted as his own.

"Long time," said Ian.

Dilip came around the counter, his eyes still wary until he was only a few steps away. And then, like the sun burning through a haze of cloud, recognition finally took hold and his face brightened. He rushed the next two steps and embraced Ian in an unexpected hug.

Ian winced but swallowed the pain, hiding it from his face as the man crushed his broken and bruised ribs. When Dilip stepped away, he looked slightly embarrassed as though he hadn't expected to unburden such emotion.

"You're looking good," Ian lied.

"You're not," said Dilip, and both men laughed.

"I'm surprised the store is still here."

"Me, too." Dilip shrugged. "Mostly lotto, beer and smokes now. The neighborhood is still here, just better hidden."

"Is your dad still around?"

Dilip grinned. "I'm surprised that's who you're asking for."

Despite the years, a blush colored Ian's cheeks. "How is Shanthi?"

"Fat and happy. Two beautiful daughters. My father claims she doesn't have a son just to spite him."

"Wouldn't put it past her," said Ian, smiling. "She always had a stubborn streak."

"That she does. So what brings you back?"

"I inherited the butcher's shop."

Dilip was dumbstruck for a moment as he tried to comprehend the information.

"Inherited? Who from? I thought that place was abandoned decades ago."

"Me, too, but apparently it still belonged to my father."

Dilip's eyes widened. "You guys were in touch?"

"No," Ian said with a sharpness that he didn't intend. "He was killed recently and the building passed onto me. I'm as surprised as anyone."

"You said killed?"

Ian swallowed. "A gangster named Zelig showed me a video. He was gunned down in a back alley. Zelig didn't say where or when, but it was recent."

"You know Mister Zelig?"

Shaking his head, Ian said, "Met him for the first time a few minutes ago. You?"

"Creepy old bastard," said Dilip. "He runs the neighborhood, been shaking us down for decades. Ever since your grandfather died actually."

"That's what I wanted to ask your father, see if he remembers anything about my grandfather. There were stories, but..." Ian paused before continuing. "I didn't want to listen back then, and my mother never talked about it. She seemed ashamed and afraid in equal measure, and maybe I was, too."

"Dad's in the back making tea, let's ask."

*

The tiny back room, separated from the shop by a bead curtain the color of leftover oatmeal, was stuffed with all the comforts of an agoraphobic bachelor. Due to the narrowness of the room, two ancient lounge chairs faced each other at an awkward angle with a kidney-shaped coffee table stuck in the middle. Resting on top of the table was a marble chessboard, the black and white pieces carved to resemble two ancient armies that Ian didn't recognize. The armchairs were so old that puffs of yellow stuffing leaked out of them like leprosy.

Beyond the chairs was a tiny kitchen that would have looked more at home inside a Volkswagen van: single sink, hot plate, microwave and kettle. Standing beside the kettle, nearly dwarfed by the farthest chair, was a frail-looking man dressed in white linen. When he turned around, Mr. Palewandram's distrustful eyes were sunk so deeply inside an ancient skull that he almost appeared to be wearing a mask. To think that as a boy, Ian was afraid of this tiny man's wrath seemed laughable now.

"Ah," said Mr. Palewandram without any hint of surprise, "the butcher's boy." He lifted his hand and wagged a bony finger in Ian's direction. "You are too late. I married Shanthi off to a good Sinhalese boy. A respectable medical doctor. Nothing like you."

An unexpected pain stretched Ian's lips, understanding now what he could never understand then: a father's love for, and protection over, his daughter. Ian would never know the heartache of a father watching his daughter stepping out on a first date, but a part of him had been dreading it from the moment Emily first gurgled in his arms.

"You were wise," he said. "I'm glad she's happy."

Mr. Palewandram shrugged. "Happiness is not everything. Soon she will bear me a grandson."

"That will be wonderful, I am sure, but I hope you are enjoying your granddaughters in the meantime."

"Are you kidding?" said Dilip. "He dotes on them like they're made of sugar and the world is full of rain."

Mr. Palewandram waved this off with a brusque, "Bah!"

When the kettle announced its boil with a shrill whistle, Mr. Palewandram poured the steaming water into a large, brown teapot.

"Sit," he commanded while reaching under the counter to a small bar fridge and removing a carton of milk. "We'll have tea and talk. I've been expecting you."

"You have?" Ian questioned.

"It was only a matter of time."

*

Over tea, Ian quickly disposed of the pleasantries and asked, "What did you know about my grandfather? Zelig mentioned that all anyone remembers is the monster, but I never heard those stories. My grandfather wasn't the doting type, but—"

"The stories are ugly," interrupted Mr. Palewandram. "And you have heard them, though at the time you may have refused to listen. That ugly boy with the unfortunate mother used to tease you mercilessly with them."

"Bo Kemp," said Dilip. "And he's still an ass."

Mr. Palewandram held up a finger to silence his son before continuing. "The stories were all based around the same set of circumstances: young women were seen entering your grandfather's shop in the evening, after business hours, never to be seen or heard from again. From there, as you can imagine, the tittle-tattle takes on a life of its own: rape, murder, cannibalism. People gossip and the tales grow taller. People will swear they heard murderous screams, others will whisper about rivers of blood flowing into the gutters. But dig deeper and none of the rumors hold root in fact. We do know women were seen entering your grandfather's shop after hours, but beyond that…" He shrugged. "No one is any more enlightened than anyone else."

Struggling to digest what he was hearing, Ian asked, "Was there ever a police investigation?"

"Not into those stories. No bodies, no crime." Mr. Palewandram squinted, capturing an old memory before it flitted away. "The police did poke around a little into your grandfather's death, but that went nowhere fast. Zelig saw to that."

"Zelig?" Ian asked. "I thought my grandfather died from an aneurism?"

"Oh, no." Mr. Palewandram shook his head in surprise. "I was there when Augustus died." He raised his hands to encompass not just his shop, but the neighborhood beyond its walls. "We all were."

"What happened?" Ian asked, barely able to breathe.

"It was the sound that made the neighbors come running. The Songs, Capellos, Wilfred Kemp, myself…everyone. Your father was on his knees in the middle of the street. I remember the look on his face and the moist blood that coated his apron. His wail was as unintelligible as it was frightening, so at first we thought there had been some kind of accident. But inside the store, we found your grandfather hanging from one of his own meat hooks." He lowered his gaze as if in shame, struggling with the memory of the experience before finishing in a whisper, "The river of blood that ran that day was his and his alone."

Ian's voice quavered as he struggled to get the words out. "Who did it?"

"You've already met him."

"Zelig?"

Mr. Palewandram nodded.

"But why?" Ian croaked.

"We never knew. At least not for sure." Mr. Palewandram sipped his tea in contemplation. "Your grandfather was a formidable man, and he protected this neighborhood from the likes of Zelig, but I can't imagine the take from a half dozen stores was worth killing anyone over." Mr. Palewandram's eyes grew brighter as if a secret long-held was to finally be revealed. "No. I believe it had something to do with the stories of the vanishing women. Whatever the truth, there is more to that than any of us know."

14

BACK ON THE street, his collar turned up against a cold drizzle that nipped at his cheeks and made his nose drip, Ian phoned Jersey and said, "Can we meet?"

"Sure," answered the detective, "but I don't have any results back on the ear yet."

"I have some information on that front that may help narrow the search."

"Oh?"

"I just watched a video of my father being gunned down."

"Jesus! Who shot the video?"

"A goon in the employ of a local gangster. You ever hear of someone named Zelig?"

"Ice Pick? Yeah, I know him. You better come in."

*

Ian plugged the meter and headed into the Portland Justice Center. The eighteen-story high-rise housed the Portland Police Bureau, four courtrooms and the 676-bed maximum-security Multnomah County Detention Center. That made it a one-stop shop for booking, arraignment and incarceration. Step off on the wrong floor, and a wide-eyed suspect could accidentally catch a glimpse of his overwashed, pink-shirted future — if he didn't cooperate.

Ian knew the building intimately as he had been through its doors more times than he liked to count, and not always for the purest of reasons.

Jersey met Ian when he stepped off the elevator on the thirteenth floor, and his first question was, "What the hell happened? You were in one piece when I left you yesterday."

Despite the breath-catching jabs of pain that caught him by surprise every time he moved too quickly, Ian had forgotten what he looked like to the outside world. He wasn't much for mirrors, and there were days when he often couldn't remember if he had combed his hair, never mind check for mustard stains on the edge of his mouth or ketchup on his shirt — or, in this case, cuts and bruises, splints and bandages.

"I had visitors last night," Ian explained.

"The Bowery brothers?"

Ian nodded.

"Why didn't you call me?"

Ian shrugged. "Their word against mine, and you know they'll have witnesses that swear they never left the wake. One odd thing though."

"They left you alive?" Jersey scolded in frustration.

"Apart from that. They wrote a note on my bathroom mirror that said *stay away*. That's not their style."

"I didn't know they could write."

"Exactly. I think the brothers were sent as a warning from this new player in town who executed Noah. He must have heard about my outburst at the funeral and doesn't want me stirring up trouble."

"You're not much of an obstacle," said Jersey matter-of-factly. "If he wanted rid."

"No, but I have a few friends who might miss me."

"Very few."

"But still."

"You should have called me."

"Yeah." Ian shrugged again. "I should have."

*

Jersey led Ian through a pair of frosted glass doors and into a cluttered maze of desks that held Portland PD's detective division. Ian recognized many of the faces from his work at Children First; others from his short time on the other side of the table.

On his escorted journey through the maze, Ian nodded to a familiar detective with a deeply tanned face that resembled well-worn leather. Dominating the space around him, the man held a passing resemblance to John Wayne in *True Grit*, minus the eye patch. With a non-regulation Stetson tilted back on his head, he was rubbing his bare feet with a hand towel while a pair of rattle-skin cowboy boots dried out on his desk. He didn't look happy, made even less so by his impeccably dressed partner in a bespoke suit who had a difficult time keeping the shit-eating grin off his face.

"Should I ask?" said Ian.

"I wouldn't," said Jersey. "When Preston's in one of his moods, it's wise to keep a wide berth."

Upon reaching Jersey's two-man cubicle, Ian was surprised to find a dangerously attractive woman occupying one of the chairs. Dressed in skintight blue jeans, killer boots, and a body-hugging black T-shirt, the athletic woman seemed far too tightly strung and far too sexy to be a cop. The badge on her belt and the shoulder holster under her arm, however, said otherwise.

"Have you met my partner before?" Jersey asked.

"Never had the pleasure." Ian held out his hand.

The woman looked Ian up and down, studying every inch of crumpled clothing and bandaged appendage, before accepting the handshake and introducing herself as Detective Amarela Valente.

"How long you been divorced?" she asked, her tongue hand-forged and razor sharp.

"That obvious?"

"Glaring."

As Ian grinned, Amarela snapped her fingers in sudden recognition.

"Wait a minute, you're that guy," she said, her words easing from between blood-orange lips as though being chewed before spoken, "from that thing a couple months back." Her smile was as disarming as it was unexpected. "I thought for sure you'd go down for that. But once Jersey filled me in on your daughter, I can't say I blame you."

"Thanks," said Ian awkwardly. He didn't see a need to mention the torment that haunted his sleep ever since 'that thing,' or the fact that he was as shocked as anyone when the case was unexpectedly dropped against him.

"Amarela's up to speed on the ear," said Jersey as he settled into his own chair. He indicated a spare fold-up for Ian. "But tell us about Zelig."

"I thought he was dead," said Amarela.

"He looks it," said Ian, which brought another ice-cold flash of smile from the female detective. Ian explained about the car ride and the video, before adding, "The beermat said McNally's."

"That narrows it down," said Amarela, sarcasm dripping. "Isn't every Irish bar named something like that?"

Jersey smirked. "Anything else?"

"The logo was a four-leaf clover—"

"Seriously?" Amarela interjected with more than a hint of derision.

"But there was a bite taken out of one of the leaves."

"Like an actual bite or was it part of the logo?"

"Part of the logo," said Ian.

"Well, that's something."

Amarela spun around to face her computer and began an Internet search.

With the female detective busy, Ian turned his attention to Jersey and said, "I also need to see what you can dig up about an old case."

"Which one?" asked Jersey.

"My grandfather. I always believed he died from an aneurysm, but I'm told that was a lie. Witnesses say he was murdered by Zelig, but the case got swept under the rug."

Before Jersey could reply, Amarela said, "Got something. There's a bar in Boston that matches your description."

"Run a check on any recent shootings in the Boston PD files," said Jersey.

"It's Boston," Amarela snipped. "Their murder rate is double the national average. You gotta be more specific than that."

Jersey sighed. "We're looking for a bullet-riddled John Doe with a missing ear who was found behind an Irish bar."

"I bet they get at least two of those a week," she said with a twinkle in her eye before picking up the phone.

"Your grandfather was murdered?" Jersey asked Ian, returning to the previous topic.

"That's what I'm told."

"And you think Ice Pick was involved?"

"Yes."

"Huh."

"And there's something else."

Both men became distracted when Amarela's voice suddenly dropped an octave, slipping effortlessly into a shimmering cloak of smoke and promise, as her flirtatious words stroked the ego of the recipient on the other end of the phone line. When she hung up, she tapped a file number into her computer.

"Google," she said as her screen refreshed, "got nothing on a lonely desk sergeant."

*

Leaning over Amarela's shoulder, Ian studied the dead man's face displayed on her computer screen. The corpse's pallor resembled a puddle of grimy rainwater growing stagnant in an alley, his mouth was slack and drooping to one side as though he had suffered a stroke, and his near-translucent eyelids were half-closed and sunk so deeply it was as if he had been dead for years.

All in all, Jack Quinn did not look at peace.

Even in death there was a deeply ingrained frown-line knotted between his eyes, and the mottled bruising of his flesh spoke volumes about his violent end. Close-up photos showed his missing ear, while other photos detailed each bullet's impact on his torso, legs and back.

He had gone down in a hailstorm of bullets, with most of them chewing him apart after the fatal shot had already hit its mark.

"*Cojeme*," said Amarela in a hushed tone. "They really wanted him dead."

"The irony is they were supposed to bring him in alive," said Ian. "He held the key to whatever Zelig wants from my family."

"So is it over?" Amarela asked, her distrusting eyes locking onto Ian's face as though attempting to peer beneath the surface of his flesh to watch how each individual muscle and ligament reacted.

"No." Ian shook his head. "That's why Zelig sent me the ear. He thinks the key was passed on to me."

"And it wasn't?"

"I don't even know what the key is." Ian turned to Jersey. "Can you dig up my grandfather's file?"

"We'll need to check the basement. Most of the archives were never transferred onto the server."

"What do you want me to do with…" Amarela swallowed the words she was going to use, and instead substituted, "…your father?"

Ian hesitated a moment before coming to the only conclusion he knew he had to. The only solution that would truly give him closure. "Is it possible to bring his body out here? We have a family plot."

"I'll check with Boston," said Amarela. "But if you foot the bill, I don't see a problem."

Ian reached out to brush the woman's shoulder in thanks, but stopped before his hand broke the barrier of her personal space. As an attractive woman she was likely prone to unwanted physical contact, and he didn't want to send the wrong message.

Instead, he simply said, "Thank you."

*

Jersey and Ian rode the elevator into the bowels of the building.

"I like your partner," said Ian as they descended. "Feisty. She must keep you on your toes."

"She does that." Jersey grinned. "She seemed to like you, too, which is unusual."

"For someone to like me?"

"Well, there is that." Jersey grinned wider, enjoying the banter. "No, for Amarela. She's not too keen on men in general. When the lieutenant put us together, I could tell he didn't think it would work. Amarela has been very vocal in the past about what douchebags her partners were, and the lieutenant was afraid we were going to end up in a messy sexual harassment lawsuit."

"So why does it work with you?"

"Isn't it obvious?" asked Jersey with a flicker of delight sparking in the corners of his eyes.

"Uh-nuh."

"She met her match in the hottie department." Jersey opened his arms to display his more than ample wares. "Women cannot get enough of this."

Both men laughed as the elevator reached its destination.

*

The basement of the Justice Center was a warren of windowless corridors filled with the droning cicada noise of large machinery secreted away behind closed doors and grated vents. At some point, however, somebody must have visited a hospital and noticed that painting color-coded arrows and follow-me lines on the wall made navigation easier.

A wide blue stripe led the pair directly to a door marked *Portland Police Department Archives — Authorized Entry Only.*

Jersey used his swipe card to unlock the magnetic latch, and flicked on the overhead lights from a bank of switches on the wall. The room pulsated as fluorescent bulbs flickered and warmed, transforming the stark white walls into a glacial blue to match the temperature.

The room was cold, its initial blast frosty enough to make Ian's breath visible. The temperature shift stopped Ian in his tracks, finding its frigidity unusually disturbing as if awakening an old memory that lingered just out of reach. He shrugged the disturbance off. It had already been a day of too many memories, and he didn't need any more added to the pile.

Along with temperature control, the storage room was unexpectedly spotless. Row upon row of white cardboard boxes were stacked on strong metal racks. Each box was labeled in bold, black ink with a series of numbers and a barcode.

Whoever had been behind the clever color-coded lines on the basement walls must have also had a hand in organizing this room.

"It's unmanned?" asked Ian.

Jersey shrugged. "We have a retired sergeant who comes in when needed, but I have no idea what schedule he's on. This room is rarely used except by the cold case crew."

Moving over to a lone computer station, Jersey logged in and typed in his search parameters. When he found what he was looking for, a tiny printer beside the computer spat out a piece of paper no larger than a fast food receipt.

Jersey took the receipt over to the rows of metal racks and soon matched the number printed on it to the correct box. He retrieved the box and brought it over to a long table surrounded by six metal chairs. With Ian by his side, Jersey pulled the lid off the box and retrieved the folders and files from inside.

*

One of the first folders that Ian opened contained crime scene photographs taken from inside the butcher shop. Most of the prints were eight-by-ten-inch, hand-developed black-and-whites on Kodak paper. Someone, however, had included a few color Polaroid snaps that surprisingly hadn't been turned into oily abstracts by the passage of time.

The photographs took Ian beyond the pristine customer area, behind the magnetic metal mesh curtain that Ian had loved to sneak through when he was a child — he remembered pretending that he was entering an alternate universe, one where gravity was lighter and he had to grip the earth with his toes or risk floating to the ceiling — and into the refrigerated processing area where the aesthetic art of butchery was practiced.

That room was where Ian first learned the skills of knife, saw, mallet, hatchet and grinder necessary to turn a hanging carcass into steaks, chops, roasts, racks, mince and sausage. But unlike when he apprenticed there, the room was in shambles.

The butcher who taught Ian, a white-haired Dutchman known as Smiling Sam who had worked under Augustus for decades, always told him how his grandfather kept as much control on sterility and cleanliness as he did on the edge of his favorite knife. One of Ian's less pleasant tasks had been to take the meat grinder apart at the end of each day and make sure it was as pristine as the day it was installed. Like a soldier cleaning his rifle, the task was finicky, repetitive and vital. The tiniest missed particle of meat could lead to a listeria outbreak. Any apprentice who messed up on the grinder, the

Dutchman told him, watched any possibility of a career vanish in the crimson haze of his grandfather's merciless rage.

The photographs showed a different rage; a tornado of pure brutality had swept through that room. Meat and steel were strewn on the floor without care; the cutting tables were overturned and dented as if an army of sledgehammers had undergone a communal schizophrenic break; and…

Ian turned over the next photograph to see his grandfather hanging from a butcher's hook.

His assailants had stabbed the hook into his back, driving deep to catch on his ribs and powerful back muscles, before suspending him above the ground. They had avoided damaging his spine, not wanting to numb the network of nerves that carried pain signals across his body.

Augustus Quinn did not die peacefully in his sleep of an aneurysm as Ian had always been told. He died kicking and screaming and suffering incredible pain.

The reason for his closed-casket funeral became obvious as the close-up of his face showed that one eye had been gouged out and left to dangle by its fibrous root; his lips were nipped, slashed and swollen; cheekbones smashed to powder; nose broken and flattened; and both ears were torn — not sliced, but *torn* — off.

Below the neck, things were even worse.

Augustus had been tortured beyond anything imaginable. There wasn't an inch of flesh left untouched from either knife, fist, hammer or flame. His stomach had been sliced open and intestines pooled on the floor; broken nubs of white bone protruded from flesh; his joints had been shattered, and the purple muscles on his legs bulged through deep, precise wounds.

Coroner notes written beneath the photographs revealed the victim had been alive through all of it before being left to die on the hook of blood loss, shock and asphyxiation.

Ian jumped in fright when Jersey placed a hand on his shoulder and squeezed. He dropped the photos and rubbed at his eyes. His voice trembled as he spoke.

"I can't even say I liked the man." Ian moved his head as though trying to shake away a hundred painful memories. "The truth is I hardly knew him, but…" He fanned the pile of photographs across the table. "No one should die like this."

Jersey squeezed his friend's shoulder even tighter before adding, "The case was dropped due to lack of evidence. But that's clearly bullshit. I found a statement from your father. It's less than a page and reads like a grade one book report. Despite being covered in your grandfather's blood, he couldn't identify the assailants. Officially, it's classified as a burglary gone wrong."

Ian shot a glance up at Jersey.

"I know," said Jersey, frustration creasing his face. "Fucking baloney."

Ian sucked in a deep breath, feeling the cold air freeze his lungs and numb his core. "Is there anything in the files about missing women?"

"No. Why?"

Ian explained about what he had been told by Mr. Palewandram.

"You think that's the reason for this?" Jersey pointed a finger at the photographs.

"It's the only thing I know of that Zelig is looking for. When I was in the car with him, he told me I had to find 'her.' But then he had some kind of fit before he could tell me who was missing or what my grandfather and father had to do with any of it."

"Women go missing in Portland all the time," said Jersey. "You know that better than most. But I haven't heard of any investigation into your grandfather on that front. Not to say one didn't exist. I'll check with cold case, but I'm thinking the officers who conducted this investigation know more than what's in these reports." Jersey's teeth clenched together before he added, "The fucked-up way this case was handled, they were obviously working for someone other than Portland PD."

"Can you find out who they were?"

Jersey's eyes hardened into irradiated plutonium. "Try and stop me."

15

TROUBLED BY WHAT he had seen in the photographs, Ian arrived at the offices of Children First in a haze of distraction. It was as if a part of his childhood had been erased and recorded over with new information without quite eliminating the static noise of the original.

Jeannie was slipping into her coat to go home for the evening when Ian walked through the door. She was excited to see him, her smile so luminous that it lit up her entire face and made her long hair glisten like electrified strands of copper and gold.

But Ian missed it, his vision barely registering her as anything more than a phantom, his lips mumbling a bland "Night, Jeannie" before brushing past her and heading into his office.

He didn't see her lingering by the door, chewing her lower lip in silent debate about whether she should leave it alone or push back, break her boss out of his inner distraction.

When Ian glanced up again, he was alone.

With a weary sigh, he walked out of his office and down the short hallway to the office of his partner, Linda McCabe. He knew she wasn't in, but she had recently purchased one of those coffee machines with the pods — designed for idiots like him who never quite figured out how to make drip coffee taste any good.

On autopilot, he made himself a strong black coffee. Sipping the brew, although barely tasting it, he returned to his desk and opened the large brown envelope that was waiting for him.

Inside was the contract to release any hold he may have on the home he had shared with his wife and daughter. The brick and mortar meant nothing, but it represented a life so precious, so vital that it had been the breath that filled his lungs. Now he was inhaling dust as though someone was attempting to erase that memory, too, wipe away that last remnant of goodness from his heart, that fragile sliver of joy.

As incentive for signing, there was a very large check clipped to the front page ready to be cashed.

Ian picked up a pen and signed everywhere there was a color-coded, sticky plastic arrow. Red arrows were for signatures, blue arrows for initials.

When he was done, he folded the check in half and slipped it into the back pocket of his jeans. He returned all the documents to the envelope. A large sticky note on the front told him to call a number when he was ready to have the documents picked up.

Ian dialed the number, spoke to someone on the other end, and waited.

When the courier arrived, Ian handed over the envelope. If you had asked him what the courier looked like or what company he worked for, he wouldn't be able to say.

Returning to his desk, Ian discovered his coffee cup was empty. He didn't remember drinking it, so he returned to Linda's office and made a fresh cup.

This time, he savored the strong brew and sip by sip tried to bring his mind back to the present.

In his front pocket, an antique key that had once belonged to his grandfather lay heavily against his thigh as though it carried a larger burden than being a simple keeper of locks.

16

IAN CLIMBED THE narrow staircase to the offices of Ragano & Associates, and knocked on the frosted glass door that bore the company's name. He was half an hour early, and didn't want to enter uninvited as he had before in case Ms. Ragano was with clients.

When Rossella opened the door, her dark curls dangled loosely around her shoulders, her scarlet lipstick imperfect with tiny grooves where her teeth had scraped it off in a nervous habit of concentration, and the top buttons of her blouse were undone to reveal a tantalizing glimpse of soft flesh straining against a blush lace bra.

"You're eager," she said with a playful chirp. "I was just wrapping up some paperwork before getting changed." She paused, becoming aware of the bruises on his face. "What happen—"

Without a word, Ian's right hand curled around the back of her neck, his fingers gliding through inky blackness to become trapped in soft entanglement. His palm cradled her skull, holding the weight of its perfect smooth roundness.

He pulled her close, his lips locking forcefully onto hers, his need palpable like a drowning man fighting for air. Rossella gasped as he steered her into the office, thumping the door closed behind them with his heel, his bandaged hand fumbling with the delicate buttons on her blouse.

He didn't have to fumble for long as Rossella caught his bottom lip between her teeth and met his challenge head on. Like two fierce warriors, their bodies came together in a match of strength and desire, lust and need.

Rossella released a moan of pleasure as Ian's hot mouth locked onto her breasts, his eager tongue exploring each rigid nipple, his teeth gently nibbling at the tender flesh. She unfastened his belt and yanked down his jeans, dropping to her knees as Ian gasped and groaned. But then his fingers tightened in her hair again, guiding her upwards, needing to consume rather than be consumed.

They found the waiting room couch as Ian finished undressing her. He kissed her feet, knees, thighs, stomach, chest, throat, mouth and face, ever drawn to her heated gaze, seeing the flame dance within and wondering if the friction of their bodies would create an inferno; if the fire department would show up to find human-shaped ash in the aftermath of spontaneous combustion.

Ian groaned from both pleasure and pain as his ribs and bruises protested, but he quieted any concern from Rossella with the heat of his mouth and the thrust of his hips.

When they climaxed, Ian's body melted on top of her like modeling clay left too long on a bedroom radiator.

Still grasping tightly to Rossella's naked form, Ian shifted their bodies so that he lay behind her on the couch. He needed to feel the length of her against him, with legs intertwined, her back pressed against his chest, her buttocks against his groin, his face buried in the fragrance of her hair like a blanket of starless night. His right hand stroked the comforting softness of her breast, while his bandaged left cradled her head.

Ian breathed her in as his lungs shuddered several times, sending a shiver down the length of his body, before finding a normal rhythm once again.

"You're still taking me to dinner," Rossella said, her voice playful.

"Definitely," said Ian, his voice lazy with surrender.

"Although I should finish with my client first."

Ian sat up, startled, his panic stopping only when Rossella's chuckle reached his ears.

"Psych," she said, a frisky pink tongue darting between her lips. "Not that you took the time to check I was alone."

Grinning, Ian softly slapped her bare ass as Rossella skipped away from the couch to a small refrigerator in the corner. From inside, she pulled out two bottles of water and tossed one over to him.

He caught it in his right hand, but before opening it, he studied the woman who had thrown it: naked, proud and unabashed.

"You are stunning," he said.

She blushed slightly and made a mock curtsy. "Thank you." Then wrinkling her nose, she added, "You, on the other hand, look a mess. What's with the bandages?"

"It's nothing," said Ian. "Ran into a little trouble, but it's under control."

"You sure?"

Ian opened the water bottle and took a long swallow before answering. "I'm sure."

Rossella crossed the room and bent to kiss him. The remainder of her lipstick was gone; her lips cold and tight from the icy water. "I'm going to grab a quick shower and get changed, then we're going out to eat. I'm starved."

After picking up her scattered clothing, Rossella strode into her office and through one of two secondary doors set between three overstuffed bookcases. She left the door partially open and a moment later Ian heard the soft clunk of a glass door followed by the hiss of a shower.

The thought of Rossella's naked body slippery with warm, soapy water made Ian's head spin, but he allowed the thought to dissolve in his mind like a rainfall of healing bliss.

With a relaxed smile, he rose from the couch, found his clothes and dressed.

*

Dinner was at a steak house on a dead-end street near Rossella's office. At one time, the road had been like any other in the down-town core, a simple connection between two main arteries. But a developer had convinced or bribed the city planner at the time to allow him to bridge two buildings he owned and create more high-traffic business frontage by sealing off the street.

While the original businesses left behind this new brick, chrome and glass wall were left to wither in its shadow, new businesses saw opportunity. They convinced, or coerced through threat of law-suits, the city to cover the tarmac with old-fashioned cobblestones, install cozy, black-iron light standards that flickered as though lit by candles, and provide economic development loans to antiqueify store frontage.

In this Victorian-era guise, the Tudor-style steak house had set up shop across from a British pub with dozens of micro and imported beers on tap. Other stores included a bicycle shop that sold vintage replicas alongside modern, battery-powered electrics with fat, four-inch tires and upscale leather grips; a gourmet cheese shop; handmade paper and card manufacturer; and several eclectic fashion outlets.

Ian sliced into his three-inch thick steak, lightly sprinkled with smoke-infused sea salt, and lifted it to his mouth. The juicy red meat attacked his tongue with flavor.

"Oh. My. God," he said aloud. "Why didn't I know about this place?"

"Obviously, you are very uncultured," said Rossella with a teas-ing smirk.

"Obviously," Ian agreed.

Sitting across from him, Rossella wore a figure-hugging black dress and a necklace of tiny, perfect pearls. Ian had always thought of pearls as something only old women wore, but their shimmering elegance added an extra touch of class to Rossella's already perfect silhouette. Unfortunately, this made his appearance even scruffier than he would have liked. It had been so long since he had been on a proper date that he had forgotten the gentlemen's basics: haircut and shave, ear and nose hair trim, clean shirt and tie, polished shoes, and most importantly, flowers for the lovely creature who was allowing him the privilege of her company.

Instead, he had arrived empty-handed and looked the same as he always did — which wasn't great.

Fortunately, Rossella didn't seem to mind.

Ian cut into a large potato, its skin charcoal black from being cooked directly in the coals of an outdoor fire. Inside, the potato was soft, creamy and delicate as though it had been carefully injected with butter during roasting.

"Oh. My. God," he said again as the potato melted on his tongue.

"I love to watch a man with an appetite," said Rossella as she dug into her own steak, which was of equal size to his own.

"Do they rent rooms here?" asked Ian. "I want to move in and never eat anywhere else again."

Rossella laughed with delight. "I'll ask the owner." She lifted a glass of robust red in a toast. "To pleasure."

Ian clinked his glass against hers.

"So tell me," she said as the meal progressed, "about your injuries."

"It's nothing, I told you."

"Mmmm, your words said it was nothing, but your actions showed something is troubling you. We don't know each other well yet, but I'm thinking what happened in my office isn't your usual seduction technique."

Ian blushed slightly before taking a long sip of wine. The

opulent, oak-finished Nero D'Avola swirled around his tongue with notes of licorice, black cherry and leather.

When he placed his glass back on the table, he released a sigh of both contentment and defeat.

"You're right," he admitted. "I'm not usually that…" He paused to find the right word.

"Aggressive," suggested Rossella.

When Ian winced, Rossella reached over and stroked his hand. "Not in a bad way," she added with a gentle smile. "I enjoyed myself. Immensely."

Ian relaxed. "It's been a long time since I've been with someone. I'd forgotten the comfort it brings."

Ian told her about his wife, Helena, his daughter, Emily, and the destruction of his family through guilt, grief and shame. Rossella listened, stroked his hand, and allowed the pain to be released.

"You still love her," she said. "Your wife."

"I never stopped," Ian admitted. "We were so damn happy together, the three of us, but…after…Helena and I lost our way and the road back has contained more bumps than we hoped."

When Ian was done with the past, Rossella changed the subject by asking, "And these new injuries?"

"Those are from last night, after I left you. A couple of punks broke into my house to teach me a lesson in manners and send a message."

"A message?"

"A warning really. Not to poke my nose into places it doesn't belong."

"Oh?"

"I attended the funeral of a young boy yesterday. He was one of my clients. I didn't take it well. His father was involved in a drug deal that went sour, and his son paid the price. His father wants it to end there. I don't."

Rossella's voice filled with concern. "Did you report the attack?"

"It's being handled." Ian shrugged dismissively. "But that's not what earlier was about. Between us, I mean."

Rossella smiled over the rim of her wine glass. "You're a complex man, Mr. Quinn."

"Not really, but I do come from a messed-up family. And it's even more messed up than I always thought."

"I don't understand."

Ian braced himself with another swallow of wine. It was as thick and dark as blood, and *damn* did it taste just right; the perfect pairing for a perfect meal.

He inhaled deeply, swelling his lungs to the point of pain, before releasing what he had to say in one gush. "Today, I watched a video of my father being gunned down in the street, and learned that my grandfather was murdered. I never knew either man, not really, but I feel the weight of their deaths like a stone against my chest." He paused, his gaze locking onto the beautiful woman before him. She was listening patiently, without judgment or comment, waiting for him to continue. "And there is a foot on that stone, pressing down, demanding that I provide answers to a question that I don't comprehend."

They were both quiet for a minute, each lifting a glass of wine to their lips, but neither really tasting, until Rossella asked, "Whose foot is on the stone?"

"His name is Zelig."

"Walter Zelig?"

Ian studied Rossella's face. "If Walter goes by the street name Ice Pick, then yeah. You know him?"

"I've met him," said Rossella, the words tiptoeing out of her mouth as though carefully chosen. "My grandfather knew everyone who's anyone in this town, but especially the criminals."

Ian reached across the table to take Rossella's hand. "Would your grandfather be willing to meet with me? I need to know what I'm dealing with, and how I put an end to it."

"I'll set it up."

Rossella's engaging smile had dimmed, so Ian asked, "Are you sure?"

Her smile returned and she squeezed his hand. "Leave it with me." She finished her glass of wine and signaled for the waiter. "I think we need another bottle after that, don't you?"

She ordered before Ian could reply.

*

"Would you like to see my inheritance?" Ian asked with a slurred thickness of tongue as they neared the bottom of their second bottle of Nero D'Avola.

Rossella laughed delightedly. "Now that's a line I haven't heard since my debutante ball."

Ian smirked. "Seriously? You were a debutante?"

Rossella flicked her hair out of her eyes and fixed Ian with a steely glare. "Do you have a problem with that?"

"No." Ian raised his hands in defense. "I just don't see you as the type to—"

"Type to what?"

Ian struggled to find the right words, and instead blurted, "To be so *fucking* demure."

Rossella tried to look shocked, but burst out laughing instead, which prompted irritated glances from other diners.

"Well," she said, the vowels losing their edge on her lubricated tongue, "you're correct. The eligible young bachelors were all rather horrified when I said I'd rather steal their money while they slept than lick their hairless little balls for housekeeping allowance."

Ian chuckled and drained the last of the bottle into their glasses. "And what did your grandfather say to that?"

"He said I'd make a damn fine lawyer."

This time, as their joint laughter filled the room to bursting, the young waiter rushed over to ask if they were quite ready for the bill and if he could call them a taxi.

"You bet," said Rossella with a wink. "This scoundrel still has a thing or two of interest to show me."

17

THE TAXI DROPPED them in front of the butcher's shop. The rain had stopped, leaving the street slick and fresh, but it would take more than a sprinkle of water to turn it new again.

Rossella stared up at the rusted tin pig hanging precariously above the doorway and saluted. "I know how you feel," she whispered to the pig.

"Come in," said Ian as he unlocked the door. "It might not be any warmer, but it's dry at least."

Inside, Ian was pleasantly surprised to find the cleaning crew had made a start. Not only was the front room beginning to look more like he remembered, but they were running several industrial-sized dehumidifiers and a couple of electric heaters to remove the damp chill from the place.

Beneath layers of dust and grime, solid hardwood floors and exposed brick walls were emerging. Ian had forgotten the subtle vibrancy of natural products. Hewn from the earth and locally sourced, the wood and brick gave off a frequency that artificial, mass-produced products never could. The wide oak planks were ingrained with rich shades of chestnut, maroon and amber, every battle scar adding to their character, while kiln-fired brick contained the rustic tones of autumn leaves.

"Cozy," said Rossella as she walked over to the large pane window that faced the street. It had been covered over by sheets of plywood on the outside when the shop went out of business, creating a canvas for creatively-stunted taggers to leave their crude calling cards in garish neon spray.

From this side, however, Rossella could read the sign painted on the glass: *Quinn Family Butchers*. And in smaller type beneath: *& Son*.

"Are you the son?" she asked.

"My father," said Ian. "But if he had stuck around and either of us had actually been interested in butchery, then, yeah, it could have been meant for me, too."

"It wasn't your calling?"

Ian shrugged. "My grandfather was a difficult man to like, so when he died and my father left, the shop became more of a yoke around our necks than anything we took pride in. I tried to take an interest, for my mother's sake, and even began my apprenticeship, but it didn't take."

"Pity," she said, her tongue playing with her lips again. "There is something cathartic about getting your hands bloody cutting up slabs of meat."

"Is that right?" Ian said with a smirk.

"Oh, trust me, butcher boy. Your senses are already tingling."

With a playful giggle, Rossella vanished through the magnetic curtain that separated the storefront from the back room. Ian quickly followed, feeling that familiar tingle deep in his bones, the childhood memory of inter-dimensional imagination, as he broke through the mesh.

As an adult, however, gravity appeared to exert equal force on both sides of the curtain.

The cleaners hadn't entered this area yet. The large room appeared frozen in time, unchanged apart from the accumulation of dust since the day men laid down their knives and cleavers and walked out the door. After his mother died, Ian made sure every employee was paid what he or she was owed. Most were grateful for the gesture, while others thought him a fool, but deep in his marrow Ian had never been comfortable with the concept of debt — even if that debt was inherited.

"Creepy," said Rossella when Ian joined her.

Her eyes were wide and glistening with curiosity as she studied the chains and pulleys, steel hooks and implements of barbarous intent.

"My grandfather died here," Ian said, crossing to one of the dangling hooks.

"Make a girl feel special," said Rossella.

"I only saw the evidence today," Ian added softly, lost in his own thoughts, missing the jibe. "I was told he died of an aneurism, but he was tortured to death right here." He grabbed the hook and made its heavy chain rattle. "That's why my father ran away. He was here, too. He saw it all."

"Okay, you're starting to freak me out."

Ian turned, his hand still clutching the chain, his mind releasing the images he had seen at the police station, bringing him back to the present.

"Sorry. Want to see the apartment upstairs?"

"Is it as nice as this?"

Ian shrugged. "Not quite."

Rossella laughed. "Okay, then, sure, let's go."

*

Rossella discovered the mother's old bedroom, and when she pulled off the dusty top comforter, the blankets underneath were still reasonably clean.

"She didn't die on these, did she?" Rosella asked.

"No. I stayed here for a week after the funeral. I remember

putting fresh sheets on before I left, as though I expected her to come back, but…"

"But?"

Ian's lips thinned to cover a troubling thought. "I didn't so much leave as run away and not look back. Not unlike my father."

"Except," Rossella said sternly, "all you left behind was a tired, old shop, not a wife and child."

Ian's smile found its light again as he shook off all melancholy and focused on the beautiful woman in front of him. "I have to warn you, the bed squeaks. Loudly."

Rossella kicked off her shoes and unzipped her dress. "Prove it."

They made love without haste, exploring each other's bodies with patience and care before falling asleep in a tender embrace.

The room was pitch black when Ian woke, but he could sense that he was alone. He stumbled to the bathroom and flicked on the light to pee. When he was done, he looked around the apartment, but the bare footsteps in the dust that led to the front door told him Rossella had snuck away to the comfort and cleanliness of her own place.

He couldn't blame her. The apartment really was a dump.

In the galley kitchen, Ian plucked a glass from the cupboard and filled it with cold water from the tap. While drinking, he realized that he had known exactly where the glass would be and how familiar its shape would feel in his hand. Not a thing had changed since the day he left, and yet it had been years. That was when he remembered he had been meaning to ask Rossella about who paid the taxes and fees on the building to keep the shop from falling into foreclosure.

Returning to bed, Ian wrestled with the pillows and sheets until realizing he couldn't find his way back into slumber. With a sigh, he pulled on his clothes and headed downstairs.

The storefront was toasty, the electric heaters and dehumidifiers working overtime to draw decades of damp from the floors and walls. The laminated posters on the wall that showed where each cut of meat came from on which animal were little more than crumbling shreds of cardboard, good for nothing but the dump.

The giant blackboard mounted on the brick wall behind the glass display cabinets, however, still displayed the faded remnants of the daily specials, including his grandfather's signature sausage.

None of the butchers' talents had stretched to chalk art, so the board was little more than a scribbled list, with one exception: someone had taken the time to draw a squiggly oval in yellow chalk around the words *Today's Special*.

It wasn't much, but it showed that someone had tried to make an effort even when the store was on its last legs. Ian felt a pang of guilt that he hadn't done more to save the family legacy, although one look at the forsaken street outside reminded him that all legacies must either adapt or disappear in time.

He crossed to the metal mesh curtain and pushed through to the back room.

*

The rear work space was utilitarian and bleak in comparison to its customer-friendly anterior. The warm oak flooring of the front room ended at the curtain's edge to be replaced with a durable vinyl sealed on top of hard concrete. Multi-colored specks patterned in the vinyl were intended to mask the inevitable scars and staining that came with mixing meat, bone and sharp implements, while industrial floor drains allowed the entire area to be washed and sanitized on a daily basis.

Today, many butcher shops installed an interior window into their workspace to allow customers to view the skill that went into creating their favorite cut of meat. It was one way of letting people know that a high standard of cleanliness wasn't lost and that a store advertising farm-raised, free-range chicken wasn't simply opening a box of pre-deboned breasts from a faceless, corporate slaughterhouse.

In Augustus Quinn's day, however, the wizard stayed behind his curtain, the quality of his product being the hallmark of his reputation. For Augustus to open a box of pre-packaged meat would be to slice his own throat.

Ian skirted the hanging hooks and crossed to the oversize, walk-in freezer. He braced himself, thoughts of mummified meat and trapped, stomach-churning odor nagging at him since spotting its sealed doors. Holding his breath, he yanked the door handle, feeling a brief moment of resistance before the vacuum pop.

Inside, the musty room was buzzing with the return of electricity, and a cloudy mist of bone-chilling air searched for something to preserve, but the shelves and hooks were bare.

Ian couldn't recall what had been done with the meat, but he was relieved to discover that someone had cleaned it out. He made a mental note to look into how he switched the refrigeration off. No point wasting electricity on something he would never need.

Studying the empty room, the hooks, chains and pulleys giving it the appearance of a torture chamber or hard-core S&M dungeon, he had a sudden thought of transforming it into a private meeting space for Children First; a place where he could mediate with clients without disturbing anyone at a nearby desk. The thick insulation already made it soundproof.

Exiting the room, he studied the open area with fresh eyes. There was more than enough space to move the entire Children First operation onto this floor, while still leaving him the apartment upstairs to live in.

The idea was exciting.

Brushing the dangling hooks aside, the iron clink and rattle of their chains a comfort in the deathly silence, Ian paced out the distance to the rear wall. The place would need to be gutted, but it definitely had potential and could save the financially hindered organization a small fortune in rent.

Along the back wall, four large, stainless steel sinks stood to one side of a van-sized garage door for deliveries. Unlike today's formed aluminum sheets that rattled in a breeze, this door was made of thick wood mounted on a steel frame, and likely took some muscle and grease to open.

Looking out of place on the other side of the door was a familiar oven-sized safe with all four corners bolted to the floor. For added security, the bolts had felt the lick of a welding torch, their iron caps permanently anchored in place.

The ancient safe reminded Ian of old black-and-white gangster flicks where the damp-browed safecracker used only skilled fingers and sensitive hearing to crack the code.

Crouching down, Ian studied the smooth black-iron face and faded gold script of its manufacturer, wondering what use his grandfather possibly had for such security. Granted, in the era when the store first opened, working men were used to being paid in small envelopes of cash at the end of each week. This allowed them to stop into the bar for a few beers on a Friday before handing over what was left to the wife in penance for sex and a hot meal. But Augustus never had more than a few employees at any one time, certainly not enough to justify the size of the safe.

On its front was a tarnished brass handle and a circular, combination lock.

Ian grabbed the handle and twisted, but it refused to budge.

He spun the combination lock, hearing it click like a playing card stuck in the spokes of a bicycle, and tried again.

It remained inert.

He wondered what the combination could be, what numbers

mattered to his grandfather, or did safes like this come with a code already programmed in?

The only numbers he could think of were the ones tattooed on his father's severed ear: 1976.

Was that why the ear was sent to me? he wondered. *Someone expected the numbers to have meaning to me beyond the year of Abbie's disappearance?*

The numbers on the dial only went up to twenty, so that left him two options. Remembering back to high school where every locker had a combination padlock, Ian spun the dial twice to clear away all previous numbers, and then entered 1, 9, 7 and 6.

He tried the handle. Nothing.

He spun the dial twice more before entering 19, 7 and 6.

Nothing.

Enjoying the puzzle, the distraction, he thought back again to his high school locker. There was always a trick to it. You spun the dial to the right for the first number, but then you had to spin it to the left for the second number and back to the right for the third.

He tried the three-number combination again, and this time was rewarded with a solid *chunk* as the lock disengaged. The twin hinges were old and rusted, any remnants of lubricating grease solidified and become clay, forcing him to put some muscle into it to swing the heavy door open.

Peering inside, Ian wasn't sure what to expect, but secretly hoped to find some small treasure that his grandfather had squirreled away. The interior of the safe contained a large cavity topped with a series of small wooden drawers. Each drawer was fronted with a delicate, hand-carved rose and a brass pull.

The main cavity was empty. No bags of gold, microfilm or bound ledgers filled with answers for what deadly rift had occurred between the Quinn family and Walter "Ice Pick" Zelig.

Ian opened the drawers, each one lined in blue velvet. In one drawer, he found a small brass key, its surface etched in green patina. Not knowing what it opened, he left it alone. In another drawer was a plain but solid pocket watch, made of steel rather than gold; a workingman's watch. Its short pocket chain was snapped in half. Turning it over, the back was engraved with his grandfather's name, A. Quinn, plus the acronym G.S.T.P and a serial number.

Ian smiled, pleased with the find. Although it was an object he had never seen before, the watch was a link to his roots, an entanglement of blood.

He opened another drawer and found a tarnished silver locket no larger than his thumbnail. There was no chain to accompany it. Ian cradled the locket in his palm and dug his nail into the tiny latch on its side until it popped. The locket opened on near-invisible hinges to reveal two photographs of smiling young women. On the left was his sister, Abbie, just as he remembered her, while the photo of his mother on the right was taken when she was very young, an age before Ian had come to know her face.

The resemblance between the two was obvious, especially around the mouth and chin. Abbie's nose, however, was his father's, his grandfather's, his own. She hadn't escaped that curse.

The last drawer was the largest and it contained another surprise. Wrapped inside an oil-stained rag was an old Army-issue Colt .45 sidearm. The gun was a brute: heavy and solid in the hand. Ian ejected the magazine, surprised to find it hadn't seized after all this time. A glimmer of brass showed it was loaded.

Ian rewrapped the gun in its greasy rag and returned it to the drawer before slipping the locket and watch into his pocket. He would study the watch later; see if he could get it working again.

Closing the safe, he spun the dial and stood. Instead of answers, the safe had, if anything, contained more questions. As a young boy, Ian had day dreamed about what his grandfather must keep in there, his childish imagination drifting from a magical, wish-granting lamp to giant bags of his favorite, mouth puckering, salted black licorice.

An image filled his mind of his grandfather bent over the safe, staring back at him angrily as though he had walked in on something he wasn't meant to see.

"Git out of here, boy."

"I'm just playing, Grandpa."

"You're too old for games. Go sweep the floors."

"That's no fun. I'm being an astronaut and this is Mars. What you doing?"

"None of your business."

"Can I help?"

"No. Go upstairs."

"Is it a secret?"

"Yes. Safes hold secrets. That's what they're made for."

"Why are you moving it?"

"Git out. Now!"

Ian replayed the image of his grandfather, the strained face, the blue vein bulging in his forehead, but there was something else. He froze the image in his mind, peering beyond his grandfather, seeing the safe tilted at an odd angle, one of the meat hooks connected to a loop on top.

Ian stood and studied the roof of the safe. The thick, metal loop was there, indented and near invisible, but that made sense. After all, how else could you move such a heavy object? However, the safe was also bolted securely to the concrete floor. Once you had it anchored in place, moving it would be an ordeal, and definitely not something one would do on their own.

Curious, Ian grabbed the nearest hook and slid it over to the safe. The hook slipped into the loop without effort, its chain gliding along a set of steel tracks with ease.

"This is stupid," he told himself, but that curious child within, the one who believed in time travel, aliens and alternate dimensions, egged him on.

Laughing at himself, Ian followed the hook's chain with his eyes, seeing it pass through several pulleys to an anchor on the wall. He removed the chain from the anchor and tugged, feeling his weight travel through the links and given extra leverage by the clever system of pulleys. The chain tightened on the safe's loop and offered a moment of resistance before…

Instead of being lifted, the angle of the chain tipped the safe onto one edge, its anchors still attached to a thick square of concrete flooring, lifting it free. The flecked vinyl coating had made the seam invisible to the naked eye.

Then, as Ian slowly released the chain, link by link, the safe was gently lowered onto its side.

Underneath, a secret trapdoor was revealed.

"Okay, Grandpa," Ian said under his breath as he released his grip on the chain, "you've got my attention."

18

IAN PEERED INTO the troubling depths of the dark hole. An iron ladder was anchored to the wall a short distance beneath the four-inch thick concrete lip. To one side of the ladder was the plastic plate of a lone switch.

Who hides a bunker beneath an iron safe? he asked himself. The answer was obvious: somebody with something to hide.

Filled with curiosity tinged with no small amount of trepidation, Ian dropped his legs over the edge, slipped his feet onto the first rung, and began his descent.

The hole was darkness absolute, swallowing the dim light from the room above within inches of its opening. The air inside was stale and cool, but didn't hold the fusty odor of mold or damp, which told Ian it had been constructed with ventilation and air flow in mind. When he was level with the switch, Ian flipped it on and was relieved to see the palpitation of bug-yellow light illuminating the darkness beneath.

The ladder descended for twelve feet before Ian reached hard ground. Releasing the ladder, he slowly turned around, not knowing what to expect but openly dreading the worst.

The room was a perfect cube, twelve feet by twelve feet by twelve feet, and constructed entirely of poured concrete. Tucked against the far wall was a sturdy metal cot with a thin mattress, sweat-stained pillow, and gray woolen blankets. Beside the bed was a small bookshelf stuffed with a collection of dog-eared paperbacks, a few magazines, and a reading lamp.

In the opposite corner was a stainless steel toilet and sink. The only other furniture was a tiny, dorm-sized fridge, an antique roll-top writing desk and a padded stool that took up a third corner.

Surprisingly, the wall closest to the ladder housed a second exit: a solid steel door with a dull finish that matched the plain gray concrete. The door had no handle, only a keyed deadbolt, and its hinges were anchored on the unseen side. Ian tested the door and wasn't surprised to find it wouldn't budge. He studied the lock, thinking of the brass key he had left in the safe upstairs. It looked like a possible match.

Crossing to the desk, Ian attempted to lift the roll-top, but it was also locked.

"What the hell were you hiding down here?" Ian asked aloud, but the plain walls swallowed his words, refusing to allow them an echo.

The room had all the makings of a prison cell, forcing Ian to wonder about the stories Mr. Palewandram mentioned of his grandfather's after-hours guests: young women who entered the store and were never seen again.

Looking at the ominous steel door, an icy dread seeped deep into his core.

As a child protection officer, Ian knew that monsters were real. He had borne witness to the horrors and depravity of man, and while it had toughened his skin and laid scales of iron across his heart, his soul was left unprotected. That vulnerability, that weakness, was the only way he could do his job, the only way he could respond when the angriest of children needed a word of praise or the most frightened needed a hug.

But if he was the spawn of such a monster?

Ian couldn't bear to think of what that would mean; how deep that wound would cut.

He began opening the few drawers that made up the desk's frame, searching for a key to unwrap its wooden shell. The drawers were littered with useless items from paperclips to rubber bands, but no keys.

Frustrated, he slammed one of the drawers closed just as the sudden arrival of voices drifted down from above. Heavy boots were accompanied by the banter of men; laughter and jovial profanity; the boom and clatter of moving machinery; the thump of hip-hop and chipper tones of a morning DJ.

Ian pulled out his phone and looked at the time. The sun had risen without his knowledge, and true to their word, the cleaning crew was back at work.

Ian sprinted to the ladder, climbed out of the hole, and returned the heavy safe to its proper upright position.

With the safe back in place, the entrance to the basement was invisible once more.

*

In need of a shower and change of clothes, Ian booked a taxi to retrieve his van and drove to the burbs. Arriving home, he found the driveway blocked by a large metal crate, and his front door open wide.

After parking in the street, Ian climbed out of his van just as two burly men exited through the door with his lone mattress between them. The sweat stains discoloring its quilted surface were both embarrassing and a testament of too many restless nights.

"You're not going to get much for that," said Ian as he walked up the driveway. "You'd have been better off with the Krugerrands under the floorboards."

Both men studied him with puzzlement, so Ian added, "You're stealing my bed."

"You Mr. Quinn?" Muscles No. 1 asked. Bald and broad-shouldered, he was a younger version of Mr. Clean from the TV commercials, except he was dressed in black rather than white. Maybe he was Mr. Dirty.

"Yeah, you want me to autograph it? Won't add much to the value."

Both men stared at him as if he had grown an extra head, and that head was trying to be a comedian.

Muscles dug out a folded piece of paper from his back pocket and held it out. "We were told to pack everything into this crate, then drop it where you need it. The crate is secure and waterproof so no need to rush unpacking. Call us when it's empty and we pick up."

Ian plucked the paper out of the mover's hand and gave it a quick read. Not one to waste time, it was signed by Helena's father.

With a sigh, Ian asked, "Have you packed my clothes yet?"

"Next on the list."

"Can you give me twenty minutes?"

"We'll finish the kitchen."

"Thanks."

Entering his home for the last time, Ian felt a swirl of panicked ghosts descend upon him. Phantom hands grabbed at his face, clutched his arms and clung to the tips of his fingers with tiny, cat-like claws. Overpowering memories of laughter and tears, joy and sorrow, pure debilitating agony…each specter weighed on him, some more heavily than others.

Gathering the restless spirits to his bosom, afraid to let any of them go, he subconsciously whispered, "You're coming with me."

*

After his shower, Ian gave the movers the address of the butcher's shop and climbed back in his van. He lifted his phone to take a final photo of the house, but stopped before pressing the button. The house was just a house, not any different than any other property on the street. It was a place where a family lived, was happy for a while, and then was not. Elsewhere in this city, this state, this country, hundreds of people were doing the same — *leaving*. Leaving out of guilt, out of pain, out of fucking misery.

He was no different except that every loss was as unique to each individual as his or her own fingerprint. His was a beautiful baby girl named Emily and she was a gaping wound in his heart that could never be made whole again.

Ian's phone rang as he lowered it from his face, his sight too blurry to focus. He wiped at his eyes as he answered.

"Ian Quinn."

"Rossella Ragano," chirped the caller mockingly.

Ian smiled. "Good morning, Ms. Ragano. You were spirited away last night."

"Hardly." Rossella laughed. "You were snoring so loud you didn't hear me stomping around trying to find my underwear."

"You don't like my new place?"

"Maybe once it's less spidery."

"Spidery? Is that a word?"

"Of course it is, I'm a lawyer. Where are you?"

Ian told her.

"Yuck. You don't strike me as the suburban sort."

"Maybe that's why the neighbors are cheering my exit. I hear they're planning a ticker-tape parade and celebratory barbecue."

"Mmmm, I love barbecue."

"We're not invited."

"Darn, it would be fun to eat with our hands, chug Crantinis or whatever suburbanites drink these days, and go skinny-dipping in the family pool."

Ian laughed. "That would be fun."

"Speaking of food. Are you free for breakfast?"

"Always."

"My grandfather is most lucid in the mornings. I'll tell the house to expect us."

Rossella gave him an address before disconnecting.

Ian took one last look around the sleepy neighborhood as if seeing it for the first time. Rossella was right, he didn't belong here, and yet this is where he found true happiness. At least for a while.

Ian punched in the number for the cleaners and asked Clark if he could focus his crew on the apartment upstairs prior to tackling the rear workshop.

"I'd like it to be less spidery before moving in," said Ian.

Clark laughed before answering, "That's our specialty."

19

THE ADDRESS THAT Rossella sent him to wasn't a house at all; it was a white marble mansion with an uncommon red slate roof. It was also situated on a landscaped acre behind a fence that made presidential security seem quaint.

Ian stopped at an iron gate — disturbing in its design that captured a cackle of demons playing hide-and-seek in a lush forest of deadly, barbed spikes — and pressed an intercom embedded in one of the stone posts.

"Mr. Quinn?" asked the post.

"You can see me?" asked Ian, looking around for the camera.

"You are expected," said the post. "You will find ample parking available at the top of the driveway. Ms. Ragano is here."

The gates swung open on well-oiled hinges, metallic gargoyles grinning and scowling as the morning light played across demonic countenances.

The lazy S-shaped driveway was made of burgundy shale that crunched under the van's tires, which made Ian wonder if it was somebody's job to rake the shale back into place after each vehicular disturbance. At the top of the driveway, he spotted a ruby BMW 6 Series Cabriolet parked near a life-sized stone lion. The license plate on the convertible read: *SP01LD*.

Parking his van beside it, Ian hoped the lion wouldn't object. It already looked perturbed.

A confident young man in his late twenties greeted Ian at the front door. He was dressed in a razor-sharp, steel grey suit, but in deference to his age had added a bright splash of color to the ensemble with a blue silk tie. The tie was ornamented with a golden tack-pin in the shape of a crescent moon.

The man held out his hand in greeting. It was so soft and smooth, Ian wondered if he nightly dipped it in coconut oil and encased it within a white cotton glove.

"Mr. Quinn, so pleased to meet you. My name is Archibald Pierce, Mr. Ragano's personal assistant."

"And how is Mr. Ragano this morning?" Ian asked.

"In wonderful spirits, I am pleased to say. He is very much looking forward to meeting you." He stepped back to allow passage. "Please, come in. Coffee is being served in the dining room."

Ian crossed the threshold into a wide lobby dominated by a butterfly-shaped staircase that could have easily been stolen from the set of *Gone With The Wind*. Everything was oversized — from the furniture to the looming chandeliers and even the art on the walls — as though designed to make every guest feel just a little bit smaller than they actually were.

"This way," encouraged Archibald as he headed down a wide hallway to a set of impenetrable French doors.

Despite the home's old-world charm, Ian spotted an abundance of discreet state-of-the-art electronic surveillance devices hidden in various nooks and crannies. When the lights were out, he imagined this lobby was an impenetrable web of laser tripwires and night-vision cameras. It was understandable. Being a mob lawyer, Mr. Ragano had every right to be paranoid.

Following behind young Archibald, Ian's head swiveled from side to side as he took in the grandeur of the place. Interestingly, all of the large oil paintings hung on the walls were nudes. Some were abstract, others heavy-breasted realism, making it clear Rossella's grandfather had a fondness for the female form — especially curvaceous black women.

When Ian entered the dining room, Rossella stood and walked over to greet him. Wrapping her arm in his, she kissed him softly on the cheek and escorted him to the far end of the table where she introduced her grandfather.

Roberto Ragano was as impeccably dressed as his assistant, except his fitting had taken place at a time when he carried more meat on his bones. Beneath an impressively wild pair of snow-white eyebrows, his flesh was soft and sallow, the wrinkles so deep that his face was a lesson in geology. But there was still a sharpness to his deep brown eyes, a glint of the giant he once was.

Ian offered his hand and the man squeezed it with unexpected vigor.

"It's a pleasure to meet you, Mr. Ragano."

The man studied Ian in return before he spoke, his investigative gaze taking in every inch of him from his overgrown haircut to his wrinkled clothes and slightly mismatched socks.

"How piss poor are you?" he asked gruffly.

"Grandpa!" Rossella chided, but Ian laughed at the candor.

"Compared to you? I was frightened to wipe my shoes in case the friction wore out the soles."

Mr. Ragano chuckled. "That's a good one." His eyes softened as he gazed down at Ian's choice of footwear. "I can see why you'd be worried."

"Grandpa, enough!"

"Bah." Mr. Ragano waved his granddaughter's protests away. "Pull up a chair, young man, let's eat. I'm sure you could use it."

Ian took a seat beside Rossella as two black maids who could have been mother and daughter brought out breakfast.

As he ate, Ian said, "Rossella tells me you knew my grandfather, Augustus Quinn."

"I did. A real stubborn son of a bitch that one."

"Gran—"

"Don't shush me, Rossella. It ain't cursing if it's the truth. August was stubborn as a two-headed mule. Quick to cock his fists, too. Man didn't know how to back down from a fight."

"Who was he fighting with?" Ian asked.

"Ice Pick, of course. Walter and August were like two peas in a one-pea pod. From the first time they met, they were at each other's throats. I tried to broker peace, but there was no point. It was all going to end badly."

Mr. Ragano stopped mid-chew and stared across the table at Ian as though seeing him for the first time. "Are you August's boy?"

"Grandson," Ian said.

"Huh. Where's your father?"

"He died."

"Ah. Your grandpa's dead, too. I remember that."

"Yes."

"Walter is a friend...well, an associate, but I always liked August. Stubborn as a mule though."

"Can you tell me what their feud was about?"

"What's any feud between men about? Women."

"What women?" Ian asked.

"Walter has a daughter. Pretty young thing. All hair, teeth and legs like a prancing colt. She disappeared and Walter blamed August. He threatened August's granddaughter in retaliation, but then she disappeared, too." He shook his head. "What a mess."

Ian's heart stopped beating as his voice caught in his throat before the words rushed out in one mad purge. "Was Zelig responsible for my sister's disappearance?"

"Huh?" Mr. Ragano seemed confused as he glanced down at his

plate and his cheeks flushed an angry red. Then his voice boomed, "Marcia! Where's my fucking bacon? Did you take my bacon?"

"You ate it, Grandpa," Rossella said.

"I did not. I'd goddamn well remember if I ate bacon." He forced out a noisy burp and waved it towards his granddaughter. "Smell that? No fucking bacon."

The older black woman came rushing out of the kitchen with a plate layered with bacon as if she had been waiting for just such a complaint.

"You hush now, Mr. Ragano," she said as she hurried over to the table. "Here's your bacon. Extra crispy just the way you like it."

"You were keeping it for yourself, weren't you?" Mr. Ragano roared. "Think I'm going senile, but I know when you're hiding things from me. Trying to rob me blind no doubt."

"Grandpa," Rossella scolded. "Don't be cruel."

The maid shook her head as if she had heard it a thousand times before and placed more bacon on his plate. As her hand moved away, Mr. Ragano grabbed her wrist. "You gonna play with me later, Marcia?" he asked in a childlike voice. "Run a bath and get the boats out? I have that new blue speedboat to play with."

"You've already had your bath this morning," said the woman as she gently broke his grip. "But you can have another one tonight if you'd like."

After the maid returned to the kitchen, Mr. Ragano picked up a strip of bacon with his fingers and sucked on it until it crumbled apart in his mouth. Returning the remaining half to his plate, he turned to Ian and said, "Are you August's boy?"

"Grandson," Ian repeated.

"You look like him. Same nose and a hardness around the eyes. You as obstinate? 'Cause that man was stubborn as a two-headed mule."

"Afraid so," said Ian. "Did Walter harm my sister?"

"Walter?"

"Zelig," said Ian.

"Watch out for him. Ice Pick is a dangerous man, especially since his daughter disappeared. He blamed August, you know?"

"What happened to her?" Ian asked, trying to keep the conversation alive despite losing the direction he wanted.

"She was a pretty young thing. All hair, legs and teeth. They named her Constance, after her grandmother. She disappeared. Must be a while ago now."

"How old was she when she disappeared?" Ian pressed.

"It was right after her twenty-first. Walter threw a big party. Pulled out all the stops. Constance looks beautiful, but there's something broken in her, a darkness that slithers beneath her flesh. I don't like to be alone with her." A visible shudder made his shoulders jerk. "That's an odd thing to say, isn't it?" He glanced at his granddaughter and smiled warmly. "Not like you, you're a good girl, always kind, but that one has something wrong. You can't tell Walter though. He worships her. Broke his heart when she disappeared. I think he's planning to hurt August."

"Why did he blame August?" Ian asked, knowing reality was crumbling around their feet.

The old man looked at Ian as if he was stupid. "Well, that's what August does, isn't it? He makes people disappear."

Staring down at his plate again, Mr. Ragano's cheeks flared crimson. "Marcia!" he screamed. "Where's the bacon? Did you steal my fucking bacon?" Tears filled his eyes as he looked at his plate. "Woman's always stealing from me. Thinks I don't notice, but I see everything."

Rossella reached out and squeezed her grandfather's hand as he began to softly weep.

*

Ian stood beside the stone lion, sipping on a cup of coffee he had taken from the table after Archibald entered the room to take care of Rossella's grandfather.

The scene had become too personal, family only, and so he had made himself scarce.

He heard the front door open, followed by the click of Rossella's heels against the marble stairs. When she was close, he inhaled her perfume.

"Sorry you had to witness that," she said. "There are times when he's so lucid, sometimes for hours, that it's easy to forget just how ill he really is."

"It must be difficult," said Ian.

"We've had deep, intellectual conversations about the law that make Supreme Court arguments sound like idle chit-chat, and then he'll call me by my mother's name and it's…it's just all gone."

"He seems to be in good hands," said Ian, draining the last of his coffee.

Rossella smiled. "Marcia is wonderful with him. She's been with us for decades, although how she puts up with his abuse, I don't know. He was never like that before…before the illness."

"It's a damn shame," said Ian. "All that knowledge, all those secrets, being eaten away." He sighed. "He knew about my sister."

Rossella squeezed his arm. "We can try again. After he's had a rest."

"Will he remember I was here? Any of the conversation we started?"

Rossella lowered her gaze. "Probably not. Sorry."

Ian laid his hand on top of hers and returned the squeeze. "Don't be sorry. I learned some things I didn't know before. It's a start."

"I'll talk with him later. See if I can learn anything more about your sister."

"Thanks." Ian squeezed her hand again, but this time it was a gesture to let him go. He handed her the coffee cup and bent to kiss her. The embrace was short, both of them distracted by the day ahead.

20

A FTER EXITING THE lawyer's demonic gate, Ian pulled over to the side of the road and parked. His van didn't belong in this neighborhood, its minimum-wage-with-a-kid-on-the-way presence likely making some of the privileged homeowners nervous. But the vehicle was pre-Bluetooth and therefore didn't have hands-free dialing.

He called Jersey and said, "Zelig had a daughter who went missing sometime before my sister disappeared. Can you check if it was ever investigated?"

"You know," said Jersey, stifling a yawn, "I preferred it when you were so skittish to ask me for a favor that you softened the blow with doughnuts. When was the last time you brought me a doughnut?"

"Sorry. Got a lot on my mind."

"Buy me lunch and we'll forget about it."

"Lunch?"

"It's the meal between breakfast and supper. Becoming quite popular with the working class I hear." Jersey paused for laughter, but when none came, he pressed on. "I have a line on the detectives who wrote off your grandfather's death. They're both retired but still tight as thieves. They meet up for a liquid lunch daily at The Crown Royal, you know it?"

"It's near work, but I thought it got shut down for a list of health violations."

"It did. New owners secured the liquor license and reopened a few months back. Still a dive though, just the way the faithful like it."

"And you want to eat there?"

Jersey laughed. "Okay, maybe we eat after."

Ian hung up, checked his rearview for traffic and slid the van into drive. Before he could pull away from the curb, however, his phone rang.

Throwing the van back into park, Ian glanced at the Caller ID and answered.

"Hey, Jeannie. I was just heading in."

"Noah's mother is here." Jeannie's voice held an edge of anxious discomfort. "She says you have an appointment, but I don't have anything written in your calendar."

"It's okay. We may have set something up before Noah's funeral. How is she?"

Jeannie lowered her voice to a notch only slightly above a whisper. "Not good. She keeps muttering to herself and can barely hold eye contact. I don't think she's slept in days, and she's certainly not showered."

"Give her coffee with lots of sugar. I'll be there soon."

*

Ian parked in his usual spot in the empty lot across from Children First. An Elvis impersonator was crooning to an audience of none on the corner, while a shooting gallery had set up shop behind a large trash container opposite. Leaning against an overloaded shopping cart, Tommy the Tink was sucking on a mixture of cranberry juice and rubbing alcohol.

Spotting Ian, Tommy shook his head in disgust at the cluster of addicts as a junkie injected his girlfriend in the neck before administering to himself. The dope was strong, taking immediate effect. As the addict nodded off, the shared needle wavered at half-mast, stuck amidst an arm's length of bruised flesh.

"Every morning," yelled Tommy, his words a slur. "Fuckin' sharps everywhere."

"You eaten yet?" Ian called back.

Tommy raised his bottle. "Got what I need."

"Make sure you get to the mission for lunch."

"Yeah, yeah."

Ian crossed at the corner, nodded to Elvis — he preferred the older one, but the youngster had better moves — and spotted Noah's mother standing on the sidewalk in front of Children First. The cigarette in her mouth was being sucked down in large inhalations, while the soiled remains of dead filters lay discarded at her feet.

Her name was Shirley and she looked as despondent as a paper doll left overnight in the rain. A clingy black dress, the same one she wore to her son's funeral, was twisted and stretched as though she had been in battle. Her nylons were ripped from ankles to knees, and her shoes, the toes split open to expose cheap plastic caps beneath a thin, pleather skin, barely clung to her feet.

When she turned to face him, her face was the color of death with dark eyeliner leaking down her cheeks.

Her thin lips curled as Ian approached. When he was just a foot away, an open hand swung up to slap him hard across the cheek. One of her fingernails, broken and chewed, caught his flesh and drew blood.

Ian took a step back, recoiling from the sharp pain.

"You," the woman screamed, "are fucking marked."

"What does that mean?" Ian asked.

"He took my son and you did nothing. So what the fuck do I care if he wants you?"

Snot bubbled at the woman's nose as she struggled to contain her grief. "Why are all men bastards? Why? The whole fucking lot of you."

The woman lunged forward again, but this time she wrapped her arms around his neck and pulled him in close. Cold lips were jammed against his ear, a sticky, wet nose tickling the back of his neck.

"My son didn't deserve this, but nobody wants to make the bastard pay. So fuck you, fuck all of you."

When the woman released him, a white paneled van pulled over to the curb and its side door slid open. Two men wearing black woolen ski masks pointed handguns at Ian and ordered him inside.

"If you make us chase you," said the driver, "they'll shoot her first."

Shirley shot the men an evil glare, but the anger only flashed for a moment before it dimmed into acceptance. This was her lot, these were the men she climbed into bed with, and the joke was on her that once upon a time she thought it was actually possible to escape.

Shirley refused to meet his gaze as Ian climbed into the van and the sliding door slammed shut.

*

Inside the van, the two gunmen dropped a black hood over Ian's head and secured it tightly around his neck. They then forced his hands behind his back, looped a plastic band around his wrists and zipped it tight.

"What 'bout his feet?" asked one of the men, his voice revealing everything. It belonged to Noah's father, Rory Bowery.

"Leave 'em," said the older brother, Ryan. "I don't want to be carrying the fat bastard. He looks heavy."

Rory laughed. "True dat."

Ian thought about asking the brothers what the hell was going on, but figured it might just piss them off even further, and he would find out soon enough anyway.

When the van stopped moving, Ian was ushered out and guided along a loose gravel path.

"Watch your step, old man," said Rory.

Ian's left toe caught a raised lip as the ground shifted from gravel to concrete. He stumbled before his escort tightened the grip on his arm to hold him steady.

"WhatdidIjustsay?" Rory grumbled. "Fuckin' retard."

Ian didn't bother pointing out that it was difficult to watch one's step when you were blindfolded.

They moved a few more paces before he was stopped and told to remain still. An overhead garage door rumbled to life and rolled into place behind them.

Once the door settled, Ian was pushed down onto a cold metal chair. The snick of a switchblade caused him to flinch, but it was only used to cut the plastic band around his wrists. Next, the noose around his neck was loosened and the hood removed.

Ian blinked in the dim light of the musty garage, regaining his focus. The smell of oil and grease added a bitter tang to the air; the remains of an old hydraulic lift still bolted to the stained cement floor. The few windows were covered in old newspapers and duct tape.

A large man with hard eyes the color of nail heads sat across from him. He had a chest like a silverback gorilla, a straining white muscle shirt showing off years spent pumping iron in the gym or prison yard. His heavily veined arms were covered in full-sleeve tatts that reached across his shoulders to lick at a short neck. Above the stubby neck was a solid square head that could have been cleaved out of a block of industrial cement. Stamped onto the head was a stubbled face that only a blind grandmother could love.

A U-shaped scar took up most of his wide forehead as though he had been kicked by a horse, and the first thought that entered Ian's mind was: *You must have been one ugly kid.*

Standing on either side of the man were the two brothers, both still wearing their full-face ski masks, white stitching around the eyes, nose and mouth attempting to make them look like spooky skeletons.

Ian glanced over his shoulder, spotted a third masked man standing by the garage door. He was skinny. The driver, not muscle.

Ian turned forward again and nodded at the two brothers. "Rory. Ryan. Who's your friend?"

"Shit!" said Rory. "He made us."

"That's 'cause you never shut your fuckin' mouth," said Ryan.

"Quiet," said the large man in the middle. "And take off those masks."

Both brothers obeyed, their eyes blazing with anger and aiming all the heat at Ian.

"I've been wanting to meet you, Ian Quinn," said the behemoth in a voice that added moisture to each word as though he had to continually suck back extra spittle, yet held more refinement than his appearance would suggest. "But it was never a priority until recently."

"Until you killed Noah," said Ian.

The man moved his large head a half-inch to either side. "That matter is none of your concern. And, no, that has nothing to do with this."

"I disagree." Ian's gaze locked onto Rory's. "What kind of man follows the monster who butchered his son?"

Rory flinched but remained silent.

"A man who prefers to live and profit rather than suffer and die," said the gorilla.

"A coward," said Ian.

"A survivor," countered the gorilla.

"Is that what Shirley calls you?" Ian said to Rory. "A survivor. Bet it's not."

"Fuck you!"

Rory broke from his position and rushed at Ian, but he moved too close to the gorilla. With a vicious backhand, the gorilla sent Rory flying onto his ass.

"Enough!" yelled the gorilla. Baring his teeth — strong, sharp and vicious — he leaned forward, capturing Ian's full attention. "You play a dangerous game."

"I don't have much to lose."

"Not much, no," agreed the gorilla. "But despite everything, you are not an island. There are still people you care about." The gorilla showed his teeth again. They needed some serious work. "Don't make me hurt them."

Ian exhaled heavily. "What do you want?"

"Tell me about Walter Zelig."

The query caught Ian by surprise. "Ice Pick?"

"Yes. You have been looking into his past. It is linked with your own, no?"

Ian shrugged. "He knew my grandfather. In fact, he may have killed him. He also knew my father, and likely killed him, too."

"And your sister?" asked the gorilla.

Ian was taken aback. "What do you know about my sister?"

The gorilla shrugged. "Nothing. Just that she is also connected, is that not correct?"

"I don't know what his connection is to my sister," said Ian. "She disappeared a short time after Zelig's daughter vanished. I've been told the disappearances may be linked."

"Who told you this?"

Ian saw no reason to lie. "Zelig's lawyer, but his testimony isn't reliable. He has Alzheimer's." Ian stopped and studied the gorilla's scar-ravaged face. "Why are you interested?"

"He's a competitor."

"He's an old man."

The gorilla grinned. It wasn't friendly. "Old men with sharpened teeth are far more dangerous than young ones without."

Ian wasn't exactly sure what that meant, but he decided not to argue. "So what happens now?"

"That is up to you."

"I don't really think it is."

"What would you like to see happen?" asked the gorilla.

Ian thought for a moment, and then said, "I would like Rory to grow a set of balls and blow your fucking head off for what you did to Noah. Then I would like him to shove the gun in his own mouth and pull the trigger again." He turned his gaze on the other brother. "Ryan and I can settle our score the old-fashioned way, only this time, I get the bat." He swiveled his head further to fix on the driver standing silently by the door. "Him, I don't have a problem with."

"Let me propose an alternative," said the gorilla. "You will leave the same way you arrived, and the brothers will be instructed not to harm you. You will continue to investigate Walter Zelig, but when I call, you will answer my questions without hesitation."

"And if I refuse?"

"You are not that stupid."

Ian had to agree, he wasn't.

*

The Bowery brothers dropped Ian off in front of Children First. True to the gorilla's word, they didn't harm him, although even beneath his hood Ian could feel the inner struggle making Rory twitch. Several times, the younger brother kicked at the walls of the van just to make some noise.

Ian knew it would take only one flint-edged comment to spark the brother's temper and ignite his fury, but decided his own body was already too battered and bruised to guarantee a worthwhile outcome.

He let it be. For now.

But, as Ian had told Rossella's grandfather over breakfast, he came from a long line of stubborn men, and that meant never forgetting an injustice, nor a beating owed.

21

IAN SPENT THE morning with clients and catching up on reams of government-mandated paperwork. He enjoyed the face-to-face work, breaking down the barriers of anger and resentment that were an inevitable part of supervised visitation, but found himself struggling to keep his focus when it came to writing reports.

The Anderson case, in particular, was a mess as both parents were so angry at each other they couldn't see how it was ripping their son's life apart.

"Maybe you guys need to get into a boxing ring," Ian suggested. "Cody and I can be judges."

Both parents stared at him in shocked disbelief.

"I don't want to hit my wife," said the husband.

"Oh, but you do," said Ian. "I can hear the venom in every word that leaves your lips. You believe your spouse's transformation is an affront to your manhood and you want to punish somebody for it. If she was having an affair, you'd know what to do. You would have somebody to hit. Well, guess what? The other person in this triangle is inside your wife and he's aching to get out. So let's step in the ring and sort this out once and for all."

"You're insane," said the man.

"I don't know," said the woman. "I like the idea."

"What about you, Cody?" asked Ian.

Cody shook his head and moved closer to his mom protectively. His mother had started on testosterone injections and her body was changing, but for the moment, she was still a she — at least outwardly.

"Okay," said Ian. "If boxing is out, then we need to talk… about *everything*. Outside of this room, I need both of you to work on your issues as parents. Resolve this anger. But in here, our focus is Cody. That will mean answering some difficult questions, but the more Cody understands about what is happening and why, the easier his acceptance of the future will be." Ian's eyes softened. "Your son loves you. Both of you. If he didn't, he would have relished the idea of watching you knock each other's teeth out. A lot of parents I work with would kill for that bond with their kids. So let's nurture that and move forward."

*

The Crown Royal had originally been shuttered by the Oregon Liquor Control Commission for a long series of complaints involving the action word 'punched': patrons punched employees; employees punched patrons; patrons punched patrons, etcetera. Naturally, this was just the tip of the iceberg as one OLCC inspector made the mistake of entering the women's washroom on a Friday night. It took twenty-two stitches to close the slash on her face.

Ian entered and headed for a stool at the bar. Interior lighting was turned low — ignoring the antiquated bylaw that illumination must be bright enough to read a newspaper — and the exterior windows painted near black so that serious drinkers wouldn't be disturbed by the passing of day. Ian walked straight until he stumbled into an empty bar stool and climbed aboard.

It was going to take a minute for his eyes to adjust before he knew if Jersey had arrived or if he was sitting here alone.

"What you drinking?" asked a disembodied voice from behind the bar.

"Something dark," said Ian, thinking he was making a joke.

"You got it."

When the bartender returned, he slid over a pint of Sinistør Black Ale — at least that was the logo printed on the glass.

A hand landed on Ian's shoulder and Jersey said, "What you drinking?"

"Something dark," repeated Ian.

"Appropriate."

"I thought so."

Jersey ordered a spicy tomato juice.

"You should always order alcohol in a place like this," said Ian.

"Why's that?"

"It's the only thing that's sterile."

"Why I add the hot sauce."

After Jersey's drink arrived, Ian paid for both and added a generous tip.

"Your cops here?" he asked.

"In the corner booth."

Ian caught the bartender's attention again. Because of the tip, he was over in a heartbeat. Ian explained that he wanted to buy a round for the two men in the corner booth.

"I'll bring it over," said the barman.

With the drinks being poured, Jersey and Ian moved in.

"Mind if we join you?" asked Jersey.

"Drinks are on the way," added Ian.

The two men looked at each other, then shifted their gaze over to the barman to see what he was pouring before nodding.

"Portland PD?" one of the men asked Jersey.

"Jersey Castle, homicide. This is my friend, Ian Quinn."

"Bill Bennett, robbery homicide," said the man. "That's Detective Jim Donald, retired."

The four men shook hands as the drinks arrived: a pint of red ale and shot of low-shelf bourbon each.

"Cheers," said Bill as he made a serious dent in the pint. When he put the glass down again, he added, "What can we help you with?" He was talking to Jersey, not the civilian.

"We're looking into an old case of yours and hoped you could help."

"Which one?"

"Augustus Quinn. He was a family butcher."

Bill's eyes narrowed as he moved his attention to Ian. "Your name is Quinn."

"Augustus was my grandfather."

Bill raised his shot glass and clinked it off his partner's before draining it in one gulp.

"That was a nasty case," he said. "Sorry for your loss."

"I saw the crime scene photos," said Ian. "Nasty doesn't cover it."

Jim's hand was shaking as he drained his shot and followed it with a long swallow on his pint. Unlike his broad-shouldered partner who seemed to be faring relatively well in retirement, Jim had the frailness and pallor of someone rotting from the inside out.

"Your report said the case was dropped due to lack of evidence," said Ian.

"That's right," said Bill.

"The place was teeming with evidence," said Jersey.

Bill shrugged. "Sure, by today's standards, but back then we needed more than science. Without an eye witness—"

"My father witnessed it," interrupted Ian.

"Without a *reliable* witness," said Bill. "Your father's statement was all over the map, and then he vanished before we could interview him any further." Bill's eyes hardened as they studied Ian's face. "That was damn peculiar."

"Did you interview Walter Zelig?" asked Ian.

"Sure we did. He was nowhere near."

"According to who?" asked Jersey.

"He had an alibi," interjected Jim, his tongue thick with drink. "Iron fucking tight."

Bill fired a steely glare at his friend. "Yeah, we had nothing to go on."

"Why did you interview him, then?" asked Ian. "If you had nothing to go on, how did his name even come up?"

Bill drained his glass and waved at the bartender for another round. He remained silent until the drinks arrived, watching Ian closely to make sure he paid before relaxing.

Bill clinked glasses with his partner and they both drained their shots.

"Okay," said Bill. "Fuck it, we know it was bullshit. A lot of stuff back then was. Zelig was a big shot in the neighborhood with the usual friends in high places. It was easy to turn a blind eye to the regular trade: broads, booze, gambling, drugs. I didn't like the drugs coming in, saw it wreck too many lives, but what ya gonna do? He paid okay, but more importantly he paid our bosses. We kick up a fuss and it's us who're out of a job, you know? We had mouths to feed."

"Did you suspect him in my grandfather's murder?" Ian asked.

"Suspect him? Zelig fucking did it, man. No doubt. We just couldn't say nothing."

"Why did he do it?" asked Jersey.

"His daughter had gone missing, right, Bill?" Jim said as though experiencing a rare moment of clarity. "He blamed the butcher. Even sent a series of goons after him, but they disappeared, too." Jim laughed as he lifted his pint to his lips. "Four fucking heavies he sent. Poof. Gone." He took a long pull of his beer. "Your grandfather was a fucking magician."

"That's why his end was so bloody," added Bill. "Ice Pick lost the plot. He carved your grandfather to pieces."

"Never got his daughter back though," slurred Jim over the rim of his glass. "That's still a fucking mystery."

22

I T WAS DARK by the time Ian returned to the butcher's shop. Driving on autopilot, he had been halfway to the suburbs before remembering he didn't live there anymore. Turning back toward the city core, he fought against a pang of loss and a craving to head to the darkest corner of The Crown Royal and wallow in self-destruction.

Two large metal containers were parked in front of the store. The sealed unit contained whatever meager possessions the packers had found in the house that morning, while the second container was open at the top and being slowly filled by trash removed from the shop by the cleaning crew. Most of the garbage appeared to consist of broken glass and chunks of rotten baseboard that had crumbled at the slightest touch.

Looking at it, Ian wished he had asked the crew to gut the apartment before cleaning since he had no attachment to anything of his mother's it might contain.

Don't think on that too long, he warned himself to keep any pangs of guilt suppressed where they belonged. *The only Quinn who didn't run away found himself butchered inside his own store.*

Inside, Ian found an envelope taped to the display case that contained a key to the moving container, a phone number to call when he had it emptied, and a scribbled note from Clark letting him know they could park the trash bin for a few days if he wanted to dump any other stuff.

There was also a P.S.

We're ready to remove the boards over the front windows, but you should look at getting a security system in place first. This neighborhood isn't what it used to be. I can recommend somebody if you want. Call me.

Ian turned to the large plate window, dark behind the sheets of plywood, and imagined this room with the reintroduction of daylight. Of all the rooms in the building this was the one he had enjoyed the most. It was also the only one where he ever remembered seeing his grandfather smile.

Despite everything, Augustus had truly loved his trade as he expertly seduced customers into trying a new cut of meat or special recipe he was excited about.

Ian phoned Clark and asked him to go ahead with getting security installed, offering to pay him a general contractor's fee to take charge of it. Clark agreed.

After hanging up, Ian pondered heading upstairs to look at the cleaned apartment, but the locked door in his grandfather's secret bunker screamed louder.

*

Descending the ladder with the brass key retrieved from the safe secure in his pocket, a nervous dread churned Ian's stomach.

Upon touching bottom, the dread climbed up his throat and squatted like a bilious lump whose main aim seemed to be in making it difficult to breathe.

The room was icy cold, and seeing it for the second time, it looked even more like a jail cell than he had first considered. The walls, floor and even the ceiling were smooth, sound-dampening concrete without a single window or natural source of light.

Somebody could be locked down here for years and nobody would ever know. Apart from the sparse furniture, it reminded Ian of the solitary confinement cells at Alcatraz.

During a family vacation to San Francisco and Alcatraz Island, a tourist guide locked him in "The Hole" for less than a minute. Helena and Emily refused to enter, but Ian's natural curiosity made it impossible to resist.

He still remembered the density of the darkness and how his imagination whispered, *This is where madness is born.*

Removing the key from his pocket, Ian approached the steel door in the corner. The metal was cold to the touch and the key needed to be forced before crunching into the lock. Once the key was flush, Ian turned the lock and pushed the door.

The room beyond was Alcatraz revisited. Looking not like a room at all, but a void of pure blackness.

Ian reached into the abyss, slapping at the wall until his hand landed on a switch. Two bare bulbs glowed to life in the ceiling revealing a larger room than the first, but with one noticeable difference. This room had been created in a rush.

The walls were rough, unfinished concrete with jagged chunks of rock sticking out in places where they had been hurriedly jammed as though to block something from getting inside.

In one corner was a collection of abandoned tools: two shovels, a pickaxe and a weighty sledgehammer. Beside the tools were two industrial-sized bags of quicklime, a common ingredient for making cement. Quicklime had other uses, too. One being the elimination of odor from decomposing flesh.

Most disturbing was the floor. An uneven covering of loose dirt and scattered gravel, the ground had settled over the years to reveal a grid pattern composed of six large indentations. Each indentation was the size and shape of a grave.

Panic clutched at Ian's chest as he took in the graves, a voice whispering behind his ear, *Some doors are never meant to be opened.*

He recalled the rumors Mr. Palewandram told him about, young women arriving at his grandfather's door never to be seen again.

Was Augustus capable of murder?

Wrong question, he told himself. The same hot-tempered blood that flowed through his grandfather's veins also coursed through his own, and Ian knew exactly what he was capable of.

Tearing his gaze away from the indentations, Ian walked the room's periphery, searching for any clue that it had served a purpose other than a secret burial site.

There was nothing.

"Shit!"

Taking a deep breath, Ian considered his options. The first was simple, lock the door and pretend to have never found the place. Unfortunately, he had been born with the curse of curiosity, making such an option impossible. Option two was call Jersey, but that felt premature. That left option three.

Ian draped his jacket on a rung of the ladder outside, rolled up his sleeves, and grabbed one of the shovels. He selected an indentation at random and began to dig.

It took some effort to crack the hard shell of compacted dirt and gravel, but soon shovelfuls of dirt began to pile up on its edge.

The body wasn't buried deep.

When a brownish ear was exposed, Ian knelt down and used his hands to carefully scrape away the dirt covering its face. He wanted to vomit, not from any stench or revulsion, but simply from fear of what he had found and what it meant.

The quicklime used to eliminate the odor of putrefaction had also inadvertently preserved the body, not unlike mummification. In Augustus's day, quicklime was a popular ingredient shown on detective TV shows as a foolproof method of quickly making a dead body dissolve. Unfortunately, like a lot of Hollywood short-cuts, the exact opposite was actually true. Quicklime was a preservative of flesh.

A large clump of clay broke away like a mask, exposing bushy black eyebrows resting above sunken eye sockets; a bulbous nose with a sizable wart over one nostril; thin, reedy lips curling away from crooked teeth…and beneath a weak chin, the decaying remains of a starched shirt collar and tie.

Ian felt a heady rush of relief.

It was a man.

Wiping cold sweat off his brow with the back of a mucky hand, Ian retrieved the shovel and moved to a second grave. After ten minutes of digging, he exposed a second face.

With stubbled cheeks, thick *Magnum P.I.* mustache, and a glaring gold cap glistening from between furled lips, it was also male.

Ian recalled what the drunken cop had said in the bar earlier that day. *"Four fucking heavies he sent. Poof. Gone. Your grandfather was a fucking magician."*

Not a magician, then, just more predator than prey.

Two of the graves were empty, as though Augustus had been expecting more trouble and decided to plan ahead. Ian wondered if one of the graves had been meant for Zelig.

Filthy, his arms, hands and face covered in grave dirt and decayed biological material that he didn't want to think about, Ian retreated from the room, locked the door and ascended out of the hole.

He would need to call Jersey, but saw no reason to rush.

The bodies had remained hidden this long, and it wasn't like they were going anywhere.

*

Slipping the brass key back into his pocket, Ian realized that a shower would be useless without a dry towel and fresh clothes to change into.

With a weary sigh, he plucked the key to the storage container out of the envelope and ventured outside. The street was quiet, almost peaceful apart from the dull roar of traffic on the overpass a few blocks east that allowed most commuters to forget this once vibrant neighborhood even existed.

Half of the streetlights had either been vandalized or simply fallen into disrepair, leaving a patchwork quilt of light and darkness that added an ominous quality to anyone hoping for an evening stroll.

Opening the container, Ian felt a stirring behind him. Turning, he saw a tall, thin man standing across the street with two large dogs by his side. It was the same man he had seen on several occasions before.

"Can I help you?" Ian called out.

The man remained motionless; his two dogs unnervingly still.

"What do you want?" Ian asked, his tone growing in anger.

The man said nothing.

"Seriously?" Ian yelled. "What the fuck is this?"

Slamming the container door closed, Ian moved to storm across the street and confront the man. But when he turned around again, the street was empty.

"Yeah, you better run," he muttered under his breath.

Opening the container again, he found several boxes marked *Clothing* and one labeled *Bathroom*. He rummaged through the clothing boxes until he found enough clean items to dress himself in the morning, placed them on top of the bathroom supplies and carried the box inside.

*

After showering, Ian walked the apartment, picking up a few of the dusted knickknacks and framed photographs that attempted to stir old, forgotten memories. Apart from the photo of his sister eating ice cream, none of the objects meant anything to him. He had never known his mother's side of the family; never met a single relative, not even at his grandfather's funeral.

Certainly nobody had shown up to lend a hand when it was just the two of them, mother and son, after his father left.

The fridge was working but empty, while all the cans in the cupboards had labels and logos that hadn't been seen on store shelves in years.

Ian crossed to the front window and peered outside. Standing to one side of a streetlight, half in shadow, half in light, was the tall man and his dogs.

A prickling at his neck made Ian head back downstairs to the cutting room. There, he opened the safe, retrieved the handgun and returned to the apartment.

Undressing in the dark, weariness took hold of his mind and body. The sheets needed washing, but he found the lingering, spicy-orchid scent of Rossella to be a welcome comfort.

Still wrapped in its oilcloth, the .45 would need a good cleaning and fresh ammunition, but, slipping it underneath his pillow, it gave Ian enough security to close his eyes and fall into a deep, exhausted sleep.

It was short-lived.

23

IAN SNAPPED AWAKE with the disturbing realization he was being watched. Rubbing his eyes to be certain he wasn't trapped in a paranoid nightmare, he took in the looming presence that filled the doorway of his mother's old bedroom.

The behemoth didn't move. He didn't need to. There was no place for Ian to run without going through him first.

"Get dressed," said the man. "Mr. Zelig would like a word."

"Doesn't he own a watch?" Ian grumbled, putting on a brave front to dampen the panic in his chest.

"Don't!" warned the man, moving deeper into the room to reveal a bandaged nose and chipped-tooth grimace. "Whatever you're reaching for, it's a bad idea."

Ian removed his empty hand from underneath the pillow and swung his legs off the bed. Standing, he dressed in the clean clothes he had laid out a short time before: jeans, maroon shirt, and—

"Don't worry about shoes," said the goon. "We ain't going far."

"I hope you didn't break anything getting in here," said Ian as they descended the stairs. "I just had the place cleaned."

Nose Bandage grunted, although whether with humor or impatience, Ian couldn't tell.

In the front room, Walter Zelig sat on a folding metal chair beside the empty display cabinets. He was hunched forward, his sparse weight supported by an elegant, silver-tipped cane that resembled the head of a bear. Ian had no idea where the chair had come from.

"I remember this place," said Zelig, his lips parting to reveal a crooked assortment of decaying brown teeth. "But I miss the aroma." He inhaled, the effort barely expanding his sparrow-like chest. "It used to stink of blood."

"I'll see if I can find a candle in that scent," said Ian.

Zelig chuckled as Nose Bandage clipped Ian around the ear.

"Show some respect."

"It was a joke," complained Ian, rubbing his ear. "Lighten the fuck up."

The goon's nostrils flared, but his leash was tugged by a simple wave of his boss's hand.

"I don't sleep much anymore," said Zelig. "Not that I miss it. Even surrounded by loyal staff in a mansion bought through sweat and toil, I never enjoyed those dark hours of vulnerability. What about you?"

"People keep waking me up," said Ian.

Zelig chuckled again as his goon slapped Ian's other ear. The infliction of pain seemed to tickle his funny bone.

"Apart from that. How do you sleep?"

Ian shrugged, unwilling to share his personal pain with a cold-blooded killer.

"Your daughter," said Zelig as though reading his thoughts. "The way she died under your watch. That failure haunts you."

Ian's fists reflexively curled in anger, but he swallowed it down.

"I understand that pain better than most," Zelig continued. "I have a daughter, too."

Ian remained silent.

"You've heard," said Zelig, reading his body language. "Good. Then you know I need to find her."

"Is she alive?" Ian regretted the question the moment it left his lips as Nose Bandage grabbed him by the scruff of the neck and squeezed. His vice-like grip sent Ian's muscles into spasm, firing jagged currents of pain across his entire back and spiking up his skull.

"She is alive," said Zelig, waving his hand again to have Ian released. "Show him the gift."

Nose Bandage reached into his jacket pocket and retrieved an inch-thick rectangular black box. At approximately nine inches in length and three in width, it was the perfect size to hold a jeweled necklace or expensive wristwatch. Apart from the shape, the packaging looked identical to the gruesome gift that had been left on the passenger seat of Ian's van during Noah's funeral.

"Another memento of my father?" Ian muttered, dreading what it might contain.

"No," said Zelig. "I receive one of these every year on my birthday." A damaged smile crossed his grayish lips. "Today is that day."

"Congratulations?"

Zelig ignored the insincere well wishes. "The first package arrived one year after your grandfather's death, and they have continued every year since. Open it."

Ian untied the black ribbon and lifted the lid off the box. Inside, nestled within a soft cushion of red velvet, was a hand-crafted hunting knife. The four-inch, spear-point blade was swirled with unique forge marks and anchored in a jawbone handle that, disturbingly, still contained the animal's teeth.

"Show me," said Zelig.

Ian tilted the box.

"That is one of the more unusual blades she has sent. Read the card."

Ian found a small black card nestled under the blade. He opened it and read aloud, "For your heart."

Zelig's lips quivered slightly as he lowered his gaze. "The message is always the same."

"And how do you know it's from Constance?"

Zelig's head snapped back to attention. "You know her name?"

"I needed to know what you were after."

"She is a beauty," said Zelig wistfully. "My beautiful, beautiful baby girl."

"And the knives?"

"She wants me to know that I am still in her heart."

That wasn't the message Ian got off the card, but he decided to keep that to himself.

"I need you to find her and bring her back to me. If you don't, you already know what I do to people who disappoint."

"Why me?" asked Ian. "I've never done anything to you."

"You inherit the debt, just as you inherit this store. Your father tried to run from that debt, but I never forgive nor forget." Zelig rose from the chair, leaning heavily on the cane, and ran a dry tongue across papery lips. "Your family took her from me. It's only right that you bring her back."

*

Alone once more, Ian double-checked the useless locks on the front door before returning upstairs. In the bedroom, he emptied the pockets of his dirty jeans, crumpled on the floor with grave dirt ground into the knees, and transferred the contents — keys, phone, cash and a slim billfold — to his clean ones.

He was still tired, but knew he would have trouble returning to sleep without some assistance. And since he hadn't been shopping yet, there wasn't even a glass of milk in the fridge that he could heat up on the stove.

Pulling out his phone, Ian found Rossella's number and touched the call button.

Not unexpectedly, she didn't answer.

He left a message. "Hey, Rossella. Hope I didn't wake you." That was a lie. He wanted to hear her voice, unguarded and sexy in drowsy sleep; to have her rush over, excited to see him, to feel her warm skin sliding across his. "Had another visit from Zelig tonight and it got me thinking again about the taxes on this place. Somebody's been paying them, and whoever that is may have answers to what happened to Zelig's daughter. Have you had any luck tracking it down? Call me."

After hanging up, another thought entered his mind.

Pulling on his shoes, Ian grabbed a large kitchen knife from a wooden block on the counter and descended to the main floor. Entering the back room, he grabbed the hook and chain, secured it to the top of the safe, and re-opened the secret chamber.

With the butcher's knife tucked dangerously into his belt, Ian climbed down.

*

Trying to ignore the locked steel door and what lay behind it, Ian moved with purpose to the antique roll-top desk. Removing the knife from his belt, he slid the tip of its blade underneath the small lock at the center of its curved cocoon and applied pressure.

It only took a few seconds for the brittle wood to snap and the lock to break. The louvered shell rolled up and away, exposing an ancient Underwood No.5 typewriter surrounded on all sides by a myriad of tiny wooden drawers. It was the perfect setup for someone with obsessive compulsive disorder; a place to put everything, and for everything a place.

Ian began opening the drawers and dumping their contents onto the desk. He found several small keys that fit the locks of larger drawers. Inside those drawers, he found several unopened boxes of over-the-counter hair dye, a simple Canon camera, boxed canisters of Kodak black-and-white 35mm film, letter-sized sheets of transparent plastic, slender art knives with blades as sharp as a scalpel, and several blank documents. The documents included a half-dozen Oregon driver's licenses and three American passports.

Ian glanced over at the empty metal cot, taking in the room with fresh understanding.

It wasn't a cell, he realized. It was a waiting station for people planning to change their identity. This hidden bunker was a perfect place to lay low, safe and out of sight, while new documents were prepared.

He thought of the women who had been seen entering the butcher shop, and then never seen again.

But why?

Why was his grandfather involved in such a set-up?

Ian rummaged through the rest of the drawers, finding little else apart from an orphan steel key that was too large to fit any of the desk's locks. A paper tag was attached to the hole in its bow. Scrawled on the tag in thick pencil was the letter D.

After returning most of the items to their proper place, Ian slipped the steel key into his front pocket, and the incriminating blank documents into his back pocket.

There were some secrets, he reasoned, that were best kept that way.

*

With no cellphone reception in the hole, Ian climbed the ladder to the cutting floor before tapping the photo icon of his friend. He had snapped the mugshot backstage one night after Jersey finished a near riotous set with The Rotten Johnnys.

Jersey hated the photo as he had been sweating like a burst faucet and his stage makeup streaked down his face in a mockery of Alice Cooper. But he didn't see what Ian did: the pure, unadulterated joy radiating from every pore. The photo always made Ian smile.

Jersey answered on the fifth ring.

"Seriously?" he grumbled. "Whatthefuck?"

"I have four dead bodies," said Ian.

"And you couldn't call nine eleven?"

"They've been dead awhile."

"What's a while?

"Couple decades."

"That could've waited 'til morning."

"I was excited to share. Besides, if you and Sally are getting serious, you may have kids one day. This is good practice for Christmas morning."

"There are some things you don't need to practice."

"Says the perpetual bachelor."

Jersey sighed. "Where are the bodies?"

"In my basement."

"What! Your basement?"

"The basement of my new digs. I've moved into my grandfather's old butcher's shop."

"Are you sure they're human?"

"Unless Augustus dressed his pigs in suits and ties, then, yeah, I'm pretty sure. Remember that cop in the bar today? He mentioned Zelig sent four heavies over to have a chat with my grandfather. I don't think Augustus liked the conversation. Either that or they asked to buy on credit. He took a dim view on credit."

"Jesus!"

"Oh, and if you're coming over, can you pick up coffee? I haven't had a chance to go shopping yet and could murder a cup."

Jersey ended the call with a brief crackle of profanity.

24

JERSEY HANDED IAN a large takeout mug of coffee along with a greasy paper bag containing a lukewarm breakfast sandwich of plastic bacon, rubber egg and a goopy substance pretending to be cheese.

"I like what you've done with the place," he said, looking around the dusty back room: stainless steel cutting tables, disturbingly large floor drains, dangling hooks, chains and pulleys. "Serial killer chic?"

"It's a work in progress," said Ian, biting into the sandwich. Unsurprisingly, it tasted as bland as it looked.

"At least it's in a bad neighborhood," said Jersey.

"With corpses in the basement," added Ian.

Jersey grinned. "Who did you piss off to inherit this?"

Ian shrugged. "Last man standing."

"Show me the bodies."

Ian led Jersey over to the hole beneath the safe and down the ladder to the secret chamber. Jersey remained quiet as he took in the concrete cell, his eyes studying every detail.

"Cozy," he said.

"I think it was designed as a safe room rather than a cell," said Ian.

"Safe from who?"

"From whoever those women who disappeared were running

from. People saw them enter, but nobody saw them leave. I think my grandfather helped them escape whatever trouble they were in."

"Why?"

Ian shrugged again. "I haven't figured that out."

"So he could have just as easily been killing them, chopping them up and stuffing their remains in his sausage?"

Ian winced. "I prefer to think not."

"Course you do. Who wants to admit they're the spawn of a serial killer? But it doesn't make it any less of an assumption. Where are the bodies?"

Ian unlocked the steel door and flicked on the lights. Jersey followed him inside.

"You disturbed six graves," he said, taking in the scene.

"I needed to be sure—"

"That none of them contained women," Jersey finished.

Ian nodded.

"Two are empty."

"How I found them. I'm guessing Augustus hoped Zelig would fill one of them."

Jersey moved closer and crouched down to study the faces of the dead before glancing over at the tools in the corner.

"Quicklime," explained Ian. "Kept the smell down but preserved the bodies. Burned most of the clothing away though."

"That's the trouble with the Internet today," said Jersey. "Back in the day people believed what they saw on TV, now they can Google to find out if it's bullshit or not."

"Unless Augustus actually wanted them to be identified at some point," said Ian. "That's possible, too."

"True. I've got a feeling these mugs won't be too difficult to track down, especially gold tooth there. They look the sort that coined the phrase 'known to police.'"

"So what's next?"

Jersey stood again and moved to the steel door. "I'll get forensics down here to remove the bodies and make sure we're not missing anything. You never know, it might give somebody somewhere some closure."

"Should I expect any blowback?"

Jersey scratched the stubble on his chin. "If these are the hired goons Jim mentioned, nobody will give a shit. However, if we find other evidence that connects to missing women, then, yeah, there'll be blowback. I also can't promise that some asshole won't leak it to the press. Your name already has chew marks on it that a reporter would love to slobber over, but I'll do my best to keep it discrete."

"Thanks."

Jersey looked at the graves again and grinned. "Your grandfather must have been one tough son of a bitch."

"Until he met someone tougher."

"Yeah," Jersey agreed. "There's always that."

*

The forensics crew consisted of a prune-faced woman in an unflattering, disposable plastic onesie and matching baby blue hairnet, plus two overly excited twenty-somethings — one of each gender.

The woman looked down the hole in the floor at the rear of the butcher's shop, sniffed loudly, and declared, "I need a cigarette."

With a nicotine-stained finger, she pointed at her two eager companions. "Guard the hole. Nobody in or out until I'm ready."

The young man with an unfortunate haircut and scurrilous shadow on his upper lip that made him resemble a young Adolf Hitler dared to ask, "Out?"

Prune Face snarled. "I'm expecting four bodies. If one's missing, I'm blaming you."

Turning her back to the assistants, a mischievous smile crept across deeply wrinkled lips, the corrugated flesh a hallmark of someone who discovered her addiction at an early age and embraced it with vigor. She caught Ian watching and winked.

Ian opened the large overhead door, allowing the woman ample exit to the rear yard. High fenced for privacy, the yard was an overgrown mess of healthy weeds, choked grass and loosely scattered gravel that had been used to fill in the low spots. At the rear was a sliding gate that led to the alley for deliveries. Like the fence, it was topped with a coil of rusted barbed wire that was ready to crumble at the slightest touch.

Sitting off to one side, beneath a tattered canvas tarp, was his grandfather's delivery van: a 1950s era Ford F-1 panel truck in original cherry and cream. All four tires were flat, and it was doubtful the engine would turn over, but it still looked in better shape than Ian's current ride. His grandfather had been a meticulous man and would be embarrassed by the state of it.

Prune Face produced a small electronic gadget not much larger than a Zippo lighter. When she touched a button on its side, a small glass tube extended and a red LED light switched on. When the LED turned green, she placed the tube between her lips and inhaled. When she exhaled, her breath was a cloud of sweetly scented vapor.

"Is that weed?" asked Ian, only half serious.

"I wish." Prune Face exhaled another cloud. "Nah, just e-juice. Half the fun of tobacco with half the guilt." She waggled the mottled yellow and brown fingers on her smoking hand. "I'm getting these puppies bleached next week. Soon, I'll be invited to all the best galas. No longer a pariah on the social scene." She chuckled to herself. "The boys can have their cigars, but Heaven forbid a lady wants to suck on something satisfying."

Holding out her hand, she introduced herself. "Babs. Full title, Dr. Mary Beth Walkerton, but everyone calls me Babs."

Ian squeezed her hand, and nodded back towards the interior of the shop. "And those two?"

"Cute, ain't they? I get new interns all the damn time. Love to fuck with 'em. Jersey said there wasn't an urgent case here, so figured it would be a good field exercise for them. They're chomping at the bit to see dead bodies in situ."

"They'll get their wish," said Ian. "I uncovered the faces, but haven't touched anything else."

"Uh-huh."

The way she said it made Ian ask, "What's that mean?"

"Nothing." Babs sucked on her vaporizer. "Just odd is all, finding a dead body in your basement and then deciding to dig around looking for more."

Ian had to admit she made a good point. "I needed to make sure they were all male."

"Oh?"

"There were rumors. About my grandfather."

"But dead *men* are okay?"

"Yeah." Ian allowed the flicker of a grin. "Dead men are fine."

Babs took one final drag on her vaporizer before sliding the glass tube back into its base and returning the unit to her pocket.

"Okay, then," she said, exhaling a large cloud of vapor. "Let's go say hello to these dead fellas."

*

When the cleaning crew arrived, Ian apologized that the rear room was off-limits for the day. He asked if they could dismantle and discard the oversized glass and stainless steel display cabinets to open up the front room instead. He had no intention of selling meat, so the refrigerated displays were taking up valuable floor space.

"I'll need to call a guy," said Clark. "Can't just dump them as the refrigeration units could still be holding Freon gas. You inhale too much of that and it can cut off the oxygen to your lungs."

"Appreciate it," said Ian.

Returning to the back room, Ian approached the dark hole and overheard the excited male intern telling his colleagues, "This is cool. His tie tack is the bottom end of a brass .45 cartridge. You can still read the writing. Federal 45 Auto. This guy was awesome."

Ian grinned. Every profession had its nerds.

He stepped back from the hole when his phone rang.

"You called me at four a.m.," said the caller. "That's too late even for a drunken booty call."

Ian laughed. "Yeah, sorry, couldn't sleep."

"Thinking of me?" asked Rossella.

"Not exactly." He told her about the four bodies in his basement.

Instead of being horrified, Rossella's first reaction was, "Do you need a lawyer?"

"I think I'm okay. Unless I was a true baby-faced gangsta, these bodies are too old to have any links to me."

"Well if things change—"

"You'll be my first call," Ian finished. "Any luck on the tax records on this place?"

"That's why I'm calling actually. There's a bank account in your grandfather's name that has been making automatic payments to the city every year. We had no record of it here, which is odd, but I managed to track it down. There's another odd thing though."

"Oh?"

"The address for the account holder isn't the butcher's shop."

That was strange. He had only ever known his grandfather as part and parcel with the store. Then again, he had never expected him to have a hidden basement filled with dead bodies and dark secrets.

Ian asked for the address, lifting his head to stare at the far wall as Rossella read it aloud.

"Are you sure?" he asked.

"Yes. All the bank statements are mailed there and none have ever been returned as non-deliverable."

*

The address was directly across the street.

Standing on the sidewalk in front of the butcher's, Ian studied the neighboring building. At street level, the Dynasty Diner was open for business. Through streaky windows, several members of the idle cleaning crew were flirting with the young waitress as they stuffed themselves on full breakfasts and pots of coffee.

As though sensing him watching, the waitress glanced over and offered a friendly wave. As he waved back, his gaze drifted skyward to the two stories that loomed above the restaurant, enough room for several apartments.

Before Ian could step off the curb to cross the street, Clark came around the dumpster and hailed him.

"Good news. I've got a guy interested in buying your cabinets. He was practically salivating when I told him what great shape they were in. He loves the whole retro thing, and he can pick them up today."

"That's great," said Ian, only half listening.

"I've also got the security guys coming down to look over the store and make recommendations. We could have the plywood off that main window any day now."

"And new locks on the doors?"

"You bet." Clark grinned. "My kids could crack these relics. Any idea when the back room will be ready for cleaning?"

"Sorry, I don't."

"Are those cops back there?"

"Forensics"

Clark raised an eyebrow, but Ian didn't feel the need to explain, so he said nothing.

"Anything we can do in the meantime?" asked Clark.

Ian turned and glanced up at the old sign dangling precariously by a lone bolt at its neck. "You could bring that pig down. She's been hanging there far too long."

"You got it."

Ian crossed the street.

Entering the diner, he was greeted with a bright smile from the waitress, Mei Song.

"Do these men work for you?" she asked, her smooth brow glistening with perspiration from the morning rush.

"They're cleaning the store," said Ian. "But there's been a delay."

"Delay is good for business. They like to eat. My grandparents are very happy."

"Can I talk to them?"

"My grandparents?"

Ian nodded.

She looked at him curiously before shrugging. "Okay."

Mei wiped her hands on her apron and led Ian through a set of swinging doors to the kitchen. The place was a clutter of a hundred hanging pots, racks of dried spices and herbs, and the cloying stench of hot grease mixed with steam.

Mrs. Song was sitting on a tall wooden stool making pork wontons from scratch. The tiny brain-like delicacies were an essential part of her famous Wor Wonton Soup. Although she was definitely Asian, Mrs. Song didn't quite look Chinese. Her skin was subtly darker, her eyes fuller, and she was tiny.

Meanwhile, Mr. Song was busy scouring the frying pans from the unexpected breakfast rush.

"Grandfather," said Mei. "We have a visitor."

Mr. Song turned around from the sink and squinted as he studied Ian from head to toe. The wrinkles lining his face made him look a century old, but he still moved with the easy grace of a man half that age.

A barely susceptible smile flickered on his lips as he raised one finger and said, "You are a Quinn. I remember you as a child, always falling down and skinning your knees. My granddaughter tells me you are planning to return across the street."

"I am," said Ian. "And I didn't fall as often as I was pushed."

The old man nodded in understanding. "Bo Kemp was a little bastard, wasn't he? I hear he's on town council now."

"I didn't know that."

"May even make a run for mayor in the next election if rumors are to be believed."

"And do you believe many rumors?" Ian asked.

Mr. Song's amused smile faded away. "Not many."

Ian dug in his pocket and produced the steel key with the letter D printed on its paper tag. He handed it over.

"Your father?" asked Mr. Song.

"Dead."

"I'm sorry."

"Zelig caught up to him."

"After all these years? The man is relentless."

"The burden has been passed onto me."

"I see." Mr. Song handed the key back to Ian. "Come."

Mr. Song led the way through the kitchen to a rear staircase. The first floor consisted of the Song's family home, a modest apartment decorated in a blend of Chinese and Western styles. Despite the age of the building, the apartment looked extremely well maintained. The number of oriental knickknacks on every flat surface, however, was tilting over the edge of kitsch into obsession.

"My wife," said Mr. Song. "She likes to collect precious things."

They continued up a second flight of stairs to a short hallway with a single apartment on either side. One was marked with the letter C, the other with a D.

"Take your time," said Mr. Song. "It is yours now."

25

IAN UNLOCKED THE door and entered the small apartment. It was unexpectedly tidy.

Against one wall was a single metal cot, sheets wrapped tight around a thin mattress with precision corners ready for a drill sergeant's inspection. It was completed with a lone pillow, so thin it barely looked worth the effort, and an adjustable reading lamp clamped to a plain, wooden headboard.

A small side table contained a collection of dog-eared paperbacks: *My Gun Is Quick* by Mickey Spillane, *A Purple Place For Dying* by John D. MacDonald, *Shadow on the Trail* by Zane Grey, and *For Whom the Bell Tolls* by Ernest Hemingway.

At the foot of the bed, a well-loved easy chair was aimed at one of two windows facing the street. The view, like Salvador Dali's *Christ of Saint John of the Cross*, offered God's perspective of the butcher's rusting, iron pig. It also allowed Augustus to monitor all comings and goings at the store.

A pocket door led to a small bathroom with sink, toilet and stand-up shower. Augustus's steel safety razor and badger hair shaving brush hung on a chrome stand beside the sink. Nearby was an iconic bottle of Old Spice aftershave, a toothbrush and a comb.

Everything had its place, standing at perfect attention and undisturbed for decades.

Against the nearest wall was what he had come to find.

Ian moved to the large desk and ran his fingers across a row of bound ledgers that lined one of its shelves. He left them undisturbed for now.

The drawers were unlocked. Inside the first one, he found more legal documents: birth certificates, death certificates, applications for Social Security Numbers, blank driver's licenses, plus several expired Canadian passports.

Another drawer contained neat bundles of cash, mostly twenties and fifties, some still wrapped in paper bands. If the amounts shown on the bands were correct, it totaled around three thousand.

A third drawer contained an opened box of .45 ammo, an unusual red butterfly knife with *Hackman Finland* stamped on the handles, and a dented metal cash box.

Ian opened the cash box to discover a collection of postcards from across North America. He flipped the top one over and read. "I'm happy." It was signed "Kc." Ian pulled out another one. "I never knew the sky could be so blue. Thank you." It was signed "Min." A third one read simply, "I feel brave." It was signed "Jb." Digging through the layers of cards, Ian noted the postmarks spanned decades.

At the bottom of the pile, a small metal loop snagged Ian's finger. When he tugged it, the bottom lifted to reveal a compartment hidden underneath.

Lifting the tray of postcards out of the box, Ian dug into the hollow and returned with a fistful of old IDs. Some were driver's licenses, others were library or voter cards. Some had their photographs intact, others had been expertly removed — most likely to be re-used on one of the blanks under a new name.

All of the cards were of women. Most appeared quite young, but not all. In the photos, very few of them were smiling.

Ian rummaged through the cards until he found the one he was searching for: Constance Arianna Zelig.

The stories were true. She was a beauty. And yet Constance looked forlorn, her dark eyes sunk deep in shadow, long bangs brushed aside for a brief moment like the accidental unveiling of an unfinished piece of sculpture. Her cheekbones were sharp, her chin blunt, her slender nose almost Persian in its perfection.

Her mother must have been stunning for she certainly didn't inherit those looks from her father.

Staring at the tiny photo, Ian felt a crack splitting the raw scar tissue of his heart. In his job, he had seen too many children with that exact same look. There were times when the palms of his hands had bled from the force of his fingernails digging into the flesh as he resisted leaping across his desk and snapping an abusive parent's neck.

And then there was the time he didn't resist. When he tracked down the person responsible for the death of his daughter. The encounter that should have meant the end of his career, and yet...

Ian wiped away an overflow of moisture from his eyes as he fanned out the discarded identities.

His grandfather had been more than a butcher, that much was clear. But had that heavy, leather apron that terrified Ian as a child actually been a knight's suit of armor? Had those bloodstained and callused hands that swung a cleaver with such force been capable of tenderness? And had Ian inherited more than stubbornness from the cold and distant man he knew so little about?

Ian picked up the postcards, reading the short messages, understanding it wasn't the words that mattered, just the acknowledgment.

Each postmark was a simple code: *I'm safe.*

*

He turned to the ledgers. A dozen of them lined the shelf, nothing unique or unusual that made one stand out from the other. Ian plucked a book from the middle and opened it.

Inside, the writing was big and blocky, letters jumping across faint blue guidelines like a kindergarten student high on sugary cereal learning the alphabet. It was the mark of a butcher's hand used to scribbling on wax paper wrapped around a joint of meat rather than in neat, uniform rows.

The clumsy writing made Ian smile. He knew how easy it was to be judged for having horrible penmanship. He still had memories, or at least echoes of memory, from when his first teacher tried to talk his parents into sending him to 'special school' because some of his words were spelled with backward-facing letters, even the simple ones like ⊠at and goD. He didn't blame the school. The diagnosis and understanding of dyslexia wasn't something teachers were even aware of back then.

Ian's mother had resisted, not wanting a child of hers to be perceived as different since in those days differences meant exclusion. Being a voracious reader, Ian soon mastered the art of fitting in, of making his words look just like everyone else's.

Unfortunately his word scramble skills were drawing a blank on his grandfather's notes. Everything was written in code.

Taking the ledger to the easy chair by the window, Ian sat as he pondered what information his grandfather would want to keep a record of. Logically, he decided the base information would be original name, age, date of first contact, date of last contact, new name and forms of ID, payment, and, lastly, destination.

New name and destination would be the hardest to crack as they were the two vital pieces that ensured the safety of his clients. And, naturally, if Ian hoped to track down Zelig's daughter, those were the two pieces he needed.

Ian thought about the postcards. If he knew Constance's new

name, then...Ian shook his head. Augustus had shown he was smarter than that. He would have asked his clients to send word they were safe, but he would have insisted they mail the postcards from somewhere other than their final destination.

One thing still troubled him, however.

He didn't believe Augustus could have done all this on his own. Manipulating the system to create a new identity took more than the creative skills of a local butcher. It required someone who was an expert at maneuvering and exploiting the maze of bureaucratic loopholes.

Augustus must have had a partner.

And Ian knew who it was.

26

IAN DROVE UP to the iron gate and pressed the intercom embedded in the stone pillar.

"Mr. Quinn," said the disembodied voice. "Are you expected?"

"No, but it's urgent that I speak to Mr. Ragano."

"Please hold while I check that we are up to receiving visitors."

Ian waited. It took ten minutes before Roberto Ragano's personal assistant, Archibald Pierce, returned.

"Sorry to keep you waiting," said the voice as the gate swung open on silent, electric motors. "Will Ms. Ragano be joining us?"

"Not this time."

Ian rolled up his window and eased the van through the widening gap. At the top of the curved driveway, he parked in the same spot as before and dashed through a light sprinkle of rain to the covered front porch. The moment his foot hit the top step, the front door opened.

"A pleasure to see you again so soon, sir," said Archibald.

The young man was impeccably dressed as before, his blue tie swapped for a soft salmon but ornamented by the same golden tack-pin.

"How is he?" asked Ian, brushing the rain off his shoulders.

The man's smile faltered only slightly. "Mr. Ragano is doing rather well today. Thank you for asking. You'll find him in the library. He so loves his books. Can I get you anything? Coffee? Tea? Brandy?"

"No, I only stopped for a short chat."

"Certainly." The man moved aside and gestured to his right. "The library is straight through those doors."

Since their first meeting, Ian had wondered how his grand-father became friendly with such a high-profile criminal lawyer. He still didn't know how the connection came to be, but Ragano certainly possessed the intimate knowledge, guile and resources to help people disappear.

The library was toasty, the cavernous space warmed by a roar-ing wood fireplace that dominated its center. It was difficult not to be distracted by the opulence; the room was the epitome of every library Ian ever imagined owning in those daydream moments when he gambled a dollar on a lottery ticket; a fantasy he stopped believing in on the day the light left his daughter's eyes, and a dark-ness entered his own.

Surrounded by oak and brass bookshelves that climbed two stories high, Ragano sat comfortably on a high-backed leather armchair. Despite the heat, a woolen blanket lay draped across his lap, while an eclectic stack of hardcover books — *The Voyage of the Beagle* by Charles Darwin, *Mein Kampf* by Adolf Hitler, and *Papillon* by Henri Charrière — was piled on a small table by his arm. He looked up when Ian entered and smiled with what appeared to be genuine recognition. But then he spoke.

"Augustus! My Lord you are looking well. How is everything? Sit, sit, tell me all."

"It's not...I'm not—" Ian silenced himself. What was the harm in playing along? He didn't know much about dementia, but perhaps like sleepwalking it was best not to shatter the illusion. Besides, Ragano trusted Augustus.

"Everything is good," Ian said, moving to an armchair facing the lawyer. "Constance is safe."

"Constance?"

"Zelig's daughter."

"Quiet, man!" Ragano barked. "We vowed never to discuss that." He looked around nervously. "One never knows who is listening."

"Zelig knows it was me," said Ian, thinking of the bodies being unearthed in his basement. "He's already sniffing around."

"Damn it! I knew we shouldn't have got involved."

"We had no choice."

"I had no choice, you mean. I'm sorry I dragged you into this mess, August, but, but—" He raised his gaze to the high ceiling, his lips moving without sound as though in silent prayer. "She reminded me so much of my own sister, of the nightmare she endured at my step-father's hand before..." He fell into silence again.

"That's what we do, isn't it?" pressed Ian, reaching for answers. "Help women escape."

"It's what *you* do." Ragano shook his head. "Even in 'Nam, you worked harder to save the damn natives than kill them. But what did I do? The exact opposite. I defended the psychopathic bastards who treated the land like their own personal Gomorrah."

"We were in Vietnam together?" Ian was surprised. He hadn't known his grandfather had done any military service. It was certainly never talked about. Then again, who was there to talk to? After his father left, his mother slipped ever deeper into her glass cage, the gin a balm that pickled her emotions and slurred her memories.

Ragano's eyes narrowed in puzzlement. "What are you talking about, man? If it weren't for me, you would still be rotting in that cell or worse. The company wanted your ass six feet under, but I got you discharged and on the first plane home."

"What did I do?" Ian asked hesitantly, fully aware that he was risking the disintegration of Ragano's delusion by his own lack of knowledge.

"You fucked up is what you did," said Ragano. "You put six American soldiers in the ground for the sake of two Gooks. And worse, you got caught."

"Two Gooks?"

"The girls. Twins."

"How old?"

Ragano's voice cracked unintelligibly as he shook his head in pain and disgust at the memory.

"Did they survive?" Ian's voice was barely above a whisper.

"Only one. You know that. Christ, you brought her back with you."

Ian hesitated for a moment, his mind whirling with possibilities, but then a smile broke on his lips as he thought of the small woman sitting on a tall stool and making wontons by hand. A woman who had lived to become a grandmother.

"Mrs. Song," he said under his breath.

If true, it would explain why the Songs guarded his grandfather's secret with such devotion.

Ragano's eyes narrowed further, his crow's feet deepening into tremulous fault lines; the Bermuda tan cracking to reveal soggy Portland underneath.

Ian changed the subject, not wanting Ragano to realize he wasn't Augustus — not yet. "Zelig sent thugs to threaten me."

"And?"

"I didn't send them back."

Ragano chuckled. "That doesn't surprise me. Does Walter suspect my involvement?"

"You know I'd never talk." Ian decided to push it a little further, adding, "But I need your copy of the code book."

"Code book? What are you talking about?"

"The code I use in my ledgers. I gave you a copy of the decipher key, didn't I?"

"No, why would you? I have my own."

"You do?"

"Of course I do. Do you think I've gone senile?"

"No, certainly not. Zelig has me on edge. Where do you keep it?"

"Oh, for crying out loud."

Ragano swept the blanket off his lap and stood up. He studied the massive library for a second before crossing the room and plucking an old hardcover off the shelf. When he returned, he handed the book to Ian. The mustard slipcover had a woodcut-style illustration of a predatory bird perched above a jewel-laden hand. *The Maltese Falcon* by Dashiell Hammett.

Ian opened the book to discover it wasn't a book at all. Nestled inside was a slim, red notebook stamped with the word *Albatross* on its cover. The circular seal of the Central Intelligence Agency was watermarked in one, easily rippable corner.

"Satisfied?" asked Ragano as he settled back into his chair and took a large swallow of brandy from a snifter hidden behind his stack of books.

"Yes, but if something happens to me, do you know how to contact Constance?"

"Of course not," Ragano chided. "I told you I never wanted to know the details. What has gotten into you? I've never seen you this rattled. Not since Walter threatened your grand—" Ragano paused in mid-sentence, puzzlement furrowing his brow again as timelines jumped their tracks and a paradox formed in his brain. "You moved her, right?"

Ian didn't know how to answer. He had always been told that

Abbie went missing, most likely ran away just as his father would do, not that his grandfather had her relocated.

"Yes," said Ian, his voice cracking. "Abbie is safe."

"They'll look after her in Boston. Good family there."

"Boston," said Ian quietly. That's where Zelig's men found and killed his father.

"What about the boy?" asked Ragano. "What's his name again?"

"Ian," said Ian.

"Any threats against him?"

Ian shook his head numbly.

"Good. Walter is a monster, but even he has a twisted set of rules."

"What do you mean?"

"Boys, of course. His peccadilloes don't lie in that direction. Until they're old enough to hold a gun, he pays them little heed." Ragano tilted his head to refocus on the man sitting across from him. "You sure you're okay? You're acting very oddly. Would you like a brandy?"

"I'm fine," said Ian. "What about your granddaughter?"

"My granddaughter?" Timelines shifted again, causing pain between Ragano's eyes. He squeezed the folds of skin to ease the pressure.

"Rossella," said Ian.

Ragano smiled and drained his snifter. "She is a beautiful baby. Takes after her mother, God rest her soul."

"Is she safe from Zelig?"

The man paled before an angry, hot flush returned to his cheeks. "He wouldn't dare. I know far too many secrets for him to ever cross me."

"Perhaps you should share them," said Ian. "For insurance."

"Hmmm." He pondered the suggestion, tucking his arms

under his blanket and turning his face toward the crackling fire. "You might have something there, gunnery sergeant."

Ian wanted other secrets, too. Why was Augustus in Vietnam? What was his mission? And was it being judge, jury and executioner following the rape of the twin girls that turned him into a secret protector of women when he returned home? Or was there something more, other secrets hidden away in the family vault of lies, abandonment and betrayal?

But before Ian could ask any more questions, Ragano released a heavy sigh followed by the near-immediate nasal rumble of deep sleep.

The conversation was over.

Tucking *The Maltese Falcon* under his arm, Ian rose to his feet and exited the room.

In the foyer, Archibald approached and asked, "Did you get what you were looking for?"

"He was very lucid."

The comment pleased him.

"He has good days and bad. One can never predict."

"He fell asleep in his chair," said Ian. "I'm rather envious. A beautiful spot for a nap."

"He does love his library."

"And why not," said Ian. "I'm sure he earned it. Does Walter Zelig still drop by to visit him?"

"You know Mr. Zelig?"

"We've met on several occasions. He's been associated with my family for generations."

"Oh, I see."

Picking up on the man's hesitancy, Ian asked, "What do you know?"

"N-n-nothing," he stammered. "I didn't know you were part of…of that social circle."

"Relax," said Ian. "I'm not. Zelig and I have history on my grand-father's side, but we don't play golf together. Does he come around?"

"On occasion."

"And how does Mr. Ragano react?"

Although there was nobody else within sight, Archibald looked left and right before answering, "I can honestly say those are some of his worst days. His agitation levels climb off the charts and it takes strong medication and massage to make him calm again."

"And Zelig. What's his reaction?"

"I shouldn't say this, but the more agitated Mr. Ragano becomes, the less prickly it makes Mr. Zelig."

"He gets pleasure from watching your boss suffer?"

"Those are not my words, but that is a fair assumption."

Ian handed over a business card with his cell number on it. "If Mr. Ragano ever asks you to deliver files to Augustus Quinn, let me know. He gets me confused with my grandfather at times, but he means for the files to be delivered to me."

"If he makes such a request, I will let Ms. Ragano know to inform you."

Ian accepted the compromise.

27

THE BOOK MADE his palm sweat, the skin moist with anticipation of breaking the code and shining light onto a mystery that had haunted him most of his life. The coded ledgers in his grandfather's secret office would contain not only the whereabouts of Constance Zelig, but perhaps the location and new identity of his sister.

How long since he had seen her? If Abbie walked past him on the street today, would he even recognize her? Would something in his brain click and make him turn, stare at the passing stranger, trying to fit her face into some abstract jigsaw of memory? Would she know him?

Every fiber of his being was on fire, but he tamped it down with measured patience. He had waited this long, but for now he had other responsibilities, other vulnerable people who required his attention.

*

"How much do I say?" asked the woman who was becoming a man.

Gender dysphoria, the anxiety individuals felt when their gender identity was at odds with their biological sex, was a condition that Ian still struggled with. He understood and sympathized with the pain and confusion that transgender individuals had to endure;

the struggle was in making his brain register the person's true gender rather than what he saw before him.

For now, Mrs. Anderson still presented to the outside world as a woman, but her physicality was changing. Hormone replacement therapy was deepening her voice and bringing the bloom of dark shadow to her cheeks and chin. She had cut her hair, bound her breasts and simplified her makeup — a light touch of lipstick and mascara, a morning routine so ingrained it was difficult to shake — but for the sake of her son was still dressing in a feminine manner. Today that meant a purple silk blouse over fitted jeans.

As the drugs and surgery progressed, even these remnants would disappear.

"You need to be honest," said Ian. "Children understand much more complicated issues than parents like to think. Hiding the truth only leads to distrust, and distrust always leads to anger."

Mrs. Anderson watched her son, Cody, playing with Legos on the short table in the corner of Ian's office. He was building a small army of brightly colored, stiff-limbed robots with long, rectangular noses and small square helmets.

Ian's large bucket of bricks contained only the essential building blocks — squares and rectangles — that were popular during his own childhood. Today, Lego was a whole other industry with specialized pieces designed to create a singular object from a movie franchise, such as *Batman* or *Star Wars*, rather than the unlimited boundaries of a child's imagination.

With Ian's blocks, he often had to ask the child what he or she was creating, and what a gift it was when the child's eyes lit up with engaged conversation about forts and robots and flying pirate ships piloted by brave captains and peg-legged first mates.

That Lego didn't have an assigned gender, it could be whatever you wanted it to be.

"Cody?" Ian raised his voice to attract the boy's attention. "Do you understand what is happening to your mother?"

Cody's eyes never left his Legos as he nodded and said, "Mom's unhappy. She wants to be a man."

"And how does that make you feel?" asked Ian.

Cody turned to his mother, his eyes damp but strong, with building blocks filling his hands. "I don't want you to be sad, Mom."

Tears dripped onto Mrs. Anderson's cheeks.

"Is it okay that your mom is becoming a man?" asked Ian.

Cody shrugged. "I guess."

"What part of this transformation troubles you the most?"

Cody wrinkled his nose. "I don't want to stop calling her my mom."

Mrs. Anderson sniffled and choked out a laugh.

"You never have to stop calling me mom, sweetie. Never. Ever."

"Even when you're a dad?" asked Cody.

"Even then. No matter what I look like, I will always, always, always be your mom."

"Okay, then," said Cody before returning to his Legos.

Mrs. Anderson turned to Ian and held out a trembling hand. Ian took hold of it and squeezed. She held on for a long time while tremors of relief made her bound chest shudder.

"Thank you," she mouthed, her words struggling to find enough breath to leave her lips with any volume.

"None of us are born with prejudice," said Ian, lowering his voice again so that it was just the two of them. "It's something we're taught by people we trust."

"My husband?"

"He'll come around. At the moment, he's hurt and feels betrayed. I'll recommend that he gets counseling, make him understand that your transformation doesn't make him any less of a man."

"He would think that?"

"Absolutely. When he's lashing out at you, the angry voice in his brain is probably screaming 'If I had only fucked her better this wouldn't be happening.'"

Mrs. Anderson gasped.

"Sorry, but you need to be aware of that part of him, that frustrated and bruised male ego. Right now, he's feeling trapped in his own emotional cage with nobody to talk to. Unfortunately, men don't share like women do. They're solitary creatures with shallow friendships that require little more maintenance than support for the same baseball team. So how do you tell your drinking buddies that your wife wants to be a man?"

Ian read the alarm in Mrs. Anderson's eyes, but he needed to continue. "I don't believe Cody is any physical danger, but you may be. Your husband's masculine pride has been hurt, and until he realizes that this has nothing to do with him, that fury could turn violent. He needs to punch something. Let's make sure it isn't you."

*

After Cody was picked up by his aunt, who he was staying with until the custody agreement between his parents could be ironed out, Ian called Jersey.

"Body removal," quipped the detective. "You find 'em, we collect 'em."

"Ha-ha," said Ian dryly. "Did your crew find anything unusual?"

"Apart from four dead gangsters?"

"Apart from that, yes."

"No. They've removed the bodies and transported them to the morgue. We'll verify their identities there."

"So just the four?"

"Yep, nothing in the other two graves and no signs of any extra bits."

"Bits?"

"Spare teeth, bones, the usual."

"Good to know."

"Many a killer has been done in by the tenacity of a tooth or two. Little buggers don't like to dissolve. Even pigs shit them out."

"Thanks for the tip."

Jersey laughed. "You owe me lunch. I'm thinking pulled pork sandwiches, hold the teeth, and a chocolate milkshake."

Ian glanced at the hardcover book on the corner of his desk. It crackled with imaginary energy.

"Take a rain check?" he asked. "I'm in the middle of something."

"Add a shot of espresso to the milkshake and you've got a deal."

"Done."

Ian hung up and grabbed the book off his desk, telling Jeannie he'd be on his cell, before heading out.

He didn't make it far.

*

A Tall Man stood beside Ian's van in the parking lot across the street from Children First. Dressed in funerary black, he gripped an old-fashioned umbrella that had been solidly crafted to double as a walking stick. By his side, sitting patiently on their haunches, were two large Doberman Pinschers. Their cropped ears were on high alert, their focus absolute.

The dogs were both terrifying and handsome, unlike their owner who appeared to be neither. Despite his impressive height, the man's frame was near skeletal, which was most evident in his face. His flesh was pallid and his cheeks hollow. The bones of his skull were prominent and sharp, while the whites of his eyes swirled with a patina of dull yellowish-green.

"You've been following me," said Ian as he approached. "Why?"

The man attempted a smile, but it was an action he had little practice at, and the result was creepy rather than comforting.

"I was asked to keep watch."

"By who?"

"You likely already know the answer."

"Zelig?"

The man shook his head, the movement barely discernible but his disappointment apparent.

"Then who?"

"Your sister."

Ian was taken aback. "You know Abbie?"

"I have had that pleasure for many years, though not under that name."

A thousand questions bubbled in Ian's brain, each fighting the other to be asked, but the first to burst forth was simply, "What is she like?"

The man smiled again. It was just as disturbing as before.

"Headstrong, courageous and fiercely loyal. I am only now beginning to understand where she gets it from."

"She lives in Boston," said Ian.

"Yes."

"Did my father know her?"

"He did, although their relationship was strained."

"Can I see her?"

"That is why I am here. She flew into town last night, but wishes to remain out of sight." The man indicated his black Range Rover parked nearby. "If you will allow me, I can take you to her."

Ian tucked *The Maltese Falcon* tighter under his arm and nodded his agreement.

"*Voraus!*" the man said to the dogs as the rear hatch of the Range Rover popped open with a touch on his key fob.

Immediately, the two dogs ran to the vehicle and bounded inside. Neither of them made a solitary noise.

"*Braver Hund!*" rewarded the man as the hatch lowered. He turned to Ian. "You may be more comfortable in a seat."

Walking around to the passenger side, Ian guessed that was humor. Or at least, he hoped it was.

*

They drove across town in near silence except for when Ian asked a question. The tall man already seemed to know everything he needed to about Ian.

"Why did my sister send you?" Ian asked.

"When your father was killed, she realized that Zelig had never given up in his search for revenge. She was afraid the burden would fall to you, and she was not wrong."

"And what were you to do?"

"For now, observe. But I also possess certain skills that could be deployed if necessary."

"Skills?"

"Your sister doesn't want to bury you, too."

"Has she known about me all this time?" An invisible hand squeezed his chest, a sensation Ian hadn't experienced in years, not since he was a child, waking up in the night, panic filling him with dread, feeling lost, alone, and afraid. "And why has she never contacted me before?"

"There are some questions to which only she can provide the best answer," said the man. "Why don't we wait and ask her. It's not far now."

And with that, the vehicle returned to silence, the air thick with the heavy sound of breathing, both dogs and man.

28

THE BOUTIQUE HOTEL was located in a quaint part of town away from the seedy hustle that attracted men like Walter Zelig. In this neighborhood, the biggest crime was not serving Fair Trade coffee.

The thin man parked outside and told Ian the room number.

"You trust me to go in alone?" Ian asked, only half joking.

The man tilted his head and his eyes became gray pebbles, revealing a dark and dangerous core.

"If she trusts you, then so do I."

Ian climbed out of the vehicle and entered the hotel.

On the top floor, he knocked on the door.

The woman who answered looked nothing like the girl he barely remembered. Slightly taller than himself, her face was thin and hard with a nose that bent slightly as if a break had never been correctly set; her hair was light chestnut and cut to frame her face in soft lines; her eyes were clear and bright, the color of a fresh water lake at dusk.

As Ian studied her, she did the same with him; two nervous gunslingers in the middle of a dusty street, neither daring to make the first move, until…

"Sprout!" Abbie broke the ice with a toothy grin. "You haven't changed a bit."

Ian hadn't heard that silly nickname in more years than he cared to remember. It had been forced on him one Thanksgiving before everything changed. Abbie had been watching a frozen food commercial on television and decided Ian was the spitting image of a character called Little Green Sprout.

Ian had naturally hated the name, but hearing it spoken with affection now chipped away more of the scar tissue deep inside his chest.

"You have," he said. "But it looks good on you."

Abbie burst into laughter, the distinctive throaty cackle breaking open a forgotten chamber in his brain, awakening a true memory. *This was his sister.*

She opened her arms to him and Ian stepped into the room, entering the embrace without hesitation, and squeezing. She was real. Not a phantom or a figment of his imagination, but flesh and blood. His blood.

After a long, silent hug, Abbie led Ian to a couch near the window. They sat facing each other.

Ian wanted to be patient, to let the questions flow naturally, but he couldn't contain them.

"I never thought I would see you again," he said. "All these years I never knew if you were alive or dead. Why did you never contact me? Why didn't our father? And why did you leave? I don't know if Mom even knew what happened to you. She never told me anything. Nobody did."

Abbie grabbed a tissue off the nearby coffee table and dabbed at her eyes. The wrinkles around them spoke of tears and laughter, love and sorrow; an entire life that Ian knew nothing about.

"It's fucked up," she agreed.

But Ian wasn't finished. "When Zelig approached me two days ago, I didn't even know who he was. How could I not—"

Abbie laid a hand upon his knee. "I know. You've been busy."

"I've been threatened," said Ian. "But it seems that's not unusual for our family."

"No, it's not."

"Last night, I found four dead bodies in the basement of the butcher shop. They were Zelig's men, and they had been there awhile. Every time Zelig sent someone to threaten our grandfather, a fresh grave was dug."

"He was formidable."

"Wish I had known that side of him. People in the neighborhood still talk about him with admiration, and yet he always terrified me."

"He loved us more than we'll ever know."

"Are you sure?"

"I am. At least one of those dead men was sent to find me. Grandfather never told him shit."

"Even when Zelig tortured him to death."

Abbie nodded and dabbed at her eyes again.

"You knew?" asked Ian.

"Father told me. Zelig forced him to watch. It broke him. I don't think he was ever a brave man to begin with, not like his father, but what he witnessed that day dissolved every ounce of backbone he had left."

Ian recalled what Mr. Palewandram had said about that day, about the neighbors finding his father soaked in blood in the middle of the street. *"His wail was as unintelligible as it was frightening."*

"That's why he ran," said Ian.

"The burden was passed onto him, but he couldn't stand up to Zelig like grandfather had. He didn't have that courage, so he ran away instead. He found me in Boston and tried to be a father, but he couldn't do that either. The only thing he was ever much good at was leaving."

"Zelig's men found him in the end."

"They never stopped looking." Abbie lowered her eyes in shame. "Father told me they wouldn't, that if I ever tried to make contact with you and Mom, Zelig would find out where I was and come for me."

"Why?"

Abbie's eyes snapped up and fire danced upon the deep, dark lake. "Because he's a sick fuck with fairytales in his head in place of truth. He abused his daughter until she begged our grandfather to make her disappear. Instead of accepting what a monster he was, Zelig demanded her return. When Grandfather refused, Zelig decided I was to be her replacement. My disappearance was always supposed to be temporary until grandfather sorted the situation, but Zelig never gave up. Whatever warped story he told himself, it became his obsession. But when Grandfather was killed and Father ran away, my bridge collapsed. There was no going home."

Ian thought of the grave his grandfather had prepared in the basement. The one that was never filled. His father ran from that responsibility, too. Maybe that was the burden his father meant in his note — not finding Zelig's daughter, but finally giving the grave its due.

"Did Mom know you were alive?"

Abbie shrugged. "I think she knew why I had to leave, but we never had any contact after I was gone. It was never meant to be permanent."

"It broke her, too," said Ian quietly. "Physically, she remained here, but whatever it was that made her a mother dissolved when dad left. I couldn't stand to look at her near the end, and then, like father, like son, I abandoned her as well. I couldn't stay in that damn shop, watching her drink herself to death." Ian choked on his final words. "She died alone."

Abbie grabbed Ian's hand and squeezed it hard.

"Goddamn shitty parents," she said.

"Yeah. Fuck 'em," agreed Ian.

Both siblings stared at each other in shock, and then they started to laugh.

*

Ian cradled a tumbler of bourbon and ginger on ice — his sister's drink of choice — while the crumbs of a simple meal littered the coffee table. Ian had barely registered he was eating as he stuffed morsels around breaks in conversation, minute by minute the years fading away until they were both children again, whispering in their bedroom about the secrets of the day.

"I've missed having a sister," said Ian.

Abbie smiled. "You wouldn't have said that when you were six. Little brothers are such pests when you're ten. I tortured you relentlessly."

"True, but I missed you the moment you were gone. How long are you planning to stay in Portland?"

"Not long," said Abbie. "It doesn't feel safe. I have a life in Boston, but I need this to end. The weight of it…" She paused in mid-sentence and crossed the room to a small safe beside the mini-bar.

After punching in the code, she returned with a small parcel wrapped in brown paper.

"Father told me that if anything happened to him, I was to give this to you."

"What is it?" asked Ian.

"He believed it was the answer to finding Zelig's daughter, but he admitted to me that he had no idea how."

Ian unwrapped the parcel. Inside was a battered red notebook identical to the one contained within his borrowed copy of *The Maltese Falcon*. It even had the same word, *Albatross,* stamped on its cover, and bore the CIA watermark in one corner.

"This was Grandfather's," said Ian, his fingers gliding over its hard-lived cover. "Part of some assignment he was on in Vietnam."

"Really? I never knew he served."

Ian lifted his gaze from the book. "He got arrested and shipped home." A smile crossed his lips. "How much of a bad ass do you need to be to get kicked out of Vietnam during the height of the war?"

Abbie laughed. "Guess we already know the answer. Do you know what to do with the book?"

Ian nodded. "But if I find Constance, what then?"

"You bring her home," said Abbie, her eyes glistening with ice. "If I know anything about surviving this bullshit, she's not going to be a frightened little girl anymore. It's time to face up to her bastard father and end this fucking vendetta once and for all. We all need to be free."

29

THE THIN MAN dropped Ian back at his van across the street from Children First.

Somebody had broken in and rummaged through the glove box, scattering expired paperwork and discarded candy wrappers on the passenger seat. There was nothing worth stealing, which was why Ian never bothered to lock the doors. Better to come back to a mess than a broken window.

Tommy the Tink wandered over and leaned against the passenger door. When Ian rolled down the window, the ripe stench of body odor, urine, rubbing alcohol and sour cranberry rolled in. It was artisanal tear gas with a fruity aftertaste.

"Weren't the fuckwits," said Tommy, indicating the mess of paper. "Sometimes one of 'em forgets you ain't got nothin' worth nothin' and goes for a rummage, but it was a big prick in a decent suit did this. Had a bloody big bandage on his nose and a snarl across his mouth like he just swallowed a shit sandwich. I was goin' to say somethin', but—" Tommy grinned, showing blackened teeth clinging to inflamed gums. "Bastard looked dangerous."

"Appreciate it, Tommy," said Ian. He dug in his pocket and pulled out a rumpled five dollar bill. Handing it over, he asked, "Did you eat?"

"Yeah," he said too quickly, before pausing and adding, "Pretty sure I did. What about you?"

Ian grinned. "Yeah, pretty sure I did, too."

Tommy glanced to the side and cursed. "Ah, shit, that's him."

Ian followed Tommy's gaze and saw the midnight blue Lincoln stopped at the lights across the street.

"I need a favor," said Ian quickly. He handed over *The Maltese Falcon*. "Hide this until I return. It's important."

Tommy accepted the book and slid it inside his clothing before scuttling off to a makeshift camp he had erected in a corner of the parking lot. Two *No Loitering* signs acted as tent poles for the rear corners of his orange tarp, while his shopping cart kept the front taut, creating a triangular canopy that kept most of the rain off while he slept.

As the light turned green, Ian took the second copy of the code book and jammed it under the passenger seat, making sure it was invisible against the mechanics. If Nose Bandage had already searched the van, there should be no need for him to do so again, but just in case, it was good to have backup.

Ignoring the approaching Lincoln, Ian returned to tidying up the mess and jamming everything back in the glove box. When Nose Bandage arrived at the open window, Ian looked up and said, "You know what the most annoying part is?"

Nose Bandage glared down at him in silence.

"They add insult to injury by not stealing my tunes." Ian held up two music cassettes: *Jumping Jive* by Joe Jackson, and *Virtuoso* by Joe Pass. "These are classics."

"Mr. Zelig wants to see you."

"You would be more likable if you at least pretended to take an interest."

The bandage covering the goon's nose flared — and not in a cute way.

"Should we take your car?" Ian asked, but Nose Bandage was already walking away, confident that Ian would follow.

He did.

*

Walter Zelig waited in the back seat, the hiss of oxygen from a nearby tank giving the air a noticeable pep. Despite the fusty old-man smell, Ian inhaled greedily, a gentle wash of oxygenated euphoria sweeping cobwebs from his brain. No wonder hospital workers used the gas as a hangover cure. It worked.

"Police were at your grandfather's store this morning," Zelig wheezed. "And the coroner spent several hours on the premises. What did she remove?"

"I stumbled across some old friends of yours," Ian said. "One sported a .45 shell as a tiepin, another had a gold tooth and Mario Brothers mustache. Ring any bells?"

Zelig was quiet for a moment. "How many?"

"Four."

"And the bodies. They were whole?"

Ian nodded. "My grandfather was very fussy about the quality of meat used in his sausage. I'm thinking your guys didn't rate."

Zelig lifted his leaking oxygen mask off the tank and placed it over his nose and mouth. His sunken chest inflated as he inhaled, and Ian had the disturbing thought of punching through his brittle ribcage and yanking out a cold, black heart. The thought made him smile, which caused Zelig's frown to deepen.

"My grandfather dug six graves," Ian added to break the uneasy silence. "He only filled four." He nodded towards Nose Bandage in the front seat. "He would've been too young back then. Who was the spare one for?"

Zelig glared at him over the transparent mask, his eyes sparking as though two electrons had collided in a miscommunication of spiral trajectory.

"Have you found my daughter?" Zelig asked as he lowered the mask, ignoring the unspoken subtext that one of the graves was reserved for him.

"Not yet, but I'm closing in."

Zelig's eyes widened.

"I'll bring her to you," added Ian before Zelig could speak. "But when I do, this vendetta against my family is over. I want to live my life in peace, and I never want to see your ugly mug again."

"Watch your tongue!" snarled Nose Bandage.

"Fuck you!" Ian snapped back. "When this is over, if you don't leave me alone, I won't hesitate to fill those extra graves. Google my history, see if I'm lying."

Zelig chuckled softly. "Maybe you are of Augustus's blood after all."

"More than you know. I'll be in touch when your daughter is ready to meet."

"I look forward to it."

The way he said it sent a razor down Ian's back, but he tried not to let it show as he exited the car and watched it drive away.

The evening was cold and dank, the coarse air a letdown for his lungs after the oxygen rich environment of the luxury vehicle. Ian shivered as he zipped up his jacket and went to retrieve his book from Tommy.

30

SITTING IN THE van, waiting for the heater to kick in and clear some of the moisture covering the interior of the windshield, Ian pulled out his phone and dialed.

"Mr. Quinn," answered the sultry voice of Rossella Ragano. "Your timing is impeccable."

"And why is that?"

"I'm hungry."

"And I'm nearby, but—"

"Don't spoil it, your answer was perfect without the conjunction."

Ian laughed. "I would be delighted to feed you, but—"

"There you go again," Rossella interrupted.

"But can we get it to go? I have some work to do and I was hoping you could help."

"Oh?"

"How are you at puzzles?"

"I'm a lawyer, puzzles are my business. Both creating and unraveling — depending on who's paying. Why, did you buy a new jigsaw?"

Ian laughed again. "I'm more of a Lego guy, but this is something that might be a little more challenging."

"Oh?"

"Did you know our grandfathers were in Vietnam together during the war?"

"I know my grandfather's history, although he rarely discusses it."

"That's where they first met. I don't know the whole story, but they both possessed the same CIA code book."

"CIA?"

"Your grandfather never mentioned working for the Central Intelligence Agency?"

"No. Never."

"I don't know what they were up to over there, but my grandfather used the code book in his ledgers here, and I'm hoping you can help me crack it."

"And what's in the ledgers?"

"The locations of women who he helped make disappear."

"Including Zelig's daughter, Constance?"

"Yes. At least I hope so."

"I'll order pizza. We can pick it up on the way."

*

"Your pig's missing," said Rossella as Ian parked the van outside the butcher's shop.

Ian leaned forward to peer skyward through the windshield. The speckled bricks beneath where the sign had hung didn't look any less ravaged than the surrounding wall. Rain and age had seeped behind the iron protector to scar them all equally.

"It was time," said Ian.

Exiting the van, Rossella dashed through the drizzle to the store entrance before Ian could stop her. When she looked back for him, he stabbed a thumb over his shoulder in the direction of the Chinese restaurant.

"We already have pizza," she said.

"Hide it until we're past the cook." Ian grinned at her confusion and explained. "That's the address you gave me this morning. My grandfather has an office there, where he kept the ledgers. The owners were old friends."

Hand in hand, they darted across the street, hiding the pizza box between them as Ian quickly introduced Rossella to the Song family before leading her up the stairs.

"They totally knew we had pizza," said Rossella when they reached the second landing.

"I suspect they also know about the bottle of wine in your purse."

Rossella gasped in mock horror. "Objection, your honor. Where is your proof?"

"Overruled," said Ian. "I can hear it clanging against your keys."

"Then we better get rid of the evidence."

"Easily done, I suspect."

"I concur."

Ian unlocked the door to the small apartment and invited Rossella inside.

*

Rossella surveyed the room, propping the bottle of wine and box of pizza on the desk before walking to the window and gazing out at the street below.

"Your grandfather liked to keep an eye on things," she said.

"I never thought of him as a man of secrets," said Ian, crossing the room to stand behind her. His hands rested on her hips and she leaned back, joining her warmth with his. "Danger, yeah. He was a powerful, looming presence in my life. A fearsome giant that I never wanted to anger, and yet these ledgers, plus the story your grandfather told me, tell such a contradictory story."

"My grandfather?" Rossella questioned.

Ian nuzzled her neck, his embrace tightening as his hands explored. Rossella pressed harder against him, her hips swaying rhythmically, their clothing suddenly feeling thick and uncomfortable.

"He told me a story about Vietnam. About finding Augustus in a jail cell with the blood of six soldiers on his hands."

Rossella gasped and stiffened.

"I didn't get all the details, but your grandfather suggested the soldiers were gang-raping a pair of twin girls. One of the girls died, but I believe the surviving twin is Mrs. Song."

"That's horrible."

"Your grandfather helped Augustus and the girl escape the country."

Rossella released herself from Ian's embrace and turned to face him.

"When did he tell you this?" she asked.

"This morning." Ian indicated the shelf of ledgers. "I stopped by, looking for a code book to decipher these."

"And what made you think my grandfather had it?" She was probing, but not angry.

"It was a guess, really," admitted Ian. "I suspected Augustus would have needed help, someone with access to the right people with the proper skills. From what your grandfather said over breakfast, I couldn't figure out their connection. How did a neighborhood butcher and a high-profile criminal lawyer become friends?"

"And my grandfather was coherent?"

"Very," said Ian, fudging the truth. "That is until—"

"Until?" A concerned spark fired in her voice.

Ian grinned. "Until he fell asleep in his chair."

Rossella's face softened with relief and her lips bent at the corners. "He does love to nap."

"Who doesn't?" said Ian. "It's the secret to a happy life."

"Oh?"

"Scientifically proven. That's why cats are the happiest creatures on the planet."

"Because of naps?"

"Absolutely."

Rossella glanced over at the metal cot in the corner of the office and began to unbutton her blouse. The heat of passion made her skin glow.

"Well then," she said, her voice growing huskier. "Perhaps we should try it."

And they did.

*

"I hope you're opening that wine," said Rossella.

She smiled teasingly as she sat up in bed. Her open blouse barely covered her ample modesty, making Ian dizzy with the sheer power of her femininity.

"As you wish," he said.

"Mmmm, I like that answer. That should be your answer to everything I ask."

"As you wish," he repeated.

Rossella laughed with delight and skipped into the corner bathroom.

"See if there are any glasses or cups in there," Ian called after her.

"As you wish," Rossella called back through a crack in the door.

The wine bottle was a screw top rather than a cork, which made opening it rather simple.

The pizza, however, would never make the cover of *Pizza Lovers Weekly* as it had endured some severe jostling on its journey to the desk. Fortunately, they weren't planning to frame it.

Ian slid the toppings back in place before ripping off a slice and taking a bite. Italian sausage with fennel, red peppers, mushroom and fresh tomato. The melted mozzarella had been sprinkled with crispy bits of bacon.

"Oh my God," he moaned.

Rossella stepped out of the bathroom. Dressed only in silk panties and unbuttoned blouse, her dark hair hanging loose and a cheeky grin on her lips, she looked far younger than she was. The image crossed Ian's mind of a college student sleeping with her wrinkled professor.

"Told you they make a great pie." Crossing the room, Rossella grabbed a slice and took a large bite, the sauce dripping onto her chin.

She picked up the bottle of wine and took a long swallow from its neck. "No glasses," she said, handing the bottle over. "Besides, this is more fun."

Ian took a swallow, the full-bodied sweetness mixing with the saltiness of the cheese, making his taste buds explode.

Rossella took another pull from the bottle and then planted her lips on Ian's, adding another indelible taste to the mix.

Moisture momentarily blurred Ian's vision as the thought entered his mind: *This is what happiness feels like.*

He had forgotten.

As Rossella's lips parted from his, cold air replaced her warmth, the art of breathing suddenly less desirable than kissing.

How does someone forget happiness?

He didn't have time to ponder the question before his phone rang. He would have ignored it, but the Caller ID showed it was Jersey.

He answered.

"Are you working with the Anderson family?" Jersey asked without preamble.

"I'm supervising visits between Cody and his parents. Why?"

"I need you over here. The dad has lost his shit."

Jersey gave him the address.

"On my way."

When Ian hung up, Rossella was already getting dressed. With her back to him, she had removed her blouse and was slipping into her bra; the garment was a spider's web upon her skin, both a distraction and silky entrapment, daring him to approach and brush it away.

"You can stay here," said Ian as he untangled his own clothes. "Or I can call you a cab. I'm not sure how long I'll be."

Rossella glanced over her shoulder at him. "Uh-uh. I'm tagging along."

"There's no need."

"Yes, there is," she said with a mischievous smirk. "I'm not finished with you yet."

31

P ATROL CARS BLOCKED the street for a block in either direction. Harsh red and blue light cut through the hazy darkness, flash freezing and distorting dozens of curious faces pressed flat to living room and kitchen windows as though demonic possession had been handed out wholesale. Some of the neighbors had swapped slippers for rubber boots and pulled heavy coats over their evening comfies to brave the elements and get a better view of whatever potential tragedy was unfolding nearby.

Every second person held a smartphone, the luminescent glow like Zippos at a rock concert.

Ian drove up to the improvised barrier and stopped as a young officer strode forward, the palm of his bare hand thrust angrily ahead of him as if it had the power of Iron Man to repel alien invaders. His other hand dropped to his holster and rested on the butt of his sidearm.

Ian rolled down his window and called out, "Detective Jersey Castle asked me to attend. The name's Quinn."

With a nod, the officer called dispatch on his shoulder-mounted radio.

After receiving confirmation, the officer instructed Ian to leave his vehicle where it was and cross the barrier on foot.

Climbing out of the van, Ian was suddenly bathed in the harsh spotlight of a broadcast media scrum as cameramen and women for the local TV stations jockeyed for position and a crumb of information. The moment lasted barely a second before the lights dimmed amidst a mutter of disappointment and chatter of "Who the hell is he?" Dressed as he was in black jeans, wrinkled shirt and civilian rain jacket, Ian looked no more important than the coffee delivery service.

One journalist was at least smart enough to ask the question, but was discouraged by Ian's unhelpful reply. Another snapped his photo on her smartphone to run his mug through Google in search of a match. She, Ian thought, had potential to go places. A match of his face would show where he worked, which would let her know there was a good chance a child was involved and potentially in danger. That angle would add excitement to the story, elevating it to a lead position and more airtime for her.

Hiding within the oversize hood of her blood red, thigh-length coat, Rossella grabbed Ian's hand as they slipped by the patrol car and headed up the block to where Jersey had established a temporary command post a short distance from the Anderson home. The demons in the windows followed their path, their open mouths fogging the glass in concentric circles like the spread of a zombie virus.

Jersey and his partner, Amarela, were huddled under a makeshift plastic awning with a heavily armed member of the Special Emergency Response Team. The SERT officer had the humorless face of someone who chewed wasps for breakfast and spat out their stingers from between a noticeable gap in his front teeth. He also sported a precisely trimmed white-blond mustache of impressive girth.

Jersey glanced at Rossella, his eyebrows asking the question he didn't have time for, before shaking Ian's hand.

"Thanks for coming."

"What's happening?"

"Mrs. Anderson called 9-1-1 in distress. Her estranged husband barged into the home uninvited. He's intoxicated, armed and distraught."

"What about Cody, their son?" Ian asked.

"All three are inside. He won't let them leave."

"And the aunt?" Ian asked. "Cody is meant to be staying with her."

"Amarela called her. She's on her way over."

"Have you talked to anybody inside?" asked Ian.

Jersey nodded. "The husband's a mess. I was hoping you could give us some insight, a way to de-escalate the situation before people get hurt."

"Who talked to him?" Ian asked.

"Only me," said Jersey.

Ian glanced over at Amarela. She was chewing gum at a rapid pace, the muscles in her jaw clenching and releasing like an alligator trying to eat an octopus. But even in baggy rain gear, her high cheekbones, deep brown eyes and caramel skin oozed Latin sexuality.

"She should talk to him," said Ian.

Amarela stopped chewing.

"He's feeling emasculated," Ian explained. "His wife's undergoing gender reassignment and that's left him questioning his manhood. He's wondering if other women will ever be attracted to him or if there is some flaw that makes him less of a man. He needs a woman," Ian locked eyes with Amarela, "an attractive woman, to find him desirable."

"You do know I'm gay," said Amarela.

"He doesn't need to know that. You just need to be nice to him, flirt a little, let him feel that everything will be okay."

"That he still has a dick?" added Amarela.

"Yes."

"And that I want to suck it?"

"Even better."

"Men, you're all the fucking same. Big babies who want their ding-a-lings played with."

"We should wait for the hostage negotiator," Wasp Face said to Jersey. "No offense, but your partner doesn't have proper—"

"What gender is the negotiator?" interrupted Ian.

Wasp Face's lips curled in what could be perceived as either a grin or a sneer. "Difficult to tell with Ralph."

"He'll respond best to a woman," said Ian. "Honestly, he's fragile and confused at the moment and it's manifesting in all the wrong ways."

"It's manifesting in a pump-action shotgun aimed at a woman and child," said Wasp Face. "My team is ready—"

"You wearing your vest under that?" Jersey asked his partner, over-ruling the officer's objection.

"Why do you think I'm so irritable," she answered. "Chafes my nipples like a bastard."

"Nips aside, you okay with this?" he asked.

"God wouldn't have given me this body if I didn't use it to make men my slaves."

"Remember to be gentle," said Ian. "Stroke his ego."

"Oh, once I'm done, he'll be wanting me to stroke a lot more than that," said Amarela.

Jersey turned to Ian. "You sure this is a good idea?"

"I'm not," said Wasp Face.

"Yes," said Ian. "He's embarrassed and frail. He doesn't want to hurt his family, but he needs to see there's a light at the end of the tunnel."

"A pussy, you mean," said Amarela.

"Touch up your lipstick," interjected Jersey before Ian could respond. "And be nice."

Amarela winked at her partner before pulling a lipstick out of her pocket and applying a fresh coat of *Spank Me Red*.

*

"Is this what you do?" Rossella asked Ian as Amarela walked across the street with her hands in the air.

The detective was alone, vulnerable, and the natural fear that would be impossible to keep off her face would, Ian hoped, keep her safe. But just in case something went wrong, Jersey had insisted she keep her backup gun, a snub-nosed .38 revolver, out of sight but within easy reach under her rain jacket.

Ian turned to Rossella. "This is nothing like what I do. Most of the time, I'm a glorified babysitter. I watch over the kids, talk to the parents, try to keep everyone safe. My priority is the children, they're my clients."

"But people trust you. Even the police. That's a rare gift."

Ian shrugged. "I try not to bullshit and I don't pretend to know all the answers. I'm a lousy liar and my many flaws are etched like warning stickers on my skin, maybe people see that."

Rossella's fingertips stroked his arm. "You have insight into the wounded soul."

"Hard earned," said Ian in a quiet voice as he looked away, his focus shifting back to Amarela as she approached the front door.

Rossella squeezed his arm and let the conversation drop. Now wasn't the time to explore what he meant.

*

Jersey, Ian, Rossella and Wasp Face listened in on Amarela's conversation with Mr. Anderson via a wireless microphone clipped under her jacket. Before long, she was sitting on the front porch, chatting through a crack in the door. She laughed and smiled, cooed, sympathized and empathized.

When Mr. Anderson finally laid down his weapon and opened the door further to share his near-empty bottle of tequila, she stroked his forearm and smiled like they were at the end of a promising first date. He didn't even seem to mind when she placed him in handcuffs and escorted him off the porch to a waiting patrol car.

"He's going to need a good lawyer," said Rossella.

Ian nodded, reading her thoughts. "Be gentle."

"You don't mind?"

"This is what you do," said Ian. "And Cody needs both his parents to get through this. His mother's transformation will be tough enough without losing his father, too. But get the man some good counseling. He needs it."

After the patrol car drove off, with Rossella catching a ride with her new client, Amarela returned to the awning and unwrapped a fresh piece of gum. Slipping it into her mouth, she grinned at her partner and rolled her eyes.

"Men," she said with great exasperation. "I don't know why we still let you idiots run the world."

32

A FTER MAKING SURE Cody and his mom were in safe hands, Ian escaped the melee and drove back to his grandfather's apartment above the Dynasty restaurant. The leftover pizza was cold, the opened wine warm, and the apartment quiet.

Settling into the armchair by the window, Ian cracked open the code book and went to work.

It took time to understand exactly what he was looking at. His only experience with secret codes had been in his childhood when he found a plastic decoder ring in a second-hand bookshop. It was laying at the bottom of a bag of old DC comics he bought for five dollars, and it used a simple substitution cipher. Unfortunately, since none of his friends owned a similar ring, it quickly lost its attraction.

After an hour of intense study, Ian began to see the logic and patterns behind the CIA code. Despite its complexity, it really wasn't that much different from his boyhood toy. He spent a second hour frustrated by his lack of progress, until he realized the codebook didn't contain one key, but hundreds. Each ledger entry began with a four-letter code. Contained within that code was a page and paragraph number that told him which key needed to be used to unlock the rest of the cipher.

When the first jumble of letters became a word he recognized — *Alice* — he practically wept for joy. In celebration, he took a slug of wine from the bottle and devoured a slice of room temperature pizza. Re-energized, he deciphered the entire first entry, breaking down its structure piece by piece. He did the same to the second entry — *Leticia* — and then compared the two.

They both followed the same basic outline.

To make sure it wasn't an anomaly, Ian began decoding the third entry — *Paola*. It fit the same pattern, which meant he could take a chance and only decipher the necessary entry on each page, the line that contained each woman's original name.

He found Constance Zelig in the middle of the fourth ledger as the morning sun brought a blood red glow to the damp and glistening streets below.

His exhausted reverie was interrupted by a knock on the door.

"Who is it?" Ian called out, his voice dry and rough.

"Mei Song, Mr. Quinn. My grandparents are asking if you would like to join us for breakfast."

"Will there be coffee?"

Mei giggled like only a young woman could. "Yes. My grandfather loves his coffee strong and black."

"I'll be right down."

*

Over breakfast in the Songs' apartment, Ian allowed himself a moment of reprieve where he listened to the family chatter of Mei Song and her grandparents, sipped coffee so strong that Mr. Song joked it could "put hair on the chest of a Chinaman," much to the chagrin of Mei, and devoured a cooked breakfast of bacon, eggs and thin Vietnamese pancakes, each one the size of a silver dollar.

The pancakes were served with butter and coconut jam rather than syrup.

"Mrs. Song," Ian said as he wiped up the last of his egg yolk with a morsel of pancake. "Can I ask how long you knew my grandfather for?"

"Very long time," said Mrs. Song.

"Did you meet in Vietnam?"

"What make you ask?"

"I'm sorry," Ian said. "I don't mean to open old wounds, but I heard a story recently about my grandfather and how he brought a young girl home with him during the war. I wondered if that girl might have been you."

"Your grandfather unusual man," said Mrs. Song as she cleared plates off the table. "He save my life, but I never know why."

"Why he saved you?"

Mrs. Song nodded. "All men want something, but your grandfather…" She paused for a moment in search of the right phrasing, failed, and went with, "He good man. Man of honor." She smiled and reached out to squeeze her husband's shoulder. "I never tell if he even like me and yet he risk life to bring me here. What is that saying about no good deed? And yet, with your grandfather, he ask for nothing. I never know another like him."

"Is that why you've kept his office for all these years?"

Mrs. Song shrugged. "The office belong to him. We do nothing but do nothing."

Ian smiled at the simple philosophy. "Do you still have family in Vietnam?"

Mrs. Song shook her head. "That story end on day Augustus find me. I have no desire to look back."

"What about you, Mei?" Ian asked the granddaughter. "Any interest in visiting Vietnam?"

"No need," said Mrs. Song before her granddaughter could answer. "Mei is American. This her home, not Vietnam."

Sensing he was tiptoeing in a minefield, Ian dropped the subject and finished his coffee.

"Thank you for the lovely breakfast, but if you'll excuse me—"

"What do you find up there?" interrupted Mr. Song. "If it is not rude to ask."

Ian thought over the question for a moment, realizing that his own intrusion into Mrs. Song's past had opened this door. "It seems your wife is not the only woman rescued by my grandfather."

"It is true," said Mr. Song. "He helped many women. They would come to him with horrible stories of woe, frightened and with nothing to their name. At first, it was women who knew my wife's story, a story she shared with Vietnamese women who had also been brought to this country but by less scrupulous men. These women thought they were escaping hell, but they were sold into another. Your grandfather became a whispered legend, a knight in the darkness."

"You helped him?"

"Where we could. When we could."

"But one of the women he helped was the daughter of Walter Zelig. You know him?"

Mr. Song's eyes narrowed as he nodded.

"Her disappearance is the reason my grandfather was tortured to death, the reason my sister vanished from my life, and the cause of my father's murder. I need to find her and put an end to this vendetta."

"What would your grandfather do?" asked Mrs. Song.

"We already know," said Ian. "But I'm not him. I won't sacrifice any more lives for the sake of one woman. I need this to be over."

*

Crossing the street, Ian entered the butcher's shop. The front door was unlocked as the cleaners were already busy on the back room, their portable boombox blaring one of the local radio stations. The front room had grown in size with the large refrigerated cases removed and its natural plank floor polished to a shine.

It wasn't perfect, the scars too deep to be covered by simple floor wax, but it was a start.

The dark sheets of moldy chipboard had been removed from the picture window, flooding the open space with natural light and revealing the painted shop sign to the absent public for the first time in decades.

"What do you think?" asked Clark as he pushed through the steel mesh curtain from the back room.

"You've done an incredible job," said Ian.

"It's a beautiful space, really," said Clark. "Pity it's in such a lousy area."

"But it's growing on me," said Ian.

"I spent a little extra on security," said Clark. "Hope that's okay?" He pointed at the large shop window. "I didn't want to block the light with steel bars, but I found this new product that's just about as strong."

He crossed to the window and wrapped his hand around one of a dozen clear plastic rods that ran the entire height of the window. The rods ran from floor to ceiling and were spaced approximately eight inches apart.

"It won't stand up to a tank, but nobody is getting through these without a ton of effort." Clark grinned. "And there's another cool feature that steel won't give you."

He crossed to the wall beside the front door and flicked a switch. Suddenly, the bars lit up in a soft blue hue.

"LEDs," said Clark. "With the rest of the lights off, it makes for a cool feature, plus it lets the outside world know your store is protected."

"And the front door?" Ian asked.

"All new locks, reinforced steel jamb, plus a four-prong deadbolt that will snap the ankle of anybody who tries to kick it in."

"Sweet."

Clark grinned. "It's been a fun project, and given me ideas about how to expand my business. A lot of the cleanup jobs we do are after thieves and vandals have broken into a place." He pointed to the wall behind Ian. "Did you notice your sign?"

Ian turned to see the rusted iron pig attached to the brick wall. Clark had hidden white LED lighting behind it to cast a soothing glow and make it appear almost three-dimensional.

"I thought about cleaning it up," said Clark. "But the oxidation and weathering just gives it so much character that I left it as is."

Ian had to agree, it looked cool. And he liked to think that his grandfather would approve.

*

Upstairs, in his freshly cleaned though still uncomfortably cluttered apartment, Ian called Jersey.

"Thanks again for helping last night," said Jersey when he answered. "Although making Amarela the hero of the hour is not a pleasant experience for any of us."

"Hey, I heard that!" Amarela called out in the background.

"You were meant to," said Jersey. "She's also unbuttoned her shirt one extra level just to make it more difficult for the officers to look her in the eye when they stop by to offer congratulations, which I might add is something they never do for me."

"I'm right here," protested Amarela. "And that button was a mistake. I was tired this morning, I already told you that."

"Uh-huh. What do you think, Ian?"

"Send me a photo, I'll let you know."

Jersey laughed and told Amarela what he said.

"She called you a pig."

"Well, I do live above a butcher's shop."

Jersey laughed again. "What can I do for you?"

"I'm trying to track somebody down. I have a name and

address in San Diego, but there's a good chance she might not still be there."

"One of your missing women?"

"*The* missing woman," said Ian.

"Oh?"

"Walter Zelig's daughter, Constance."

"Okay. And what are you going to do when you track her down?"

"Bring her home," said Ian coldly. "It's time for her to settle up with her father and get my family off the hook. There's been too much blood spilled for this to have a happy ending. He's an old man now, she can take him."

"I'll see what I can do."

33

IAN SAT AT the small kitchen table, sipping a coffee and talking to Birdie, the rack-thin brunette who had patched him up
last time he brought Molly to visit her uncle. Birdie simply listened and nodded.

Molly held the large ginger tom in her lap, the cat's delighted
purr loud enough to be heard from the kitchen.

The armed biker on the porch outside kept glancing in the
window as though to remind Ian that he wasn't part of the broth-
erhood, and thus couldn't be trusted.

"You expecting trouble?" Ian asked Gordo as his fellow gang
member glared through the window again. "Your guard dog is acting nervous."

"Nothing we can't handle," said Gordo. "New player in town
is spreading his oats, testing the boundaries, you know how it is?"

"You have a name?"

Gordo shook his head. "No name. Not yet. He's sticking to the
shadows, making a few moves but still testing the waters."

"But he's about the size of a gorilla?"

Gordo grinned, surprised by Ian's intel.

"That's what I hear."

"The Bowery brothers are working for him."

Gordo nodded. "Heard that, too. What's your interest?"

"He killed one of my clients."

Ian winced as Molly looked up in horror. He tried to back-pedal. "Sorry, Molls, I shouldn't have said that. It was—"

"It's okay," said Gordo. "It's good for her to know the dangers of this world." He turned to his niece and stroked her hair. "But don't you worry. Anybody tries to hurt you, they'll have to go through me first, and that ain't gonna fucking happen."

Gordo turned back to Ian. "Who was your client?"

"Noah Bowery."

"Rory's boy?"

Ian nodded.

"And the stupid prick is working for his son's killer now?"

"Both brothers are."

"Fucking addicts, man. They'll sell their own mothers for a hit." He turned back to Molly. "If you learn anything from me, learn this. Drugs destroy from the inside out. They take your dignity, they rot your soul, and they turn you into a cancer that shits on everyone and everything you ever cared about. You want to get high? Smoke a little weed; take a shot of Jack, that's fine. But I ever hear you're into anything more than that and you'll wish you were never born. You got that?"

Molly's eyes were the size of dinner plates as she nodded.

"I've lost too many friends to that shit," Gordo continued. "Plenty of coin to be made without it." He turned back to Ian. "You know this gorilla?"

"Met him once."

"Where?"

"Don't know. I was blindfolded. The Bowerys took me to him."

"What's his interest in you?"

"It's complicated. He's actually interested in Walter Zelig. Zelig is interested in me. He wanted to ask about it."

"Zelig ain't much no more."

"Maybe not to you."

"What's that mean?"

Ian explained a slice of the story. When he was done, Gordo scratched his nose and said, "Old man still has teeth. Impressive."

"Not if it's your ass he's got in his sights."

"You're a complicated dude, man." Gordo rubbed Molly's head. "No wonder Molls here likes you."

"Mr. Q's alright," said Molls.

Gordo grinned. "Straight from the horse's mouth."

"Hey!" complained Molly, putting up her fists. "Who you calling a horse?"

Gordo dropped to his knees on the floor, placed one hand behind his back and cocked his left fist in challenge. "You," he said with a broad smile. "What you gonna do about it?"

Without a moment's hesitation, Molly feinted with her right to make her uncle block it with his left, and then planted a solid left fist in her uncle's eye.

*

"Sorry again, uncle," shouted Molly sweetly as Ian led her to the van.

Standing on the porch, with Birdie by his side, Gordo held a bag of frozen peas against his eye.

"I hope he's not mad," Molly said to Ian as she climbed inside. "I told Birdie to kiss it better once the swelling goes down."

"He seemed more amused than angry," said Ian. "He underestimated you."

"Yeah," agreed Molly. "People do that all the time."

"That they do, Molls."

*

After dropping molly at her foster home, Ian pulled into a

drive-thru to order a burger. He was just enjoying a second bite when his phone rang.

"I've got a number for you," said Jersey. "She's moved around a bit, but stayed mostly within the San Diego area. Four years ago, she changed her first name back to Constance, but kept her adopted surname of Silver. Her last move was only two months ago, so the number is fresh."

"Did you call it?"

"Didn't want to spook her. You sure you want to do this?"

"I don't have a choice."

"We always have a choice."

"Not this time. Not anymore."

"Okay."

Jersey gave him the number.

Ian took another bite of hamburger, but it sat heavily in his mouth until he spat it back into the wrapper. After throwing the meal away, he took a deep breath, composed what he was going to say, and dialed.

The phone rang four times before an answering machine kicked in. The recorded message wasn't what he expected.

"Congratulations, Ian, you did what Zelig never could, you found his daughter." The voice was deeply moist, male and familiar. A visage of the gorilla's horseshoe-shaped scar filled Ian with icy dread. "The Bowery boys bet against you, which shouldn't come as any surprise, but I knew you possessed an iron streak of resilience. I could see it lurking deep behind those stubborn blue eyes the first time we met. Most people shit themselves, as they should, but you...you barely flinched." The gorilla chuckled. "Unfortunately, you're too late. Constance is my pawn now."

There was no beep to leave a message as the line went dead.

34

IAN DROPPED HIS phone and slammed both hands against the steering wheel.

"Son of a bitch!" he screamed, ignoring nervous glances from neighboring vehicles as occupants froze mid-bite.

He wanted to hit something...*someone*. Instead, he punched the center of the steering wheel, making the horn howl in protest.

The vehicle directly beside him started its engine and drove away, the driver's strawberry milkshake frozen halfway in its journey between lap and lips as though his elbow had locked in terror.

This isn't the end, Ian told himself as the horn fell silent and his breathing resumed. The gorilla may have a different endgame, but that didn't mean Ian had to be cut out.

If Zelig was to suffer, Ian needed to be part of it.

All he had to do was convince the gorilla that a partnership was valuable.

And to do that, they needed to meet.

*

Unwrapping his grandfather's .45 from its oily rag, Ian sprayed the gun with a lubricating cleaner and dragged a bore-snake through the barrel. For its age, the gun had been kept in incredibly good shape and showed no signs of rust or burnt powder build-up.

This didn't surprise Ian as he had many a memory of his grandfather slaving over the sausage grinder and meat slicers, cleaning every razor sharp tooth, blade and gear until they glistened better than new.

Once the gun was cleaned, greased and oiled, Ian dug back into the bag he had purchased at a local sports store and opened a fresh box of ammunition. Keeping one eye on the house across from where he was parked, Ian loaded the magazine with seven jacketed hollow-point rounds. If he needed to reload, that left thirteen fresh rounds in the box, but that would also mean he was in a deep, deep pile of trouble.

Resting the gun in his lap, Ian lifted the small pair of binoculars he had bought and focused them on the house.

The dwelling was exactly as he had imagined it would be: a dull colored, side-by-side duplex with a dead square of lawn and a bruised front door that looked to have been opened with a kick more often than a push. Inside, a large flat-screen television flickered and flashed though nobody seemed to be watching.

Ian cracked his window to stop the glass from fogging as his warm breath mixed with the cool, damp air.

Rory Bowery, his face flushed with anger, stepped in front of the living room window. He was waving his arms in the air and thick spittle flew from between dry, cracked lips. Whoever he was yelling at was out of sight. It took a long time to get his point across as every second and third word was a profanity. In Rory's world, toast wasn't just toast, it was goddamned fucking useless fucking burnt fucking toast.

The target of his rant burst through the front door and made sure to slam it behind her. The flimsy barrier rattled in its frame, tired hinges barely strong enough to keep it attached.

Ian hadn't spent as much time with Noah's mom as he had with Rory as she wasn't the one whose visits needed to be supervised. She looked so young and yet so completely depleted at the same time. Her gray skin and limp hair blended with the rain, toil and grief having smothered the embers of life.

Part of him wanted to go to her, to say he wasn't angry with her, and explain all the ways she could improve her life by asking for help. Assholes like Rory were a dime a dozen, which was why there were so many tireless organizations set up specifically to help abused and ill-treated women.

But Ian stayed where he was and watched her walk away. Her shoulders were hunched tight and her back was curved as though the storm clouds added more weight to her burdens. But today, he was not the healer, nor the protector; today, he was fire and rage.

Ian waited until Shirley disappeared around the corner before taking his gun in hand and opening the van door.

*

Rory yelled "Fuck off" through the closed door when Ian knocked. So he knocked again.

"Godfuckindammit!" Rory screamed. "I don't want to see yer fuckin' ugly bitch of a face—"

He stopped talking after yanking open the door as Ian wasn't who he was expecting to find.

"What the fuckin' fuck do you—"

Two bloody teeth went flying out of Rory's mouth as the cold, steel barrel of the .45 sliced through his cheek. This was followed by a bruising pain in his chest as Ian's left hand shoved him roughly inside. Rory stumbled and fell onto the stairs with a crunch of tailbone as Ian entered the home and back-heeled the door closed behind him.

The attack was more brutal than Rory deserved, but Ian knew he had to make him frightened for his life or this would all be for nothing.

"Anybody else here?" asked Ian. "Your brother?"

Rory raised his hands and shook his head. Blood poured down his chin from the gash in his cheek and his broken mouth.

"Wha'thefuck—"

"Shut up," snapped Ian. "I'm trying to decide whether to kill you or not, and flapping your gums isn't helping your case any."

"You can't fu—"

Ian thumbed back the hammer, letting Rory hear the loud click as it locked in place.

"What did I just say? You can talk when I ask a question, not before."

"But you—"

Ian rushed forward and pressed the barrel of the gun against Rory's left eye, pushing it deep into the flesh and twisting slightly so the steel rim bit in and drew blood.

"How fucking dumb are you, Rory?"

"Okayokayokay."

Ian stepped back and took a look around. The place was a dump, except for the TV. It stood like a golden idol amidst a clutter of poverty and neglect.

"I can make this easy," said Ian. "Take me to see the gorilla and I'll let you live."

Rory's eyes widened in panic.

"I can't do that—"

Ian shot the TV, the hollow-point widening on impact and pulverizing the glass into a million pieces.

Rory whimpered at the sight.

"Imagine what that would do to your kneecap," said Ian. "Because if you don't take me where I need to go, that's where I'll start."

Snot bubbled out of Rory's nose as he reluctantly hung his head in defeat.

"You ready to go for a drive?" asked Ian. "Without a hood this time."

Rory glared as Ian helped him to his feet.

35

"WE CAN STILL turn the fuck back," Rory whined as he pulled the van onto a gravel driveway surrounded on both sides by an overgrown laurel hedge. A weather-beaten and bullet-pocked sign hung from a metal pole advertising *Buddy's Garage*. A large vinyl *Foreclosure* sticker had been slapped across it when the garage went under, but there wasn't much left that was readable.

"You worried about me or you?" Ian sat in the passenger seat with the .45 pointed at Rory's side. From this distance, a squeeze of the trigger would pulverize his liver, sever his spine and make a hell of a mess of the driver's seat.

"Don't give a fuck 'bout you," said Rory in a rare moment of honesty.

"That's what I figured." Ian clenched his teeth. "Drive."

Rory drove, jamming it into park only when the van reached the end of the driveway.

Pulling the keys out of the ignition, Ian shouldered open the passenger door and told Rory to join him outside.

The garage was a small, two-bay handyman special attached to a ramshackle bungalow that wore its years of neglect like a mossy cloak. Once upon a time this would have likely been a thriving family business, bringing in just enough income to make life comfortable without having to report to a sociopathic boss or endure a long, stressful commute. It was the type of business that could shut up shop for the afternoon when the kids had an important hockey game or school play, or even when a nap after lunch seemed like a particularly great idea.

But, not unlike his grandfather's butcher shop, those days were gone, lost to the bulk-buy corporations with loss-leader oil changes, Chinese-made tires, and vehicles that contained more computer chips than pistons.

The garage door trundled open to reveal the gorilla and a skinny sidekick Ian reckoned was the hooded driver from before. The driver didn't look particularly surprised to see them — then again, he had one of those slack faces that only ever sported one expression: ambivalence.

The gorilla, however, was clearly enraged.

He was also gripping a short-barrel, pump-action Defender shotgun.

Rory immediately held up his hands. "I-I didn' fuckin' want—"

Without a word, the gorilla raised the shotgun, pointed it at Rory's face and pulled the trigger.

Rory's head vanished in a bloom of blood and brain, pieces of his skull flying like the skin of a burst balloon. Ian flinched as a chunk of bloody jawbone slashed his cheek, but he was too shocked to move.

The gorilla spoke to his skeletal sidekick. "Bring Quinn inside, then clean up this mess. Call his brother to help."

The sidekick raised a chromed Beretta and gestured to the interior of the garage. It took a moment for Ian's trembling legs to obey, but he found the strength when the man didn't seem to notice him slipping his own .45 into the waistband of his jeans and covering it with his blood-peppered jacket.

*

the interior of the garage was exactly as it had been during Ian's first visit: starkly utilitarian with the familiar reek of grease and oil that helped mask the fresh metallic tang of splattered brain.

The gorilla paced back and forth in the shadows, muttering indecipherably to himself, as Ian stood awkwardly a few steps inside the door.

"I—"

"Not yet!" The gorilla slammed an open hand into a large file cabinet with enough force to dent the metal.

The large man returned to pacing and muttering before flipping a switch that caused the garage doors to rumble closed.

Ian glanced over his shoulder at the diminishing light, wondering if he should run while he still had a chance. Then something soft hit his cheek and he instinctively turned back to catch it. The overhead doors closed behind him as he stared at a clean, white rag in his hands.

He looked across at the gorilla, who was using a similar rag to wipe ruby freckles from his face. Ian followed suit, surprised at the amount of gore that had spattered his own face and neck.

"You surprise me," said the gorilla, the pacing of his words slowing as he regained control of his temper, "coming here. I gave you credit for being smarter than that."

"You have something I need."

"Well, that is the nature of my business. I deliver what people need and take what I want."

"You have Constance."

The gorilla shrugged. "I have lots of women."

Ian ignored the sloppy evasion. "I need to deliver her to Zelig. What happens after that doesn't concern me."

"I don't believe you."

"What part?"

"Your lack of concern. That's not how you're built."

"Meaning what?"

"I've watched you." The gorilla grinned, his badly crooked teeth glistening with saliva. "You're the kind of man who helps old ladies carry their groceries across the street, the soppy idiot who rescues kites out of trees for wailing children."

"Once perhaps."

"Bullshit. I know what you did to those responsible for your daughter's death, but that doesn't make you a tough guy, it only makes you a grieving father. Face it, that wound you cling onto is scabbing over. Underneath, you're still a soft touch."

Ian bristled, but the gorilla wasn't finished.

"You know I battered little Noah just to make a point. You know I made his father work for me, to lick the boots of his son's killer every day. You know exactly what I am, but you're not going to do a damn thing about it." The gorilla paused to show his teeth again before adding, "Even with that gun hidden in your waistband, you're fucking impotent. That's the difference between you and me."

The gorilla raised his shotgun, pointed it at Ian's chest and chambered another round. The deadly *click-clack* made Ian's heart wither in fright, but his face kept it hidden. Ever since his daughter died, life had become a daily decision rather than a necessity.

"Why shouldn't I kill you right here, right now?"

"Because you need me," said Ian, attempting to sound braver than he felt.

The gorilla's grin twisted and a rivulet of drool escaped the corner of his misshapen mouth.

"And why do you think that?"

"Because I'm still alive."

The gorilla laughed and lowered his gun.

"See? You're a clever fucker, but don't confuse brains with

balls." He indicated a table in the middle of the garage. "Leave your gun and we can continue this discussion inside."

To show his sincerity, the gorilla placed his shotgun on the table. Reluctantly, Ian placed his .45 beside the shotgun and followed the man through a door to the interior of the attached house.

*

A pale woman sat at the kitchen table in a room that had known better days. She was dressed casually, but definitely not cheaply. Ian had never understood the difference between a regular pair of jeans and those with a designer label on the pocket, but he had a feeling that Constance did.

She had taken good care of herself and the years were as kind to her as time could be. In a flattering light, she could easily pass for the same age as Ian rather than the decade or so she had on him. The kitchen's light, however, was unjustly harsh. When she lifted her chin and brushed platinum hair from her face, the dark bruise under her left eye jumped out in sharp contrast to her pale skin.

"Constance, this is Ian Quinn," said the gorilla. "Quinn, this is Constance."

"Quinn?" said Constance.

When she moved her arms, Ian saw that her left wrist was attached to the chair with a pair of old-fashioned steel handcuffs, although they hung so loosely on her wrist, she likely could have slid right out of them without much effort.

"You knew my grandfather," said Ian. "Augustus."

A sad smile glistened upon her lips. "He saved my life."

"And now his grandson is here to end it," said the gorilla.

Ian's eyes flashed in anger, which made the gorilla laugh.

"See!" he proclaimed. "Your resolve is weakening already. One look at a damsel in distress and all your tough-guy attitude melts like butter on toast." The gorilla slammed his open palm against the table, making both Constance and Ian jump. "But it's time to be the bastard you say you are."

"What's he talking about?" asked Constance.

Ian had trouble meeting the woman's gaze as the gorilla said, "He's going to deliver you back into the bosom of your far-too-loving father."

"What? No. Why?" The woman looked terrified.

"He made a bargain," said the gorilla. "Tell her."

Ian lifted his gaze and fixed it on the woman. "I'm sorry," he began. "Zelig tortured and killed my grandfather, gunned down my father, and sent my sister into hiding. The only way I can make his vendetta stop is to return you to him, but—"

"There's no but," interrupted the gorilla. "Where your grandfather died with honor, you're choosing to live with shame. Nothing wrong with that, you're human. Who the fuck is she to you anyway?"

Ian stared at the gorilla with pure hatred, but that only seemed to amuse the beast.

Unexpectedly, the woman reached her free hand across the small table and latched onto Ian's closed fist; paper smothering rock.

"It's okay," she said softly. "I've grown tired of hiding, of looking over my shoulder and being afraid every time a stranger pays more than a passing interest in me. It's time I faced him once and for all."

"Awww," mocked the gorilla. "Don't let the sap off the hook. It's fun watching him squirm."

Ian glared at the man. "Why do you need me?"

"Zelig is already expecting your call. He won't have his guard up when it finally happens."

"And what do you get out of it?"

"You get your life back, I get everything else."

"Which is what?"

"Once his daughter is back under his roof, Zelig won't have the heart to put up a fight when I take his empire from him. Nothing makes a man weaker than family."

"I didn't think his empire was worth taking," said Ian. "Not anymore."

"You'd be surprised. A man like Zelig doesn't stay alive and out of jail without considerable influence and assets. I need those assets working for me."

Their conversation was interrupted by a sudden howl of pain as though a stray dog had been kicked in the balls.

As all three heads turned toward the kitchen window, the gorilla flashed his teeth again. "See? Family. Rory's brother's here, should we go out and tell him what you did?"

Ian balked. "Me?"

"If you hadn't made Rory betray me, I wouldn't have had to kill him. His blood is on your hands. Besides, who do you think Ryan would rather go up against? You or me?"

The gorilla had a point.

Fuck, thought Ian, *fuck, fuck, fuck.*

36

RYAN BOWERY STARED fiercely at the two men as the garage door rumbled open. He was slumped on the ground in a puddle of gore with the lifeless body of his brother in his lap.

"What the fuck have you done?" he screamed at both of them.

The gorilla stared back impassively, his shotgun resting against his leg. He had returned Ian's gun to him also, but Ian stuck it in his waistband rather than hold onto it.

"Your brother brought Quinn to my home," said the gorilla. "I don't take betrayal lightly. You both understood that."

Ryan's heated gaze shifted to Ian. "Why the fuck would he do that?"

"Quinn forced him," said the gorilla before Ian could speak. "I was as surprised as you are. Your brother didn't strike me as such a little bitch."

Ryan dropped his brother's body and sprang to his feet. His eyes flicked toward the gorilla, but his rage remained focused completely on Ian.

"Pull a gun and I'll end you," warned the gorilla. "I have use for him, but..." The gorilla paused before adding, "I don't need him whole."

Ryan splayed open the fingers of his right hand to show their lack of gunpowder malice before using his left to remove a large hunting knife from a sheath on his belt.

"Oh dear," said the gorilla, winking mischievously at Ian. "Didn't see that coming, did you?"

"I'm gonna carve out your fuckin' eyes," said Ryan.

The gorilla held up a lone finger. "One eye. I still need him to see."

Ryan licked his lips. "One fuckin' eye and one fuckin' ear, but that's just to start. When the boss is done with you, I'm taking the rest."

The gorilla looked over at Ian. "So, tough guy, what are you gonna do?"

"Can we talk about this, Ryan?" Ian asked. "I'm not the one who shot your brother."

"Fuck you, you fuckin' fuck," yelled Ryan. The sharp knife danced between his hands in nervous anticipation.

"Can't argue with that rebuttal," said the gorilla as he moved off to one side, an amused smile on his scarred face.

Ian stood alone in the garage doorway.

"You're gonna fuckin' scream," said Ryan.

Ian braced himself as the brother's grip on the knife tightened, his knuckles turning white while bloodlust veined his face in angry streaks of beet. A primal, agonized howl of rage and revenge tore from the man's throat as he rushed forward.

A dozen calculations went through Ian's mind simultaneously, but he couldn't find any other choice.

Snaking a hand into his waistband, Ian drew out the .45 and fired three times. All three bullets hit center mass, punching open the brother's ribcage, pulverizing his insides, and exiting out his back in fist-sized holes.

The power of the .45 knocked Ryan off his feet to land on top of his brother's corpse, dead before his body stopped twitching.

"See," said the gorilla as the sound of gunfire faded, "that's why Ryan was never going to go far. A clever man would have asked if I needed him alive, too."

Ian's elbows were locked in rigor, his shoulder muscles trembling, and his stomach churning with sour bile.

Christ, he thought, *what have I done?*

*

The gorilla's large hands smothered Ian's to unlock his grip on the gun. When the weapon was free, he handed it to his skeletal partner who had barely blinked during the exchange.

"You got this?" asked the gorilla.

The man nodded. "Furnace is hot enough to melt steel, should take care of these morons easily enough. Not that anybody'll miss 'em."

One of the gorilla's hands moved to Ian's face, pinching his chin between large fingers until Ian's shocked eyes found their focus.

"We've got business to discuss," he said. "Don't go maudlin on me."

Ian's chest shuddered violently as he suddenly exhaled and began to breathe again.

"There you go," said the gorilla. "Let's head back inside. I believe there's even a slice or two of pie left in the fridge."

*

Sitting at the kitchen table, Ian slowly ate a slice of homemade apple pie. The flaky crust was sprinkled with brown sugar and he savored every sweet kernel as it dissolved on his tongue. His coffee had also been laced with spoonfuls of sugar. It wasn't the way he normally liked it, but he lapped it up.

The gorilla barely said a word as he poured the drinks and served the pie. He didn't ask either of his guests how they liked their coffee, but simply served it the way he wanted to.

Nobody complained.

Once Ian and Constance finished their pie, the gorilla cleared the plates and refilled their cups. This time he didn't add extra sugar.

"You thinking clear?" the gorilla asked.

Ian wiped his mouth and nodded.

The gorilla produced a scrap of paper with a phone number written on it.

"Call Zelig," he said. "Tell him you've found Constance and want to meet. Don't let him run the conversation. Sly old bastards like him get suspicious if everything's too easy."

The gorilla turned to Constance. "Unless he wants proof of life, you just sit there and keep it zipped."

Constance tugged her hair to cover the bruise around her eye and silently lowered her gaze to focus on her coffee, but Ian could see she was hiding a rebuttal beneath the furl of her lips.

"You ready?" asked the gorilla.

Ian dug in his pocket for his phone, thankful he had retained control over his bladder when his body went into shock, and placed it on the table. After tapping in the number, he hit the speaker button and waited.

The phone rang four times before a voice answered. Ian recognized it as belonging to Zelig's goon with the bandage over his nose.

"I need to talk to your boss," said Ian, his voice quaking slightly with the last tendrils of shock.

"Who the fuck is this?" asked Nose Bandage.

"Ian Quinn. He'll want to take my call."

"How did you get this number?"

"Who cares? You think your boss is the only one with friends in this town?"

"What if I told you to go fuck yourself?"

"Then you better dig your own grave," Ian snapped, allowing his own self-loathing to fuel his words. "I have your boss's daughter. You don't want her, fine by me, but when Zelig finds out—"

"Hold on!"

The phone was muffled as the goon walked across a room and opened a door. It took a few more minutes before Zelig's aged voice came on the line.

"You have my baby girl?"

"I'm looking at her right now," said Ian.

"How does she look?"

"The years have been kind."

A smile flickered in the corner of Constance's mouth as an audible sigh escaped her father's lips.

"Where are you?" asked Zelig.

"Right here in Portland."

"Has she been here all this time?"

"No. I brought her back with me."

"You didn't harm her, did you?"

"What do you care?" said Ian. "You're the reason she left."

"You know nothing."

"Wrong." Anger frothed on Ian's lips. "I know everything and I've had to live with the fallout my entire life."

"Let me talk to her."

"Fuck you."

"How dare you talk to me—"

"Shut up! It's my turn. I have something you want, but I need a guarantee this will be the end, that your goddamned vendetta against my family is over."

"Return my darling daughter to me and you have my word."

"And what's that worth?"

"It is everything."

Ian glanced over at the gorilla. He shook his head and mouthed, *"More."*

"Sweeten the pot," said Ian.

There was a short pause before Zelig answered. "How much?"

It was a language every gangster understood: greed.

"Quarter million. Cash."

The gorilla nodded. It was a respectable number.

"Deal," said Zelig. "Can I talk to her?"

Ian looked across the table at Constance. She nodded.

"One question," said Ian. "She's listening."

There was a longer pause this time before Zelig said, "I have missed you so much, Constance, my darling. Have you missed me?"

Tears sprang to Constance's eyes and she covered her mouth with her unchained hand. She began to tremble and shake her head, struggling to find a voice. Until the moment her father spoke directly to her, she had been stoic and strong, likely believing she possessed the strength that she had been telling herself was within her all these years.

"Constance?" Zelig pressed.

"Give her a moment," said Ian. "This is difficult on everyone."

Finally, Constance lowered her hand from her mouth and spoke.

"Father," she said. "Did you receive my gifts?"

"Yes," said Zelig, his voice light with joy. "Every one."

"We'll be together soon."

"Yes," enthused Zelig. "Yes, yes, yes."

"Touching," said Ian dryly.

"If you harm—"

"Don't! You've terrorized my family long enough. It's over."

Zelig began to cough, his chest spasming as the snap of elastic and hiss of air told Ian that he was sucking on his tank of oxygen.

"We'll meet tonight," said Ian. "You hand over the money plus an assurance that my sister can return home unmolested, and I'll deliver your daughter. After that, I never want to see your ugly mug in my neighborhood again. Is that clear?"

"Where?" Zelig gasped, still struggling to breathe.

"Where it began," said Ian. "My grandfather's shop. Don't come inside. I'll meet you on the street. Ten p.m."

Ian hung up the phone and turned to the gorilla.

"How was that?" he asked.

"Cold," said the gorilla, his lips parting in a smirk. "Stone cold."

37

IAN DROVE AWAY from the garage with his gun on the seat beside him. He stopped at a gas station with an automatic car wash and drove inside. The white foam turned pink as the brushes washed away a sticky film of blood, sending the last remains of the Bowery brothers down the drain.

As the brushes spun, Ian removed the clip from the .45 and loaded three new hollow-point cartridges. His hands trembled slightly as he pressed the fresh brass into the clip.

His conscience quivered also, struggling to answer the nagging question: *Could I have done something else, anything else?*

The truth was, when he squeezed the trigger he hadn't even been sure the gun would fire. The weapon had been out of his sight before being returned, and the gorilla didn't strike him as a trusting soul.

But now, with blood on his hands, the gorilla had leverage over him, and that was something Ian didn't need.

Ian exited the car wash and drove home. He only had a short time before everything came to a head, and he needed to prepare.

38

IAN'S HEART LEAPT into his throat when the gorilla banged the flat of his hand on the front door of the butcher's shop.

Unlocking the door, Ian spotted a dozen heavily armed men staring back at him from the darkness. Two large black Escalades had formed a V in the middle of the road, blocking any traffic from entering the street from the west.

"Isn't that going to spook him?" Ian asked as the gorilla escorted Constance inside the store.

"He won't come alone," said the gorilla. "This will make him think twice about going back on his word."

"I don't like it."

The gorilla showed his teeth. "Like I give a fuck."

The mesh curtain separating the back room from the front parted and a tough-looking man with full-sleeve tattoos and dark ginger hair stepped out. A ragged scar ran across half his face, and one of his eyes was swollen from a recent punch.

The gorilla barely blinked. "Who's this?"

"A friend," said Ian. "Just in case you go back on your word."

"And you think he would be enough to help you?"

"He didn't come alone," said Ian. "And his friends will lay down their lives, and a lot of firepower, for him."

As the two large men sized each other up, Ian turned to Constance. "How are you?"

The unshackled woman shrugged, her gaze taking in the room as a way of avoiding eye contact.

"It looks so different." She pointed to the tin pig hanging on the wall. "I remember that. Are you living here now?"

"So long as we make it through the night."

She turned to the large picture window. "The neighborhood's changed."

"Maybe I can help change it back."

Constance offered up a brief smile. "Optimism. A rare quality."

"We're nothing without it."

The gorilla turned away from the biker and snorted. "You armed?"

Ian nodded.

"I'd keep it cocked and locked if I were you."

"Zelig's not going to try anything with his daughter here."

"That's why chumps like you die in the street. When a shark shows its teeth, it's not because he's being friendly."

The gorilla handed Constance a slim, rectangular black box. "A gift for your father. Just in case he doesn't recognize you. It's been a few years."

Constance lifted the lid to reveal a commando-style dagger with a hand-forged handle and black ceramic blade. The handle was wrapped in ebony parachute cord.

"It's beautiful," she said, her voice barely above a whisper. "He'll adore it."

"Almost kept it for myself," said the gorilla.

The woman unexpectedly touched the gorilla's arm, her fingers grazing the thick hair on his forearm before retreating.

A radio on the gorilla's belt crackled, and a voice said, "He's here. Lincoln Continental, dark blue. Slowing down."

The gorilla moved away from the door and locked eyes with Ian. "It's your show, don't fuck it up."

Ian turned to Gordo. "Anything happens to me, shoot him in the head."

Gordo grinned, the scar on his face turning white from the strain. "Be my pleasure."

The gorilla barely acknowledged that anyone had spoken.

Ian took Constance by the arm. "You ready?"

Constance inhaled sharply and clutched the black box to her bosom. Without a word, she reached out and opened the front door.

*

Walking out to the middle of the street, Ian struggled to keep his breathing regular and his legs strong.

This was the man who had butchered his grandfather, terrified his sister, and gunned down his father. What the hell made him think he would be treated any differently?

His grip tightened on Constance's arm as they moved in front of the roadblock and faced the approaching vehicle. The Lincoln stopped a short distance away, its headlights blinding.

The front passenger door opened and Nose Bandage strode forward into the light. He was carrying a small duffel bag.

"Send her over," he ordered.

Ian shook his head. "This is between your boss and me, not his hired goon. I need to see it in his face that this ends things."

The hired goon spat on the ground to show his disgust before tilting his chin in the direction of the blockade. "Who've you brought?"

"Hired men," said Ian. "No personal interest. Just here to keep me alive."

"No need. Zelig gave his word."

"Let's call it my own insecurity," said Ian.

"Yeah," said Nose Bandage, the corner of his mouth creaking open in a smile. "I get that."

The goon raised one arm and a team of men fanned out from behind the Lincoln. They moved up to stand on either side of him, three abreast.

Nose Bandage's grin widened. "Little insecure myself."

Ian glanced off to the side and saw the Song family at the window of their restaurant. Two of Gordo's men were standing with them, offering protection. Ian shook his head at them and they retreated back into the darkness.

"We all good?" Nose Bandage asked.

"I'm good," said Ian. "Constance is nervous. It's been a long time since she's seen her father, but if he's not prepared to join us…"

Ian let the sentence drift as the woman trembled in his grip.

Nose Bandage turned his head as the Lincoln's driver exited the vehicle and opened the rear door. After helping the passenger to become steady on his feet, the driver stepped back and waited by the door.

Walter "Ice Pick" Zelig strode forward into the light. He had washed and dressed for the occasion in a sharp, charcoal suit beneath a dark tweed overcoat. The silhouette was broken by a coral blue scarf wrapped once around his pale throat, while the fresh polish on his shoes reflected the light with rich abandon.

Tonight, he looked younger than his advanced years, especially without the oxygen mask strapped to his face and the tank in his lap.

Constance gasped at the sight of him and her hand latched onto Ian's arm, squeezing so tightly that he had to grit his teeth to hold in a yelp.

"Is that you, Constance?" Zelig asked as he stopped at the head of his small army. "Come closer. Let me see you."

Releasing Ian's arm, Constance straightened her shoulders, sucked in a deep, cleansing breath, and began to move forward.

Despite a burning pang of guilt in his chest, Ian let her go.

*

Constance kept walking until she was but a few steps away from her father.

"Is it really you?" asked Zelig. "After all this time?"

Constance lifted her chin and stared deep into her father's eyes. "It's me."

Zelig swayed on his feet, clearly overcome with emotion.

Constance held out the black box.

"A final gift."

The old man smiled as she lifted the lid and showed him its contents.

"For your heart," she said.

Tears poured down the man's wrinkled cheeks.

"My beautiful, beautiful baby girl."

He opened his arms, inviting her into his loving embrace.

Stepping forward, Constance removed the knife from its box and plunged it deep into her father's chest.

*

Gunfire erupted as Ian dived to the ground, bullets flying in both directions as the street turned into a war zone. Ahead of him, Constance lay atop her father, her face spattered in blood, the knife still plunging over and over as a look of pure psychosis shone in her eyes.

Beside her, Nose Bandage was struggling to break her grip, but failing, as his boss's last orders were to keep Constance safe. Around him, his team was returning fire, but the gorilla's gang was better prepared and better armed.

One by one, his gunmen were reduced in number until he saw no other escape.

Ripping Constance off her dead father's corpse, Nose Bandage hauled the woman to her feet and used her as a shield until he was the only man on his side of the street left standing.

The duffel bag stuffed with cash lay off to one side, forgotten and ignored.

Lying on his stomach in the middle of the road, Ian sensed the gorilla approaching. Glancing up, he watched the large man stride past him without a flicker of fear. His hands appeared empty of weapons except for a small knife, its triangular tip peeking from between enormous fingers. The knife's sharp blade cut into his skin, turning his clenched hand red with blood.

"You should let her go," said the gorilla. "End this like a man."

"Fuck you," said Nose Bandage.

"Okay. Kill her, then."

Nose Bandage winced, clearly not expecting that response.

"We delivered her to your boss," said the gorilla. "Her value to us is done."

"If I let her go—"

"You face me," said the gorilla. "That's the only way you live."

Defeated, Nose Bandage knocked the bloody knife from the woman's hand and released her. She didn't run away. Instead, she leaned back on the hood of the Lincoln and smiled. Her face was a mask of blood, glee and madness; her body taking on a posture and strength hidden until this moment.

"Are you okay, Mother?" asked the gorilla.

"Never better, darling," replied Constance.

Nose Bandage spun back around, suddenly realizing his horrible mistake in letting his hostage go.

But he was too slow.

The gorilla sprang forward, grasping the man's head in his

hands and squeezing. Nose Bandage screamed as the knife in his attacker's hand pierced his skull. With a twist of the blade, the split in the goon's skull widened as the gorilla put all his strength into the vice-like grip until a sickening crack changed the shape of his combatant's head.

Nose Bandage dropped to the ground, his eyes locked open wide, but there was nothing left to see.

The gorilla offered a bloody hand to his mother.

"Should we visit our new home?" he asked.

"In a moment," said Constance, her voice light and dreamy. "It's such a lovely evening. Let's soak it in."

In the distance, the sound of sirens began to converge.

"Just for a moment, then," said the gorilla as he joined his mother on the hood of the Lincoln and took in the stars.

In the middle of the road, Ian rose slowly to his knees before strong arms grabbed him under the arms and helped him to his feet. Holding Ian's weight, Gordo grinned over at him and whispered, "Holy shit! You get more interesting every time we meet."

Ian felt a dozen pairs of eyes following their staggered path as he was helped back to his store and stumbled inside.

Locking the door behind them, Ian slumped to the floor and covered his face.

Zelig's reign was over, he told himself, but what in hell had he helped create in its place?

EPILOGUE

ROSSELLA HUNTED FOR a fresh shirt while Ian finished washing his hands and face. The man in the mirror looked older than he should with uninvited strands of white in his hair, deeper wrinkles around his mouth, and a weary hardness in his eyes.

"It needs ironing," Rosella said, appearing in the bathroom doorway with a shirt in her hands, "but it's clean."

Ian accepted the shirt and slipped it on.

"You ready for this?" she asked.

"Truthfully?"

Rossella nodded.

"Is it too late to climb out the back window and run away together?"

Rossella smiled. "In this dress, you've got to be kidding."

Despite the lateness of the hour, Rossella was dressed to kill in a dangerously short and distractingly tight black dress, plus lethal high heels with cobalt blue soles.

"I hope your date didn't mind the interruption," said Ian, attempting not to sound jealous.

"Only when I said I'd rather be with you."

"Ouch."

Rossella smiled wider. "Do you have your story straight?"

"Straight as I can get it."

"Stick to the facts, don't fill in any blanks, and when they stop talking, you stop talking. Don't try to fill the silence."

"Wow," said Ian with a grin. "You sound just like a lawyer."

"Smart-ass."

Downstairs, Detective Jersey Castle stood by the front window and watched the flashing red and blue lights that illuminated the organized chaos outside. The coroner had to call in a favor from the local hospital to help transport the number of dead to the morgue.

"Your neighbors opened their restaurant to make coffee for everyone," he said when Ian and Rossella arrived in the front room.

"They're thoughtful like that around here," said Ian. "One of the reasons I'm moving back."

"I asked them if you were part of this, but they claim they didn't see you. That right?"

Ian nodded.

"I find that hard to believe," said Jersey.

"Me, too," agreed Ian. "But I guess I'm not the only one with a hate on for Zelig."

"Turf war?" asked Jersey.

Ian nodded again. "New player in town wanted a bigger piece of the pie. Guess negotiations went south."

"He the same one who killed Noah?"

"Be my guess, although I didn't get a good look at anybody."

"Hiding under your bed?"

"Behind the sofa actually."

Jersey kicked a duffel bag that was laying at his feet. "Found that lying out there in the blood."

"What is it?"

"Cash. Around a quarter million."

Ian let out a low whistle.

"Any ideas?" Jersey asked.

"Drug deal gone bad? Or it's meant to look that way."

"Meaning what?"

"A new player in town sets up Zelig to make a buy, drugs, weapons, whatever, only there was never going to be any deal. They simply wanted to get Zelig out in the open and take him out."

"Zelig got sloppy?"

"Man was getting old."

"Not anymore." Jersey stared hard at his friend. "You being straight with me?"

"Straight as I can be."

The detective nodded. "No civilians were hurt, so the Gang Violence Task Force will take it from here. They'll likely have more questions, so it won't hurt to keep your lawyer close, just in case."

"Does that mean she should sleep over?" asked Ian.

Jersey grinned. "I recommend it."

With a nod, the detective left the store, duffel bag in hand.

"Sleepover?" asked Rossella.

"We can lay head to toe if you don't trust me," said Ian.

Rossella punched him in the arm.

*

The phone rang in the middle of the night. Rossella was snoring gently beside him when Ian answered.

"I like this new place better than the mechanic's," said the gorilla. "It has two swimming pools, can you believe it? All those years Mother and I spent working our way up from nothing, and he had two goddamned swimming pools."

"They're yours now," said Ian.

"Yes," said the gorilla. "He left everything to his daughter. Makes things so much easier for the bastard son."

"I said nothing to the police."

"Didn't expect you to."

"Where does that leave us?"

"You worried I'll change my mind?"

"Yes."

"I'm a man of my word. So long as you don't get in my way, I've no need to see you ever again. Besides, my mother has a soft spot for your family. So in honor of your grandfather, I owe you one."

*

Ian held his breath as he placed the phone to his ear.

A sleepy voice answered on the fourth ring.

"Hey, sis," he said, his voice cracking with emotion. "It's safe to come home."

— The End —

ABOUT THE AUTHOR

Grant McKenzie is the internationally published author of five edge-of-your-seat thrillers, plus an ongoing mystery series set in San Francisco. His riveting thrillers *Speak the Dead, The Fear in Her Eyes, Switch,* and *K.A.R.M.A.* are available from Polis Books. Under the pen name M. C. Grant he writes the Dixie Flynn series that began with *Angel With a Bullet,* continued with *Devil With a Gun,* and returns with *Baby With a Bomb.* His short story "Underbelly" appeared in the *First Thrills* anthology edited by Lee Child from Tor/Forge. As a journalist, Grant has worked in virtually every area of the newspaper business, from the late-night "Dead Body Beat" at a feisty daily tabloid to senior copy/design editor at two of Canada's largest broadsheets and editor in chief of Monday magazine. He lives in Victoria, British Columbia. Follow him at @AuthorGMcKenzie.